Praise for

WHAT I SAW AND HOW I LIED

"A gripping story, beautifully paced"
The Times

"Has the intensity and claustrophobia
of a stage play or thriller"
Daily Telegraph

"A dark and thrilling novel…
Will send a tingle down the spine"
Daily Mail

"Beautifully written and paced …
a dark, captivating tale"
Independent

"A real thriller to impress"
Daily Mirror

"An extraordinary story … gripping"
Wall Street Journal

Judy Blundell is the author of *What I Saw and How I Lied*, winner of the National Book Award and an ALA Best Book for Young Adults and *Strings Attached*. She lives in New York with her husband and daughter.

www.judyblundell.com

STRINGS ATTACHED

JUDY BLUNDELL

■ SCHOLASTIC

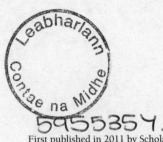
First published in 2011 by Scholastic Press, an imprint of Scholastic Inc.
First published in the UK in 2011 by Scholastic Ltd
This edition published in the UK by Scholastic Ltd, 2014
Euston House, 24 Eversholt Street
London, NW1 1DB, UK
A division of Scholastic Ltd.
Registered office: Westfield Road, Southam, Warwickshire, CV47 0RA
SCHOLASTIC and associated logos are trademarks and/or registered
trademarks of Scholastic Inc.

ISBN 978 1407 13038 5

A CIP catalogue record for this book is available
from the British Library.

Printed in the UK by CPI Group (UK) Ltd, Croydon, CR0 4YY
Papers used by Scholastic Children's Books are made from wood grown in
sustainable forests.

1 3 5 7 9 10 8 6 4 2

This is a work of fiction. Names, characters, places, incidents
and dialogues are products of the author's imagination or are used fictitiously.
Any resemblance to actual people, living or dead, events or locales
is entirely coincidental.

www.scholastic.co.uk

For Neil

One

New York City
October 1950

The second act curtain was one chorus away when I spotted him. Third row on the aisle, smack in my sight line. I missed the beat and almost sent Shirley into the orchestra pit with my hip.

To get me back, Shirley gave me a pinch underneath the frothy short skirt, so hard it made my eyes water. Brush step, kick, shoulder roll. Mascara stung and my vision blurred. Ball change, pirouette, as he swam in and out of focus.

I could feel my heartbeat slam, even though the routine wasn't hard. Hold the note, arm up, finger pointed at Millicent March, the star, small and delicate with a thin soprano in constant quest of pitch.

Applause trickled over the footlights. Dust spiralled and settled. I saw his palms hit a few times, then stop. The question of why he was here made my nerves jangle.

1

Shirley turned on me in the wings as Millicent brushed by, drained of light and energy and comedy, just a thirty-eight-year-old beaten down by the effort of appearing as a coed onstage in a terrible musical with a half-empty house.

"What do you think you're doing out there, leadfoot?" Shirley spat the question at me like a wad of chewed gum. "There could have been a Hollywood scout out there, you know!"

Shirley thought there could be a Hollywood scout out there every night. As if they'd be cruising the chorus line of *That Girl From Scranton!* instead of the Copa Girls or the Lido Dolls. Shirley paid me a dollar a week to wash out her dance clothes and tights in the sink, because she didn't want the imaginary Hollywood scout to see chapped hands when he took her out to El Morocco after the show. *They won't be looking at your hands, Shirley,* I wanted to tell her. But I kept my mouth shut, because I was currently sleeping on her mother's couch. Ten bucks a week she charged me.

Even though I talked back to Shirley in my head, I envied her, too. Faith seems to grab people and not let go, but hope is a double-crosser. It can beat it on you anytime; it's your job to dig in your heels and hang on. Must be nice to have hope in your pocket, like loose change you could jingle through your fingers. Christ, I found myself jealous of everyone nowadays, even dimwits like Shirley.

The roses arrived as we all started in with the cold cream and tissues. The assistant stage manager stuck his arm in with the bouquet. Newly married, he wasn't allowed to peek. The girls loved that and razzed him every chance they got.

"George, hand me my brassiere, will ya?"

"Georgie, zip me up, be a honey!"

"Come on in, we're decent – we just ain't dressed!"

Nancy, the quiet one with the fiancé, handed me the flowers. "Pretty," she said. "He didn't buy these in the subway."

No flattery, no snow job on the card.

I'd like to take you to dinner. Nate Benedict

No pleases or thank-yous, either. I tossed the card on the counter and bent over to fasten my stockings. I didn't want them to see my face. I'd get enough teasing as it was. My fingers were shaking and I couldn't manage the garter.

"Ooooh, Kit's got a hot one," June said.

"What about that boy you're still sweet on? The one in the army?" Edie asked. There was a hard edge to the question. Edie stared at herself in the mirror, leaning forward to reapply her lipstick. She was older than all of us, probably thirty, some of the girls whispered, but she would only admit to twenty-four. I was seventeen and told everyone I was twenty-one.

"Anybody got a pen?" Shirley trilled. "Kit's got to write a Dear John to the poor sucker."

I'd only been slapped in the face once in my life, but I still remembered the shock of it. If only I could've passed on that feeling to Shirley, special delivery. On one long cold

3

ride home to the Bronx, I'd mentioned Billy to Shirley, and had regretted it every minute since. Shirley had blabbed to the rest about my sweetheart in the service. Most of the girls respected that – you didn't razz a girl if she had a guy in uniform. They knew he'd be shipped to Korea after basic training. But Shirley didn't believe there was a topic you couldn't poke at. It could be the day of your mother's funeral, and she'd tell you to change your hat.

"Nah, I dropped him for your boyfriend," I said. "He says that when he turns on the light he gets spooked, because you look just like his mother."

Shirley's face got red as the girls laughed and catcalled – "Oooh, good one, Kit."

Dumb move. There went Mrs Krapansky's couch.

I grabbed my jacket and on the way out tossed the roses at George to take home to his pregnant wife. If only I'd learned to save my scene-stealing for the stage, maybe I would've actually been going somewhere.

Nate waited by the stage door. I couldn't tell by his face what he was thinking. I'd known Billy's mood before he said hello, if he was happy or sulky or crazy to see me. Nate's face was as clean as if he'd just scrubbed his feelings off with a washcloth. He was nothing like his son.

Why was he here? I sucked air into my lungs and stood with my chin up, braced for the hit.

"Billy?" I asked.

"No word," he said. "He hasn't shipped out yet."

I blew out a breath while I slowly pulled on my gloves. The pull of fear eased. I could talk now.

Nate waited while I adjusted each finger. I dressed older now, trying to look mature. Nylons and heels and my hair still pinned up the way I wore it in the show. "All dolled up," Aunt Delia would've said in a disapproving way. I did feel like a doll, painted and false, under his gaze.

He turned and we started walking east down Forty-fifth Street. It was almost eleven o'clock and the streets were still crowded. Every once in a while we had to separate to let a group of happy theatregoers through, then come back together again, like a dance. When I'd arrived at the theatre it had been a warm October evening, but now I could feel the chill through my jacket. I'd given my old winter coat to my sister before I left Providence. Muddie had probably already replaced the buttons and sewn velvet on the collar. Unlike me, she planned ahead.

"Lousy play," he said. "For this you left home?"

"Yeah," I said. "The bright lights of Broadway."

Broadway wasn't looking so good just then. A drunk across the way chose this moment to blow his nose in the gutter.

I wondered what the plan was. A steak on a big white plate would be grand, even if I had to make conversation for an hour or so. If I could get down a couple of bites, it would be worth it.

"So where are we going, Mr Benedict?" I asked finally, because the silence was driving me nuts.

5

"Here you are, all grown up in New York. I think you can call me Nate."

We kept walking, all the way crosstown, passing one restaurant after another. COCKTAILS AND SPAGHETTI blinked in cheerful, lipstick-red neon at me from a window. A man held the door open for a woman, and I heard her laugh as she walked in, her chin buried in a fur collar. I felt a blast of heat and noise. We kept on walking.

I sneaked a look at him. Back in Providence he was called Nate the Nose because his nose had been smashed in a fight when he was younger. It should have wrecked his looks, but it hadn't. Sometimes the papers called him "dapper gangster Nate the Nose Benedict", but he wasn't in the papers much. "I'm just an attorney," he always told the press. "I'm in business, not rackets." I wondered if any gangster called himself a gangster. Maybe even a famous mobster like Frank Costello called himself a businessman, for all I knew.

"You ever hear of a taxi? They have them here," I said after the fourth empty cab had streaked by. I'd never mouthed off to him that way, but I was cold and ticked at the way he expected me to fall in line. We were on a side street now, no restaurants in sight.

"Any minute now we'll be in the river," I said. Which, on second thought, was not the right thing to say to a gangster.

He looked at his watch. "Fifteen minutes from Times Square, if you walk fast."

6

"Twenty in heels," I said.

"Not bad."

He stopped in front of an apartment building. I stayed put. "This doesn't look like a restaurant," I said.

Instead of heading towards the front door, he motioned to me. There was a black iron gate that led to another door directly to the left. "I want to show you something," he said, his hand on the gate.

I wanted to just walk away, but I couldn't think of a reason. He pushed the gate and held it open for me. I followed. He put a key in the lock and went on, "This is what's called a maisonette. An apartment with its own entrance. You can go in through the lobby, or this way."

He pushed open the door and held it for me. It was just an open door. Nothing to be scared of. I'd known him most of my life. There were neighbours all around me, windows next to windows next to windows, all with people behind them. I could hear a dog barking. So why did I have the heebie-jeebies?

He hadn't told me one word of why he'd shown up or what we were doing, and now he expected me to follow along like a duckling. And look how he held the door open, not even seeming impatient or pleading, just waiting for me to do what he wanted.

I walked towards him, lengthening my stride on purpose, hitting my heels down hard like I had my tap shoes on. As I went by, he reached out and switched on the light. I tried not to flinch as his sleeve brushed mine. We were standing too close. The door shut with a click as I walked further into the apartment.

The warmth hit me first, the radiator hissing heat. The living room was off the foyer, a pretty room with the lamps lit, nice but not fancy – a rug, a green couch, a table, two armchairs near a fireplace. Thick gold curtains on the windows, shielding us from the street. Through an archway down at the end of the apartment, I could see into a kitchen. A breakfast table with yellow legs was right up against the window where it would catch, I was sure, the morning sun.

I stopped in the middle of the rug, keeping my back to him. I was done with the chatter and the questions. It was up to him to start.

"I made a mistake with Billy," he said. "I should have understood him better."

"Seems like you should be telling *him* that, not me," I said. I kept on looking at the table with the painted yellow legs. It made you think of sitting there with a cup of tea on a Sunday afternoon.

"I tried," he said. "I wrote him a letter. Three, in fact. He sent them all back, unopened. So I'm sitting there at home, wondering how to make it right. I want to set things up for him so when he comes back he doesn't have to worry. I know what the two of you wanted. I heard him say it enough times – he was going to marry you and make a life for you both, here in New York."

"We don't want anything from anybody," I said. Leaving

8

out the part about my saying to his son *I never want to see you again*.

"So, the war interfered with your plans," he said. "That's what wars do. I got this apartment a while ago. I needed a place for business, but I don't need it any more. So now it's yours."

"Mine?" The surprise made me turn.

"Yours and Billy's. For when he gets back and you get married. You'll be eighteen soon, so you won't need permission. You might as well take it now."

"Now," I repeated, feeling dumb. Then I saw where he was going. "No." I was suddenly warm, so I stripped off my gloves and jammed them in my pockets.

"Where are you living now, some rooming house?"

"I have a room with one of the girls in the show." Mrs Krapansky coated herself with Vicks VapoRub every night before she went to bed. She charged me for everything – towels and hot water and a spoonful of sugar in my tea.

"OK, you ran away from home – that's your business. My business is my son."

"So leave me out of it!"

I saw his chest swell as he took a breath. What was he expecting, that I would thank him?

"I'm saying this wrong. I'm trying to give him a dream, you see what I mean? The dream he had. So he'll have something to think about. I know about war – I know you need something to come back to. So, please, Kit. Take the key. No strings. You wanted this, too."

I shrugged. "Everybody wants something."

"That doesn't mean they can't get it."

"You know this isn't right."

"No," he said, anger in his voice now. "This *is* right. It just doesn't *look* right. So don't tell anybody, and nobody has to know."

"Not even Billy?"

"Especially not him."

"So you want me to keep a secret from him."

"I think you can. If it helps him." He eyed me. "You have before."

"What about you?" I looked at him, gripping my gloves inside my pockets. "Don't you ever give anything up?"

"I gave up my *son*!" Nate slammed out the words, and I saw a flash of what he would be like if he let out that rage full on. I saw Billy in him, the way you could never tell when he was simmering until he blew the pot lid off.

"So I can trust you," I said. "That's what you're telling me."

"You know you can," he said. "For God's sake, Kit, you've come to me before. You know I'm looking out for Billy, and that means looking out for you."

"You weren't so happy with me or my brother a couple of months ago."

"I wasn't so happy with Billy, either."

"Yeah. Me, too. But I didn't go blaming anybody for it." I held his gaze, and he was the first one to drop his eyes. He knew I was talking about Jamie.

10

"Let's forget about that day. We were all upset. You can tell Billy that you got a job, that you have a place to live, a nice place. He'll have a furlough before he ships out, so he can see you here." He took a step towards me, and in that quick eager step, I saw Billy in him again, and this time tears suddenly were behind my eyes and I shook my head, hoping that would clear them.

He thought I was shaking it at him and he said, "After a while, you'll forget about our deal. I'll never knock on your door." He held up his hands, like he was surrendering.

I thought of telling him that Billy and I had argued that night. That the fight had been so bitter and terrible that I couldn't remember words so much as broken glass and a heart so twisted in pain and fear that I threw up in the bushes. If Nate could see a future, all I could see was a past that blocked it out.

He walked closer and slipped the key in my pocket, looking at me while he did it. I felt his hand brush mine and could smell his soap. I had to fight not to step back.

"I can't afford this place," I said.

"What, you think I'm going to hand you a bill?"

"You might. What if things don't work out the way you want?"

"I'm giving it to you, you got that? Till Billy comes back. The rent is nothing. I own the building – it's an investment. I won't call. I won't bother you. You have someplace to stay, pursue your dream and whatnot. Who knows – maybe you'll be a star, after all."

I didn't know any more if I had enough for that. It was one thing to dream of something and another to come and test it.

He could always read faces. "Don't sell yourself short."

"I'm not," I said. "But what's good in Providence isn't so special in New York City."

"Don't ever think that, Kitty," he told me. "You were something else when you were twelve, and you're something else today."

Even for a girl who was used to compliments, there were some that delivered the goods. I didn't want him to see the pleasure on my face so I turned and pretended to look around. I wished I could stop thinking of our apartment in Providence, crammed with beds and tables and pillows and shoes, or Shirley's lumpy couch and the smell of Vicks that I couldn't get out of my nose. I wished I could stop thinking of how swell it would be to pack my suitcase and tell Shirley I'd found my own place.

"So what do you say?"

I held out the key to him and shook my head.

"You know the favour I did your family," Nate said. "I didn't want to have to mention it."

"That's funny, because you just did."

"I told you back then, even when you were a little girl, you'd owe me a favour. And you shook on it."

"You're calling in a promise I made when I was *twelve*?"

Did I owe him this much?

I owed him this much.

"C'mon, I promised you dinner. How about a steak? There's a place around the corner that's good."

I wanted the steak. My mouth watered for it. The steak, and this place, and the radiator blasting heat, and the radio, and the pillows. I could see myself here, and I could see Billy knocking at the door in his uniform and me opening the door in a dress and heels and lipstick, welcoming him home.

Maybe I'd been dead wrong about Billy. Maybe the decision to stop seeing him was the latest in the long line of bad Corrigan luck. Wasn't it true that I was still crazy for him, that I had to stop myself from writing him every single night? That there were plenty of nights I left the theatre, hoping he'd be at the stage door in his uniform, with that hungry look in his eyes before he lifted me into his arms? How many times had I played that scene in my head – how I'd shake my head at him, telling him it was still over? Didn't it always end in a kiss?

There was too much going on in my head, and I was afraid some of it would spill out in front of Nate Benedict.

"I never eat after a show," I told him.

When we walked out, the wind hit us, cold and damp from off the river, and leaves crunched under our feet as we walked to First Avenue.

"I'll put you in a cab," he said.

He raised his arm and directed his next remark to the street. "You said a lot, but you never said you didn't love him."

13

The cab pulled over, and he handed in some bills to the driver. He cupped my elbow, helping me over the kerb. Our heads were close together when he murmured, "You and me, we want the same thing. His happiness."

I slid a bit in my heels and almost fell into the cab. He closed the door. I crashed back against the seat, looking through the window at him. He stood on the corner, bareheaded in the wind, hands in his pockets. It was like we'd made some kind of bargain. Another one, like the ones we'd made before.

In my pocket, my fingers closed around the key.

Two

New York City
October 1950

I hadn't expected it to be easy to come to New York, but I hadn't expected it to be so hard, either. Doughnuts and peanuts for a diet, rooming houses so far north in the Bronx that it took me an hour on the subway to Times Square. The green stain in the sink, the toilet that wouldn't flush. The sounds from the other rooms – the fights, the crying, the rhythmic thumping that made me put my pillow over my head and hum "Skylark". The discovery of bedbugs. I'd bounced from one bad rooming house to another.

Then I got smart, and lucky. I found out where all the actors ate lunch, at Walgreens in Times Square, and I squeezed out my dimes and ate lunch there every day, just a bowl of soup I could eat real slow. One day a blonde in a tight red sweater started talking to her friend about a girl leaving a show. In the chorus and had quit right there and

15

then, saying she had appendix trouble. The blonde had snickered, said in a high squeaky voice, "That's four months' worth of a swollen appendix if you ask me." I slapped down my coins and left.

I went straight to the theatre and my luck was still holding, because the man at the door was Irish, and he actually remembered the Corrigan Three, the performing triplets from Rhode Island. He waved me through the door and said the director and choreographer were both onstage, right then.

I picked up routines fast. You could show me once and I could do it, straight from the top. And I was strong. That was training. Then there was luck. This time I had the right height and the director didn't need a blonde. I guess he knew the show was a dog and would be closing soon, and he didn't really care. I think he patted himself on the back for giving a kid her first break.

I was in a Broadway show. Lights and glory. But it wasn't much different from summer stock. It was a bunch of girls razzing each other and helping each other, and there was always a mean girl, too. It was "Would you lookit that, I got a run and I just bought these at Woolworth's yestaday" and "My feet are gonna fall off my legs one day, I swear to ya" and "Christ, I'm getting married as soon as somebody asks, as God is my goddamn witness" and making lewd comments about the state of the lead actor's trousers when he looked us over. Pin curls underneath their rayon scarves when they got to the theatre, and after the show half of the girls going out with dates, the other half home to their mothers.

Luck doesn't last, I knew that much. Sometimes over my cup of coffee I'd think about the Corrigans – a long line of lunkheads going straight back to County Galway. One dumb choice after another. The family had sailed to America in 1883 and they were still greenhorns. Always looking at their feet, never up at the sky. We went down in ships, we died in childbirth, we drank or worked ourselves to death, we disappeared without a trace. What chance did I have to break that chain of misfortune?

Where did the bad luck start? Maybe you could trace it back to the night in '23 when sixteen-year-old Jimmy Mac Corrigan offered to help unload some whiskey on a boat from Canada. Or a Sunday morning in '32 when, after three days of rain, Jimmy convinced Maggie Corrigan to skip church because he had a better idea of how to pass the time. Who knew that would result, nine months later, in twenty-year-old Maggie's last breath as three babies came into the world?

"All those falls from grace," Aunt Delia would have said in that thin-lipped Irish way. Lust, liquor and legs – that's where I came from. That's who I was.

For a minute when I woke up, I thought I was back in Providence. Maybe it was the sound of the whistle on the tea kettle. By the time I'd fallen asleep, the light had been just coming up. I glanced at the clock on the mantel, an ugly big brass number that looked like the first thing you'd grab to bean a burglar.

It was after ten. Four hours' sleep would have to do. I could hear Shirley and her mother in the kitchen, talking in loud whispers so that they could claim they were trying to be quiet. I didn't know if I could get up the oomph to be polite this morning. I didn't know if I could face Mrs Krapansky flipping through the newspaper with her furrowed dark red nails, the shape of her toes showing through the worn leather of her slippers. Each time she turned a page she'd lick her dry finger. Turn, lick. Turn, lick.

And today, Shirley would have told her mother that I almost messed up the line last night. Not to mention the crack about her age. Shirley was twenty-six and thought she was over the hill. No confidence, no brains. All she had was a mother with her hands at her back, pushing.

I sat up. Hell to pay. No question about it.

"She acts all high and mighty and sneaks around behind her boyfriend's back. And him in the service and everything! I swear to you, it *lit-rally* makes me sick."

I felt bored already; I knew every step of what was going to happen next, how I'd have to go into that kitchen and pretend I hadn't heard, maybe hum on my way to make tea, ignore it when Mrs Krapansky complained about the cost of sugar. And then the remarks would begin, little pellets of contempt, putting me in my place.

18

I got up and stretched, a dancer's stretch. I could feel Shirley watching from the kitchen so I held it, knowing I was pulling my nightgown up my legs, almost posing now, because my figure was better than Shirley's, and Shirley knew it, too.

"You'd better get that bedding straightened up quick today. I've got guests coming later this morning," Mrs Krapansky said.

Guests. Please. That meant Mrs Maloney from next door. I yawned as I made my way to the bathroom and brushed my teeth and hair, then packed away the brushes and my things in the little pouch I'd bought at the five-and-dime. Shirley had given me one drawer in her dresser and a tiny space in the closet. I packed quickly and pulled my best cardigan on, along with my navy skirt, the most becoming one I had. I wriggled into high heels.

Then I walked out and laid the key and ten dollars on the kitchen table.

"If you think you can just walk out of here—" Mrs Krapansky said, her potato nose glowing red. "Good riddance to bad rubbish!"

It was easy enough to keep going, right out the door and down the stairs. It was when I hit the sidewalk that I lost my nerve. I looked down at my cheap suitcase with its broken latch. Everything I owned was in it, and it wasn't much. The chill wind twined around my ankles, and my legs already felt cold in my nylon stockings.

19

I only had one place to go. But maybe that made it harder to take the first step towards it.

I woke up alone the next day in fresh, flowered sheets. I sat down at the kitchen table with the yellow legs. The sun pooled on the tabletop, just the way I'd known it would. In one of those dramatic changes of weather that seemed to happen all the time in Manhattan, the October day felt like spring. The wind had blown the grey clouds out to sea, and when I threw open a window I was sure I could smell the river. It reminded me of home, but that was all right today. I was the product of rivers – you couldn't walk a half mile in Providence without bumping into one.

Steam rising from my teacup. Buttered toast on a plate. The sweetness of being alone. The radio on, softly. Everything would be perfect if I could just stop thinking. Nate had given me Billy's address when he'd given me the key. I'd tried three letters, one after the other, and they were sitting in front of me.

Dear Billy,
I guess you'll be surprised to get this. I never thought I'd be

Dear Billy,
How is everyth

Dear Billy,
You'll never guess where I am!

I put down the pen. I'd never lied to Billy – even when I'd told him I never wanted to see him again, I had genuinely never wanted to see him again.

And now . . . I'd made a promise to his father. But I hadn't promised *when* I'd write to him, had I? I didn't have to write the day I moved in. I could wait a few days to find the right words. I'd find a way to fill the letter with so much truth that one little lie wouldn't matter.

A pair of sneakers appeared on the fire escape stairs outside the window. The ladder came shuddering down with a clang. I flinched, spilling the tea across the letters I'd tried to write.

A boy, tall and lanky, jumped down the last two steps. A thick book was tucked underneath his arm and he held an apple in his teeth. His gaze slid past the kitchen and then stopped. His mouth dropped open, the apple fell out, and I burst out laughing.

I walked over, tying my robe tighter, and leaned out. I looked down at the ground, where the apple had fallen into the dirt of the scraggly yard.

"I think I owe you lunch," I told the boy.

"I didn't know the apartment was rented – it's been empty for years." He stammered out the words, blushing up to the tips of his ears.

I recognized the blush. I saw it on teenage boys all the time.

"I'm Hank," he said.

"I'm Kit. I just moved in yesterday," I told him.

The book was a textbook, *American Prose*. I'd left textbooks behind when I'd left home, and even though I'd hated every day of school, the book made me feel hollow, like I was missing out.

"I study outside sometimes," Hank said. "For the privacy." His hair was light brown and matched his eyes perfectly.

"Lots of brothers and sisters?" I asked.

"No. Just parents." He shrugged. "That's enough, sometimes."

"So who's the piano player?" I'd heard the music that morning, through the ceiling over my head.

He blushed again. "Me, I guess. Is it too loud? I can—"

"No, it's nice."

There was a pause. I began to feel stupid, standing there in my nightgown and robe.

"I go to Stuy. You?"

It sounded like another language at first – *igotastyu?*

"Stuyvesant High?" he said. "I'm a senior."

I was used to people thinking I was older than I was. But my face was scrubbed clean, and I must've looked my age. A girl in high school. I was suddenly annoyed at him, at his earnestness, his sneakers, his book.

"I just moved," I said. "From Rhode Island. I'm not in high school; I work. And I've got things to do, so. . ."

"Sure." Embarrassed, he started back up the ladder, then paused. "With the move and all . . . do you and your parents . . . I mean, do you need help with anything?"

22

"I don't need any help," I said, then shut the window.

Empty for years, he'd said. I found myself wondering: if Nate had bought the building as an investment, why hadn't he rented it out?

He called that night about five minutes after I got home. Almost as if he'd timed how long it would take me to get back from the theatre.

"Did you send the letter?" he asked.

"You said you wouldn't call."

"Did you send the letter?"

"You said you wouldn't call."

"We had an agreement."

"Exactly. You said you wouldn't call."

The stand-off. I leaned against the wall, the receiver against my ear. I couldn't believe I was talking to an adult like this. I'd only been here a month, but New York had sure taught me not to waste time being polite.

He let the silence hang there stiffly, frozen clothes on a line. I looked down at the carpet. The pretty carpet that wasn't mine, that I really didn't have a right to dig my bare toes into.

"I haven't sent it yet," I said. "It's not so easy. I can't find the words."

"Tell him you're here. He'll have to leave soon, before he's shipped out. If you don't mail it now, he won't come."

But I don't know if I want him to come.

Inside me lived a million versions of yes – all of them for Billy. Part of me couldn't refuse him anything. Part of me was scared of him. But all of me loved him.

I didn't say yes and I didn't say no. Quietly, I put down the phone.

It wasn't until the next week, tired and worn out after the final performance of *That Girl From Scranton!*, that I sat down at the table again, in my stage make-up and robe. It had turned cold again, and I had a blanket wrapped around me. It was one in the morning.

Dear Billy,
I don't know what the right thing is. All I know is that it shouldn't have ended like that. I felt the breath go out of me when I heard that you'd enlisted. I don't think I've breathed since.

Here's my news. I left, too. I dropped out of school. (My teachers probably threw a party.) I moved to New York City. It was hard at first, but I actually got a job in a Broadway musical! Now I have a nice apartment on the East Side. I can walk to Times Square or the river. I'm right near the new United Nations headquarters.

Everything we talked about – I'm living it. I'm still not sure whether talking about it was better.
Love,
Kit

I added my phone number and address, then put my coat on over my nightgown. I walked to the corner and mailed the letter that night, afraid that if I waited, I would tear it up.

Three

Providence, Rhode Island
September 1950

Jamie didn't come home that night. Da was furious. He banged on my door and asked me where my brother was and I said I didn't know. Muddie looked over at me, scared, and I only shrugged. I hadn't confided in my sister since I was four years old. I'd learned the hard way that whatever I'd done or felt would be too big for Muddie to hold, like an overstuffed grocery sack that kept spilling oranges. Only it would be my secrets dropping to the floor.

My face in the mirror looked wrecked. I had cried so hard that my eyes were swollen. I had been sick last night in the parking lot. One of the waiters had brought me a napkin dunked in ice water to clean my face.

I didn't know how I would get dressed and go through this day.

Last night, Jeff Toland had come to, foggy and still

drunk and lying flat out on the rainy pavement. Sammy and the waiters helped him into the kitchen. He kept asking for a doctor, or for the cops, and they kept saying they'd called them, but they hadn't yet. They were putting ice on his nose while he threatened to sue the entire city of Providence.

Nate arrived as Jeff was sipping Scotch for the pain. He came with two big men I didn't recognize, who took Jeff's agent off to sit at the bar. Nate and Jeff sat talking in the kitchen, and I knew everything would be all right when Nate put his arm around Jeff's shoulder.

"What happened with your brother last night?" Da asked me when I finally had to come out and face him. My father was a mild man, but when he was in a temper, you didn't want to be near him.

Muddie hovered in the background, already dressed for church in her blue skirt and white sweater, her strawberry blonde hair brushed and shining. Out of all of us, she was the only one who still thought missing Mass was a mortal sin.

I didn't say anything, but Da closed his eyes and sighed. "I told you that no good would come of it. You've cried so many tears for that boy, it's a wonder we don't have a fourth ocean."

"Sixth," Muddie said.

"Oh, please, just leave me alone, the both of you," I said.

"Listen, Kitty girl, I've left you alone, and look what's happened. You get your heart broken, just like—"

27

The pounding on the door startled us all. Da swivelled. "Is that him?"

"How should I know?"

"Open the door, Muddie," Da said.

Muddie crossed slowly in her stocking feet and opened the door. Nate Benedict strode in, hatless, his face red.

"It's on your head, Jimmy!" he shouted. "It's on your head, I'm telling you. It's your fault they did it."

"Did what?" Da turned his guileless blue gaze on Nate. "What are you talking about? I don't know anything except my daughter's crying her eyes out for your boy, and it's not the first time, either."

"They enlisted. Billy and Jamie. Last night."

This was not what any of us were expecting to hear.

"Jamie's underage—" Da started.

"Well, apparently he was able to convince them he's nineteen." Nate shook his finger at Da. "This is his fault. It's your pansy of a son, wanting to be around other boys, and dragging my Billy along. . ."

For a moment, we all stood staring at Nate, as though if we tried hard enough we'd be able to read his words in the air and have them make sense. Confused, Muddie looked at me. I shook my head, not understanding, either. Jamie? He was saying that Jamie . . . I couldn't get my mind around what he was saying. Jamie wasn't one of those milquetoasts from school. He was strong and big and athletic.

Da's skin was mottled. "Get out of my house! You can't

28

be saying that about my boy!" Da started towards Nate, furious, and got his hands on his lapels. Smaller than Nate, not nearly as strong, he was still able to shove him back towards the door.

"Open your eyes! Your boy has corrupted him! He doesn't know what he's doing!"

"My boy has corrupted *yours*?"

"I can't get him out of this, do you understand? He's lost." Nate was in the doorway now, staring at us blindly. "I've lost my boy!"

Da pushed him out the door and shut it. Then he sagged against it. He seemed to be gathering himself for the simple act of breathing. Eventually, he looked up and met my eyes.

"What do you know about this?" he asked.

"About what? I don't understand."

"He's saying that . . . your brother" – Da seemed to have to force the words out – "is unnatural."

"It's stupid," I said. "Jamie is Billy's best friend. That's all."

Muddie, pale and trembling, backed up against the wall. "It was a terrible thing to say. We should pray."

"Go ahead and pray – it won't change anything," I said. "Da, I don't know what he meant. Billy and I had a fight last night. I sent Jamie after him to help him. They're pals, they're friends – you know that."

"So there's nothing in it."

"Of course not. Billy's in love with me! Mr Benedict is just crazy, and he's taking it out on Jamie. Did you hear what he said? They *enlisted*. You have to go and tell the army he's only seventeen. You can get him out. Go to the enlistment office and tell them. You can fix this for Jamie."

Da didn't nod, or say a word. It was like he didn't hear me. He went off to sit at the kitchen table.

"What are we going to do?" Muddie whispered.

"It'll come out all right in the end," I said. "We'll straighten it out, and Jamie will come home."

"Did you break up with Billy? Oh, Kit. And you were going to marry him!"

I didn't want to see Muddie's tears. I went back to my room and dressed quickly, pulling clothes out of the closet without looking at them. When I returned, Da was sitting at the table, hands clasped around a mug of tea. I filled the kettle and put it back on the burner. My thoughts clattered and clanged inside my head, slamming against my worry for Jamie and my anguish over Billy.

The front door opened and closed. I hurried out of the kitchen. Jamie leaned against the door, dressed in the same clothes as the night before. He looked exhausted and pale. His tie flapped from his pocket. When he saw me, he shrugged in a helpless way.

"Nate was here and told us you enlisted," I said. "Is it true?"

He swallowed. "I couldn't let him do it alone."

And there were the eyes of my brother, that same honest blue. I couldn't imagine him in a uniform. I couldn't imagine him with a gun.

"We'll get you out of this. You're only seventeen."

He didn't say he didn't want to get out of it, and that gave me hope.

"Why?" I asked. "Why did you do it?"

"It seemed like a good idea at the time," he said. "Get away from everything."

"What do you have to get away from? What, damn you? I'm the one with the broken heart!"

We stood in the dim light, staring at each other. There was a red crease across Jamie's cheek, as if he'd slept on something that had pressed against his skin. He rubbed it slowly. "And you're the only one, aren't you?" he said.

"You mean Billy? It seems like he can take care of himself. How could you let him do that, Jamie? You could have stopped him!"

"How?" Jamie asked. He smiled without any humour in his eyes. "Maybe I just don't have your charms, Kit."

It was a nasty crack, even though I wasn't sure what he meant. I nearly pounced on him, just like I would when we were kids, fighting over marbles.

I don't know what would have happened if Da hadn't stamped out from the kitchen and barrelled down on us.

"How could you do this?" he bellowed.

Jamie looked down at his feet.

"From the time you were a boy, you were like a soft day – all mist," Da went on. "Delia used to say, spend more time with the boy, he's with his sisters too much. I guess I should have. Too busy with work and worry. And now I reap what I've sown. I never knew what to make of you. Well, now you'll make something of yourself."

"What are you talking about, Da?" I asked. "You're going to get him out of it."

"He's claimed his manhood," Da said. "May it make him a man. Let him pack his suitcase and go."

"No!" I shouted.

Jamie shook his head hard, back and forth, back and forth, as if to drive out what he heard behind Da's words. Then he turned around and went to pack. Da stood over him, his arms folded, watching until the suitcase closed. Then he shook his hand and told him goodbye.

He left a note for me.

Kit,
Sorry for all.
J

As if he didn't even have the heart to sign his whole name.

I knew Billy was gone when I read his name in the paper along with Jamie's and all the others who had joined up to fight in Korea to defeat the Communists.

Also in the paper, in a gossip column about Hollywood, I saw this:

> We hear . . . that Jeff Toland is back in Hollywood
> and raring to go after his automobile accident on

Cape Cod this fall. Don't worry, girls, that gorgeous profile is still intact! Word is he's inking a new contract with Paramount and in talks for the lead role of Harry Manning in "Manning Makes Good".

Is that what Nate could do? Reach all the way to Hollywood and get Jeff a job? How many favours had he called in for that?

My last argument with Da had us standing toe-to-toe, screaming into each other's faces.

"Let them make a man of him, let the army do it. God knows I couldn't!" Da yelled, his face beet red with anger. "And you – no more working in nightclubs. What was I thinking, allowing that? No, from now on, it's home after school and studying like a regular girl. I've lost control of this household. Thank the Lord that Muddie has a head on her shoulders."

"That's no thanks to you," I said. "You didn't raise us. We just lived in the same house as you."

"I did the best I could—"

"The best you could. Delia was right – you lived off us and you lived off her."

The words were out and I couldn't take them back. Da turned away.

I went on. "So now you want to catch up, prove you're a good father? You're going to let Jamie go to war just for that?" I hurled the words down the hall. "Well, say a prayer for yourself, Da. You just might have killed him!"

That afternoon I made my plans. Ironed my blouses. Packed my suitcase. Muddie begged me to stay, with tears in her eyes, and I told her I'd write, that I would be leaving when I graduated anyway, and she was the smart one, so why should I stay just for a diploma? She brought in her blue chiffon scarf and put it in my suitcase and then ran back out to the hall so I couldn't say no.

Every once in a while Da came and stood in the doorway, saying, "And don't think you can come back!" and "You'll be back once you realize how hard it is to keep a roof over your head!" and "Please, Kit, I can't bear to lose you, too."

I let him talk, and I didn't answer. I was right there, and I was already gone.

Four

New York City
October 1950

I heard the piano music in my dreams. He played early in the mornings, probably before school, and I was half awake. I started thinking of him as Mr Broadway. He'd play a classical number, something I didn't recognize, of course, and then he'd swing into "Embraceable You" or "I Could Write a Book".

I'd lie in bed, listening, and for a while the piano would chase away the blues. I was out of work, and even though I didn't have to pay rent, I needed money for food and stockings and toothpaste. I was getting down to my last dime, and it was plenty thin. I'd been hoping to step into another chorus job, but none of my auditions had panned out. Today I would look for a waitress job to tide me over. I tried not to think of this as defeat. Plenty of girls had jobs and managed to take classes and go on auditions, too.

I was up and circling want ads when the phone rang. I didn't want to answer the phone, afraid it would be Nate, but I was waiting for a callback. If you're a dancer, you've got to pick up the phone.

"This isn't about Billy, so don't blow up at me," Nate said. "I know that your play closed. I've got a job lead for you." He talked fast, like he was afraid I'd hang up. Before I did, he said, "At the Lido."

"A nightclub?" I said this automatically, even though my heart raced at the sound of the name.

"Not just a nightclub. The Lido. You know what that means."

I knew. The Lido was class. The girls on the line were chosen as much for their elegance as their legs. Frank Sinatra played the Lido, Ethel Merman, Johnnie Ray, all the big names. And Hollywood movie scouts constantly dropped in, looking for the girl who stood out, the one they'd offer a Hollywood contract to. Lido girls were on the cover of *Life* and *Look*, they were in Walter Winchell's and Cholly Knickerbocker's columns.

"Why are you doing this?" I asked.

"Because you need a job."

"You can't just fix everything, you know."

"Don't make a federal case. I've got a new client in New York, he's got a connection, I heard something, I'm passing it along. Look, the auditions are going to be on Friday. If you go tomorrow, you can get a jump on the competition. Just go see Ted Roper – he's in charge of the shows. Two o'clock tomorrow. He's expecting you. All I can do is get you in the door. I can't get you the job, so relax."

Nate hung up with a soft click. No chance for me to say no. It was like he knew whatever I'd say would be a waste of his time. He knew I wouldn't turn this down. He knew I'd be crazy to say no.

I didn't like him knowing all that. I didn't like how staying here suddenly made me available to him whenever he felt like calling. I hadn't counted on that.

I didn't have cab fare, so I'd have to walk to the Lido. When I got to First Avenue, I picked up a newspaper from the corner store. I flipped the paper in half so that I couldn't see the screaming headline ALLIES PUSH ON PYONGYANG, FIGHTING STILL HEAVY. I wouldn't read the war news, but I'd need to skim the want ads if the audition didn't work out.

The owner took my nickel and smiled. "You're back!"

"Back?"

He looked at me closer. "Oh, sorry. I thought I recognized you. Enjoy your day, miss."

I tucked the paper under my arm and headed west towards Second Avenue. One thing I hadn't realized about New York was that it was a city of neighbourhoods, and not just big ones, like Greenwich Village, but tiny ones, made up of just blocks. You went to the stores right near your apartment, and after a while people knew you. Soon that man would know my face and not confuse me with anyone else. Then I'd feel at home.

Nightclubs shouldn't be seen in daylight. I loved being in a theatre at any hour, loved it especially in the daytime, with its smell of coffee and cigarettes and dust, but the glamorous nightclub I'd read about for so long and dreamed about just looked dingy and sad when the sun was up. It smelled like watered-down drinks with cigarette butts swirling in them, a bunch of sour reminders from four in the morning.

A man checking receipts at the front told me to go on through to the dressing rooms, so I headed for the stage. The floors were being cleaned, and the furniture had been shifted around into clumps. Chairs and tables seemed to conspire against me on the way. I slammed a hip into a chair back, then bounced off the edge of a table.

"Doesn't bode well for the dance routines," a man said. But he smiled at me in a friendly way.

"Don't tell the dance captain," I said.

"Good smile." He wasn't flirting, he was judging. "Joe didn't say you were a redhead."

I didn't know who Joe was, but I said, "Born with it, sorry to say."

"It's OK, kid, you've got a look. I'm Greg. I'll be playing your music."

"Kit Corrigan."

"So you want to be a Lido Doll, huh?"

"Doesn't everyone?"

"I'll tell Ted you're here."

A tall, thin man in horn-rimmed glasses and khakis walked out onstage. He looked like a professor, but I could tell he was a dancer from the way he moved, elegant and easy. "This the girl?"

Yeah, I was the girl. I was used to being *the girl*. I was used to the look he was giving me right now, sizing me up. Not in a personal way; in a way you'd size up a horse if you were a jockey.

"Did you bring rehearsal clothes?"

I nodded.

He hadn't introduced himself, but he was obviously Ted Roper, and I was expected to know that. "Let's see if you can dance. You can change in the dressing room."

I knew about nerves, and I could make them work for me, but I felt rattled by Ted Roper's obvious irritation. Maybe he was ticked off that Nate had pulled strings to get me in to audition early.

In the dressing room, an ashtray full of cigarette stubs sat beneath a NO SMOKING sign. The light bulbs in the wire cages washed out my skin. I fumbled in my purse for rouge. I pushed aside bobby pins, a comb and a lipstick to clear a space on the counter. Quickly, I wriggled out of my skirt. I was already wearing my leotard. It was cold, so I kept on my sweater and tied a scarf tightly around my waist.

A stout woman with iron-grey hair came in, her broad

39

hands full of an explosion of tulle. The wardrobe mistress, I guessed.

"Audition?" she asked in some kind of European accent.

I nodded while I patted on a little rouge.

She dumped the skirts on a table next to a sewing machine. "You should wear higher heels. What are you, a seven?"

"Yes. . ."

She walked over to a shelf full of shoes – pumps, sandals, gold and silver and an array of colours. She slammed a pair of black pumps on the counter. "Use these."

I slipped out of my own scuffed shoes and into the higher heels. I straightened my shoulders and looked at myself in the mirror.

Back in Providence, Florence Foster, my dance teacher, had taught me everything, including how to walk. I'd been studying dance since I was eight. By the time I turned fourteen, she was telling me that I'd have to leave town. "You're not getting anywhere in Providence, dolly," Flo had told me. "Shake the dust of this town off your shoes and get yourself to Manhattan. White mink and diamonds, kid. That's the big time. Don't ask me if I think you should. And don't come by and say goodbye. Just drop me a postcard."

Now I heard her croaking voice in my head. *It's not just the feet, it's the arms, it's the neck, it's the goddamn elbows and the goddamn knees. Keep your face strong. Don't simper like*

*an idiot beauty queen. You're a dancer. A dancer. Got it? You
can't forget about your pinky finger, for godsake, you've got to
know what every muscle is doing, even your eyebrows. You're
a dancer.*

I'm a dancer, I told myself.

"No time to be late," the heavyset woman said. "He's
waiting to see how fast you dress. Around here, the clock
hands move for Ted."

"Thanks. And thanks for the shoes."

I hurried back onstage, but I was careful to slow down
as I got close. I knew he'd be watching how I walked.

The trick to auditions? You've got to not mind that
they're bored, or that they're thinking about the last girl, or
that they're dying for a smoke. You've got to think about
your own joy.

So I danced. He threw combinations at me, and I kept
up. It was like he wanted a reason to flunk me, just like old
Mrs Babbitt back in American History.

But he couldn't. *There's nobody I can't please. Nobody.*

Finally, he signalled for Greg to stop playing.

"So," Ted Roper said, "you can dance."

I waited.

"Three shows a night – I presume you know that? You
come at six thirty and you get out at three a.m. And you
have to be available for promotional pictures during the
day, or special shows. You're a replacement, so you've got
to catch up fast. You'll work with me for the rest of the
week."

"Yes, Mr Roper."

"You might as well see Sonia now – she's the wardrobe mistress. She'll tell you about your fittings. And hair. Every girl wears an upsweep. You'll have to handle some headpieces in that dance."

"That's not a problem."

"It better not be. Dress rehearsals on Saturday – look at the schedule in the dressing room after you talk to Sonia. If you're late for dress, even a minute, I dock your pay."

He looked at me over his eyeglasses. I didn't see contempt any more, just . . . what? Like he felt sorry for me? "One more thing. I don't stick my nose into the personal lives of my girls. But there's no special treatment, no matter whose friend you are. Got it?"

"I've got it, Mr Roper."

"All right, Miss Corrigan, you're hired."

When I walked out of that place an hour later I wasn't just another pretty girl. I was a Lido Doll. I was somebody in New York City. I could feel my whole body adjust to the change. I used my hips in my walk now, challenging every man on the street not to notice me. They all did. When I smiled at a businessman walking by, he couldn't stop looking and slammed right into a mailbox.

I'd made it. It seemed impossible, glorious. I thought of all the dancers sitting at drugstore counters, out of work. That wasn't me any more.

Would it have happened without Nate Benedict making

42

that call? I knew I'd danced well, but the fact that someone had paved the way took some of the pleasure out of it. That was the thorn on the stem of the flower, the lemon in my dish of cream.

Five

Providence, Rhode Island
September 1950
This was how the act at the Riverbank Club had gone: Tony
Carroll would call for a glass of water in the middle of the
act, and I would bring it. He would make eyes at me, and I'd
ignore him, and then he'd say, "What you need is a love
song," and I'd say, "What you need is a muzzle." He'd act
offended and stomp off the stage (straight for the bar to
down a drink) and I'd be alone up there. After a beat, I'd
take a sip of the water, cue the orchestra, and sing "Powder
Your Face with Sunshine". Right after the applause, he'd
come back and say, "No need to steal the show, kid," and
together we'd sing "Baby, It's Cold Outside". More applause.

I even got a mention in the paper:

CORRIGAN TRIPLET GROWS UP SWELL CROONER

One night as I carried the glass of water up to the stage, I
saw Nate sitting at the corner table, alone. Probably there

to check out that I could actually sing, I figured, or maybe that my material was clean. He slipped out after my number with Tony, without saying a word.

It was a hard September rain that night, but it didn't stop people from coming. I had been back and forth, back and forth, seating people all night. I stood near the door, waiting for the late-night crowd to trickle in from the theatre or the movies. The band was playing, and the dance floor was packed.

About midnight the door opened, and two men walked in, dressed in snappy suits and hats. I saw the hat-check girl's face as one of them handed her a tip, a folded bill that obviously pleased her. Some swells from Boston, I guessed. Then one of them turned around and it was Jeff Toland.

"Providence!" he called. He strode over, smiling, and took my hand.

"Mr Toland!" I couldn't believe he was right there in my hometown. "We don't see a Hollywood star in here every day."

"Call me Jeff – you did this summer at the theatre. Hey, you promised to come and see my show."

"I'm sorry, I was planning to. . ."

"It's all right – it was a dog, and we're closing out of town. The producers pulled out, the skunks." I could tell he was a little drunk.

The other man slipped a twenty in my hand and asked for the best table. I showed them to a booth that gave them

45

the best view of the dance floor but was still private, so Jeff couldn't be seen from the door.

"Perfect," he said. "Now if you dance with me I'll feel even better. You should see this girl dance," he told the other man. "I'm not kidding."

I remembered the last time we'd danced, outdoors at midnight underneath a big fat moon, showing off for the cast.

"I'm not allowed to dance with customers," I said. "Sorry."

The opening chords of Tony's act began, and I hurried towards the bar for the glass of water to use as a prop. I gave the high sign to Sammy, the manager, that there was a VIP in the house. Then I waited through the beginning of the act for my cue.

"Sorry, folks, I'm a little hoarse tonight. Anybody got a glass of water for a dying man?"

The couples in front held up a glass of water if they had it. Some drunk usually yelled out that water went better with Scotch. I made my way through the tables, holding the glass high and throwing out my first line. I could feel the pleasure of the audience and hear their laughter, and I could tell by Tony's upstage wink that the night was going well.

I sang my first song, and then we did the duet. I looked over at Jeff's table and saw him applauding madly. He beckoned to me. I looked over at Sammy and he nodded. A Hollywood star was in the house, and he would get whatever he wanted. Including me.

46

I walked over to the table and he stood. "That was terrific, kid."

I realized that he was calling me "Providence" and "kid" because he didn't remember my name.

"You were really something. And you look like a million bucks. Did you grow up or something?"

"Or something, maybe."

"Sit down and have a drink. OK, not a drink – a soda. Meet my friend here. This is Mr Tommy Fabian. He's a very big agent, so smile at whatever he says, and maybe I'll forgive him for talking me into the turkey that's closing tomorrow. Tommy is from Providence, how do you like that, so he's showing me the town. Just to get my mind off my misery. We've got a room at the Biltmore. He's paying."

Nervously, I slid into the booth. Jeff appeared to be drunker than before, but I guessed he was blowing off steam after a bad show.

He waved at the waiter, and I saw Jamie enter with Billy. Billy scanned the room and I shrank back, but he saw me.

Of course, I thought. *Just my luck.*

Billy registered that I was squeezed in next to Jeff Toland. Even from here I could see how he stiffened.

"If you'll excuse me," I said quickly, "I have to get back to work."

"Ah, duty calls. Well. . ." Jeff slid out of the banquette and stumbled a bit just as I got out. I reached out to steady him, my hands on his arms, and he leaned over and kissed me on the lips. "Sorry to get fresh. I'll regret that in the morning. But then, I'm going to regret the whole last six months. Ten years ago I was golden, and now I'm doing stock. And schlock."

"You'd better sit down, Mr Toland." I pushed him back down.

I hurried towards Billy and Jamie. "We can go," I said. "Is it still raining outside?"

"You don't want to leave your boyfriend, do you?" Billy asked sulkily.

"C'mon, guys," Jamie said. "If we don't leave soon, we'll have to build an ark."

Billy pushed past us and stalked back towards the rear exit. Jamie started after him, but Billy kept going, slamming out the outer door. I saw him for one moment illuminated against the neon and the glitter of rain.

"Go," I said to Jamie. "I have to tell Sammy I'm leaving." It was a few minutes before my shift was over, but I quickly went for my coat and signalled I was going. Sammy beckoned to me but I pretended I didn't see him. Probably asking me to stick around, but he'd forgive me if I left.

The rain slapped my cheeks as I opened the door. At first I didn't understand what I was seeing and hearing, the crunch and squeal of metal, the shattering glass. Billy was in his car and had rammed into a yellow Cadillac with New York plates. He backed up and then floored the accelerator, ramming into it again.

I ran across the parking lot. Jamie was soon at my side.

Billy's car stopped. He slumped over the steering wheel. I ran towards him, afraid he was hurt.

The car door opened and he slowly got out. Then he fell to his knees.

"Billy. . ." I ran forward, holding him up by the shoulders. "What are you doing? Are you crazy?"

He shook me off and I stumbled and almost fell. He wasn't hurt. He stood up again and lifted his face to the sky, his eyes closed. With all the rain, I couldn't tell if he was crying. His white shirt was plastered to his chest. My heart ached to see the pain on his face. "Billy. . ." I whispered his name and the sound was swallowed up by the drumming of the rain on the hood.

Suddenly, he slammed his fist into his car. I cried out. He could have broken his hand.

Jamie put his arms around him from behind and held him fast. "You've got to stop it now, Billy," he said. "Billy, do you hear me?" Jamie tightened his hold and rested his forehead against Billy's back, restraining him. "It's all right. It's all right."

"It's *not* all right!" I yelled, pulling back. "Look at Jeff's car! What are you doing?"

"What were *you* doing?" Billy spat back at me.

"My job!"

"What – did he pay you extra for that kiss, or did you just throw it in for free? Do you know what you looked like in there?"

I could see the murder in his eyes. That rage. It wasn't

surprising me any more. There was no way around it. At this moment, he hated me. When he got angry, he couldn't even see me any more. He saw a different girl, a girl who was deliberately grinding his heart into the ground.

"I can't take this any more!" I had to shout the words over the rain and wind.

"You?" He laughed. "*You* can't take it?"

"Do you think I could ever marry you, stay with someone like you?" I asked him. "Why do you keep doing this to us? What is *wrong* with you?"

I saw him register the shock of the question. He smiled at me, an empty smile. "Everything, I guess."

"I never want to see you again," I said. "This time it's over. I'm *afraid of you*!"

He pushed out of Jamie's grip and fell back against the car, his wet hair in his eyes. "That makes two of us," he said.

I almost went to him then; I even took a step forward. But just then, Jeff Toland displayed the worst timing of his career by coming out of the back door, fumbling with an umbrella, and splashing right into a puddle.

Billy looked over at him and I saw the change in his face, how the fury came roaring back. Now he had something to fight that would fight back. I saw it all, but my reflexes let me down. Before I could stop him, he pushed away from the car and raced towards Jeff.

Jeff looked up, the umbrella half open, as Billy's fist connected. The blow was so hard I heard it, the sickening sound of the sudden rearrangement of bone. Jeff fell back. I heard the thwack of his head against the concrete.

Jamie and I ran. Jamie grabbed Billy while I knelt over Jeff. His eyes were closed. His skin looked so white. With shaking fingers I tried to feel for a pulse. I looked up at Jamie. Billy's eyes were wide with horror.

"Get Billy out of here!" I screamed.

They stood frozen for a minute. Then Jamie half carried, half dragged Billy to his car. Billy kept staring back at Jeff. Jamie pushed him into the car and went around to the driver's side. I heard the engine start and the car pull away.

"Jeff!" I yelled the word into his face. "Please. Wake up. Please, please don't be dead." I started to cry, and I tried to shield the rain from his face while I talked to him.

The rain was washing away the blood on his mouth. I looked around frantically. I couldn't leave him like this, but I had to get help. I ran inside. Sammy was at the end of the bar, and I plucked at his sleeve with wet fingers.

"Jeff Toland is outside, passed out. . ."

He took one look at me and hurried away, back towards the rear door. I walked unsteadily to the phone behind the bar. I willed my shaking fingers to dial Billy's number. It rang only three times and I heard Nate's voice, sounding alert and awake.

"I need you to fix something," I said.

Six

"Dancing in a nightclub? Da will blow his stack!" Muddie said. "Oh, Kit, are you sure?"

"It's not just a nightclub – it's the Lido!" I was already starting to regret splurging on a long-distance call. I could feel my money draining with every exclamation Muddie made, from her first squeal "*Kit!*" to her "*Isn't this expensive?*" and her "*Where are you calling from?*"

Walking home, all I could think of was telling someone my news. I hadn't been lonesome until that moment, when I had nobody to tell. I'd been dying to brag, to let my family know that not only did I have a job, it was a real job, a job to envy, something glamorous, exactly the kind of job a girl from Providence would dream of getting in New York City. And who else to call but my sister? Every Sunday night we'd listened to *Manhattan Merry-Go-Round* when we were kids, listening to "all the big night spots of New York town".

I sat on the couch, wedged into a corner. The telephone cord stretched just far enough. Sitting here one day, I'd realized that the mirror on the far wall was hung high for a reason. If the curtains were open, you could catch a flash of the East River.

"He'll only know if you tell him," I added.

"I can't lie to him, Kitty."

I sighed. "I'm not saying lie. Can't you stretch a commandment once in a while? You can say you talked to me. Say I'm fine, I have an apartment now and a job. You don't have to tell him what it is. Oh, hell, I don't care if you tell him. Let him blow."

"You said *hell*."

"Damn right I did."

"Kit!" I could hear Muddie try to stifle her giggle. "You're a caution. It's so quiet here without you and Jamie."

We were both silent for a moment.

I looked at the sliver of river in the mirror. Home. It came back to me then, the apartment on Transit Street. Cramped and damp, street noise coming through the window, along with the smells of Portuguese stew and someone playing the radio. Kids down the block playing a game on the street, yelling out instructions for One Flies Up. And me, grabbing for privacy in the bathroom, tapping out shuffle ball change and time steps on the tiles while I looked in the full-length mirror Da had hung on the back of the door so I could practise. Over the years, my taps had pitted the tiles, but he'd never cared. Would he really blow his stack if he knew I was dancing in a nightclub? Probably . . . but then wouldn't he in the next breath twist it around and be proudly proclaiming to the neighbourhood that I was a Lido Doll?

"You're still mad at him?" Muddie asked.

I thought of that morning when Jamie came home, of the thin line of Da's mouth, of the way disgust had made my handsome father look ugly.

"He hasn't done a thing since I left, has he?"

"No," Muddie said, drawing out the word. "But, Kit, he feels it. Do you know, he stopped drinking. Not even a slug of whiskey from the bottle when he gets home. He's here every night on that couch, just sitting. When I come in from work, he's there. Sitting like his heart is breaking."

"I have to go, Muddie," I said.

I had to be off the phone, doing anything but talking to my sister, thinking about our father sitting, just sitting.

She either didn't hear me or ignored what I said. "It's worse than when Elena left him. Oh, that reminds me! She's back! I mean, she's back in Fox Point. She got a divorce." Muddie whispered the terrible word. "And her father won't take her in. So she's living with her sister. I ran into her yesterday; she's still so beautiful. . . Da knows she's back, I can't imagine a man feeling worse. I think he doesn't care any more what he does. . . Say – have you heard from Jamie?"

"How could I have heard – he doesn't know where I am. Have you?"

"No, not since he wrote and told us where he was. I look

54

every day for a letter. I've written him every week – I'll send you the address. Oh, I don't want to use up your money. Goodbye, then, and I'll tell Da you're settled. He'll be glad, no matter what he doesn't say."

"Bye," I said, then hung up the phone and reached for the teacup I'd balanced on the wide rolled back of the couch. As I stood, the phone cord scraped against the cup and I just barely caught it before it fell. The spoon slid off the saucer and I heard it clatter behind the couch.

I put down the cup and the phone, happy I hadn't stained the couch. I laid myself flat to fish for the spoon. I could see the glint of it and I stretched, fingers splayed, to find it. My cheek flat on the floor, I groped through the dark. My fingers slid over metal and I pulled it out.

It wasn't a spoon. It was a woman's compact, slim and silver, something you could buy at Woolworth's. That's what I thought at first. I turned it over in my hands and felt the weight of it and realized it was expensive. I opened it and saw that the mirror was cracked. The powder had dried. I snapped it shut, turned it over and saw the initials in curlicue script: *B.W.*

It had belonged to the woman who'd lived here before. Or could it have been someone else, a woman Nate had brought here? Someone with a sophisticated name that clanged with brass. Barbara, or Brenda.

I wasn't very bright, but I was starting to get wise, just by keeping my ears open. I was beginning to realize how New York worked, how the men chased their secretaries or the

Broadway dancers and brought them to discreet hotels or apartments they kept without their wife knowing. I figured Angela Benedict didn't know about this apartment. And how would she find out, if she never left the house back in Providence?

I leaned back into the pillows and looked out at the gathering dusk. I held the compact in my hand. Suddenly, I could feel someone else here, a presence. Another woman had sat here, had hung that mirror at an awkward height just so she could see the river. I shivered. I didn't know why it should have spooked me, but it did. With the compact still in my hand, I went around the apartment and turned on all the lights.

Chorus girls' dressing rooms had their own rules and their own comradeship. We were there to make ourselves beautiful, borrow lipsticks, complain about our aching feet and our boyfriends. I'd noticed a certain frost in the air during my week of rehearsals, but after my debut on Saturday night, I settled into a chair at the mirror and felt the atmosphere shift. I hadn't tripped into someone's drink, I hadn't lost my headdress in the "Hoop-De-Doo" number, and I hadn't stolen the show. I was OK.

At first, I hadn't been able to attach names to faces. Polly, Mary, Edna, Darla, Mickey, Barb, Pat. But after a week I knew them all.

"So how old are you, kid? Twenty-one, you say?"

"Yeah, and you have the papers to prove it, right?"

56

"Leave off the kid. I started when I was fifteen. Said I was eighteen."

"When was that, honey – in 1933?"

"Hardey-har-har."

"I like your hair. Is it natural?"

"You're lucky, only redhead in the line. People will remember you."

"Don't say that or Pat will dye her hair again."

"Dry up. I get more dates with blonde hair. You think I'm going to go changing a good thing?"

"Is the coffee still hot?"

"Anybody got an extra pair of stockings?"

Music to my ears. I hung up my costume and pulled on my clothes. I'd been careful to keep quiet during the week. I wanted to see how things worked. Everybody called the owner Mr D, for Dawber, which almost sounded friendly, but everyone was terrified of him. If he saw a problem, he'd tap his pinky ring against the table and someone would come running. The day before, I'd seen him throw a cabbage head at a waiter.

But Ted Roper was in charge of the Lido Dolls, of our hair and our make-up and the way we walked and even the way we smiled. "Lick your lips and show some TEETH!" he'd yell in rehearsals.

By the time I said goodnight to the manager, Joe, it was after three in the morning. I hadn't been paid yet, so I couldn't afford a taxi. The blocks stretched ahead of me and I couldn't believe how tired I was.

But after a while I got into the rhythm of it. The streets were quiet, grey and silver, and the sky was like a pearl. My footsteps echoed down a river of bluestone. Every once in a while I'd see a light in a house or apartment, and I'd wonder if someone was awake, reading, or rocking a baby.

I rounded the corner, fumbling for my key. Under the awning the door swung open and Hank and an older woman in a robe and slippers walked out. She must have been his mother. They both gaped at me.

"Hi," he said.

"Morning," I said. I was at my private entrance now, key in my hand. Hank's mother was frowning, her face tight as she took me in. I was still wearing my make-up from the show, powder and dark red lipstick and mascara. I could suddenly feel my eyelashes, thick and curled like a cartoon cow's. Just what did she think I was?

I turned my back on her, feeling the snub in my shoulder blades. I opened the door, went in and slammed it shut. Hard.

I tossed my coat and went straight to the bathroom. I creamed off the make-up, scrubbing hard. Wriggled out of my skirt and stockings and left them on the floor as I fell into bed in my slip. No. I didn't owe anybody anything. I wouldn't accept disapproval like that, ever again. I'd been there before.

Seven

Providence, Rhode Island
November 1949

Love had entered my life like a thunderclap, but it didn't knock me off my feet. I was too busy for that. I wasn't like other girls, with time on their hands to be dreamy-eyed when they discussed their Joes or Mikes or Mannys. I didn't shriek, "Turn it up!" when "Forever and Ever" came on the radio. Billy just became part of my days, woven into the time between school and my job at the luncheonette on South Main. Providence was a small enough city that he could walk me to my dance lesson downtown and then walk back to the East Side in time for his own class at Brown. After school he'd sit studying at a table while I kept him supplied with cheeseburgers and soup and sodas and cups of coffee. On Sundays we'd take off, often with Jamie, to find parks and beaches, stretches of sand and grass where we could be alone and feel as away as it got in Rhode Island. Billy always had his camera and Jamie his sketchbook, but I'd just lie back and dream.

When I emerged from school and he was waiting in his car, I didn't linger, drawing out the moment so that the other girls could see that I, only a junior, was dating a college man. I didn't draw hearts in my notebooks. The first time he told me he loved me, I didn't swoon. I laughed.

It was November. We said goodbye right by my front door. He turned and jumped off the porch on to the sidewalk. I was about to open the door when he turned back and called to me.

"Hey, Kit! I love you, too."

I walked over to the railing and leaned over. "What do you mean, 'I love you, too'?" I asked. "I didn't say I love you."

"You were thinking it."

"I was not."

A slow grin started on his face. "Fink."

"Snake."

He walked slowly back towards the porch. I walked down a step and stopped. When he came up the stairs he stayed on the third step so that he was just a bit below me. "Aw, you're just chicken," he said.

"Try me."

He put his hands on my cheeks and gently guided me down to his mouth. The kiss started, stopped, started again and kept on going. I put my hands on his shoulders so I wouldn't fall. Da would hear about this the next day at Sullivan's Bar.

From then on, we were together. He introduced me to the best spaghetti restaurant in Providence, to fried clams at the beach at Misquamicut, to lobster rolls in Watch Hill. He introduced me to the complicated rhythms of jazz and the photographers he loved, like Henri Cartier-Bresson, whose name I could hardly pronounce but whose pictures I could understand.

Unfortunately, he also introduced me to his mother.

"This is Kit, Mom," Billy said.

I held out my hand to shake, but she turned to take Billy's coat. I pretended to gesture instead. "You have a lovely house," I said.

"You're letting in a draught," she told me. "Close the door, Billy."

Her hair was tightly curled, and a bit of lipstick had been applied, an orange-red that was the wrong colour. I could still see the indentations from the bobby pins that had anchored the curlers to her scalp. She was dressed in dark green with a gold pin near her shoulder.

"We've met before," I reminded her. "In the lobby of *Carousel*."

"I don't recall," she said, and I could see not only that she was lying, but that she knew that I realized it, and she didn't care.

Nate came forward to shake my hand. "It's good to see you, Kit. How is your father?"

"He's fine, thanks."

61

There might have been a blinking sign above Angela Benedict's head reading YOU ARE A POOR IRISH GIRL – GO AWAY. She turned and led us into the living room, where tiny sandwiches had been set out with the coffee. The plan was to have a snack and go out to the dance, where we'd meet Jamie. There were four tiny tea sandwiches on a silver plate. Obviously, we were supposed to eat and run.

Billy perched on the edge of the couch. I'd never seen him so nervous. "Kit just got a job at the Riverbank downtown," he said. "She's a hostess on Saturday nights. And last night Tony Carroll, the headliner, asked her to sing, and she's become a regular part of the show! That's how good she is."

"That's wonderful," Nate said. He lit a cigarette and poured some coffee.

"I guess you enjoy being looked at," Angela said. "Me, I think a lady should stay at home. Take care of the family."

"I've been performing since I was two," I said. "You get used to it."

"I suppose so, if you're that type of person."

"What swell sandwiches," Billy said. "I love a devilled ham sandwich."

"You have a lovely home," I said to Angela. Then I remembered that I'd said it already. "Beautiful furniture."

"Angela knows exactly what she wants," Nate said. "She describes it and sends over fabric, and Greenaway's makes it up for her."

"When I was little, we did an advertisement for

62

Greenaway's Department Store," I told them. "My da had lined up the endorsement: The Corrigan Three Love Greenaway's Goods! They promised to pay us in trade, so we thought we'd get a new bed or two, or a kitchen table. They gave us pillows instead, the ones that didn't sell. For a while we didn't have a couch, but we had pillows. Ugliest pillows you ever saw."

Billy forced a chuckle, but nobody had anything to say about that. I don't know why I'd just blurted out that story. This was supposed to win them over?

"Billy, pour some coffee for yourself," Angela said. "Warm yourself up before you go."

We sipped our coffee and nibbled at the sandwiches. I couldn't think of another thing to say, especially since the woman was willing me out of the room.

After barely ten minutes, Billy stood and said, "We'd better be going, we don't want to miss the fun."

"Now be careful driving," Angela said. "There's supposed to be snow tonight."

"Oh, Billy's a great driver," I said.

A strangled silence fell. Billy pulled at his tie, looked at his shoes, then his watch.

I stood up quickly. My skirt brushed against the coffee cup and it rattled in the saucer. Angela jumped.

We got our coats and scarves and said goodnight and escaped into the frosty air.

"Sorry," he said once we were out of earshot. "That was awful."

"I bombed," I said. "Was it the pillow story?"

"I loved the pillow story." He took my arm and pressed it against his side. "Tell it again."

It was a relief to laugh. "Why did everyone freeze up when I said you were a great driver? Should I be bringing a crash helmet?"

Billy gripped my elbow as he led me around a patch of ice. "She doesn't trust my driving. Ever since Michael was killed."

I wanted to kick myself down the street. Billy's cousin Michael had died in a car crash when he was sixteen.

"No wonder she hates me," I said.

Billy sighed. "She hasn't left the house in five years," he said. "She went to my cousin's funeral and then she never left the house again. At first we didn't notice it. She'd always make me run errands, buy the groceries, and told me not to tell my dad. She even sent me to the dress shop a couple of times. I almost got beat up on the way home, carrying that bag. But my dad figured it out. Now everybody pretends it's all right. All the family – they say she has headaches, poor Angela. The doctor comes to the house, the food is delivered, her clothes, they just send them over, all the stores on Federal Hill know Angela Benedict. God forbid she gets a toothache, she'll rip it out with pliers. So don't take it personally."

But I did. It *was* personal. I'd seen hatred in that woman's eyes. "I guess she doesn't want to let go of you."

"She won't let go of anything." We reached the end of

64

the driveway and stopped by the car. He stepped back from me and jammed his hands in his pockets. "I just want to punch something."

"That's why you're on the boxing team."

"I quit."

"You didn't tell me. Don't you like it any more?"

He swung open the door and held it for me. "I started to like hitting the other guy a little bit too much."

The interior light illuminated his face, his full mouth so taut. I touched his arm. "It's all right. It's just family. We'll make our own one day."

"Not here. Not in Providence. We'd never have a life here." He looked back at the house. "You never talk about what my father does."

I shrugged. "He's not you."

"We pack away lies in that house like you pack away Christmas. We put them in boxes and tape them over. My mother is a great hostess – that's what everyone says. She never comes to anybody's house, but she cooks like crazy on holidays. My father is a stand-up guy, defending people in the neighbourhood. You should see the fruit baskets we get at Christmas, the liquor, the presents . . . for what? For getting some murderer acquitted? Do you think he sleeps at night, my dad? I hear him walking around. . ."

"Billy—"

"Can you honour your father if you think he's a louse? And he wants me to be him! Benedict and Benedict, that's his dream."

"It's OK if it's not yours."

"I want to take pictures, I want to travel the world—"

"You can do anything." I said the words firmly. "Anything you want."

He dipped his head and rested his forehead against mine. "You put up with a lot from me. I don't want you to have to put up with my family, too."

"They're part of you."

"No." He shook his head, back and forth, his cool forehead moving against mine. "You're my family."

When he kissed me, his lips were so cold they made me shiver.

"I hate devilled ham," I whispered.

We laughed, and something eased in him. He took my arm and helped me into the car, even though I didn't need it. The upholstery felt stiff and cold through my coat. He closed the door and walked around to the driver's side. I watched him through the windshield. I never got used to how beautiful he was. I had watched him box once – only once – and I'd seen how the elegance of his movements translated to a ring. He had been a beautiful thing to watch – until the blood began to flow, and I had to run out of the room.

Later, at the dance, we held each other closer than we ever had. All he had to do was touch the small of my back and I shuddered. With his lips close to my cheek, he said, "Thank you for tonight."

"For what?"

"For not kicking the tray of sandwiches over. For not dumping your coffee in her lap. For not insulting her the way she insulted you. For trying to tell a funny story. For making me feel OK."

"Just OK?"

"For making me feel like I can do anything." His arms tightened around me. "As long as I have you."

Eight

New York City
November 1950

The call came in the morning while I was deeply asleep. I stumbled to the phone and said hello.

"Will you accept a collect call from Virginia?" the operator asked, and that woke me up.

"Yes, operator, put it through."

"I got your letter." Billy never said hello. I'd teased him about it so many times. He just opened with what he wanted to say. Over the hiss of long distance, I could hear the nervousness in his voice. "I was so glad to get it."

"I wanted you to know where I was."

"I was thinking . . . I have leave. Before we ship out. I could come up to New York. Maybe around Thanksgiving."

My heart was thudding, banging. I put my hand over it.

"Would that be all right?" he asked.

"Yes. That would be all right."

"I'll call back with details when I know. Kit?"

"Yes?"

"I woke you."

"It's all right."

I hung on to the receiver, picturing his face. I closed my eyes, remembering how his mouth moved.

"There's so much to say. I can't talk. I'm in town, in a drugstore. I just have a minute. Thought I'd grab it before I lost my nerve. I have to go."

"I'll be waiting for you."

"I like the sound of that." He stopped, and I listened to the hiss of the line. I wanted to hear his breath. His voice sounded so far away and yet it hit me in every muscle, every bone. "I'll let you know."

The phone clicked. He never said goodbye, either.

I put down the receiver and sank down on the floor, hugging my knees. I stared at the phone. I would have to call Nate and tell him. I'd thought that would be easy, picking up the phone with the simple news that Billy was coming. But now that the moment was here, I couldn't do it. This was my news, not Nate's.

But he had made it his, somehow, and I had let him.

I was sitting in the kitchen in the early afternoon, stretching out the kinks in my hips and back, when I saw a fishing line bobbing down, down, outside the window. A hook dangled, a piece of paper stuck in the barb. I threw open the window and reached out, detaching the paper carefully. Then I looked up. Hank sat on the fire escape above. He didn't look down. Instead he pretended to be absorbed in his book, the fishing rod held casually in his hands.

I read the note.

Sunday Dinner with the Greeley Family 5 p.m.?

I lived on canned soup and melba toast and cottage cheese, tea and toast and apples. There was nothing in my icebox for supper but an orange.

I'd thought on my day off I'd be roaming the streets, travelling down to Greenwich Village, exploring the parts of the city that Billy and I had talked about, the museums and jazz clubs and coffeehouses. But instead I stayed inside, reluctant somehow to go on my own.

I thought of Hank's mother, the way her eyes had narrowed when she'd seen me close to dawn in my stage make-up. What had he had to do, to get her to agree to ask me to dinner?

Well, let her cook for me, then.

I scrawled *Gratefully accepted* and sent it back up. This time when I looked up, Hank was reading my note. He looked down and grinned.

The Greeleys' apartment was stuffed with books. Bookshelves in the foyer, in the living room, even in the dining room. I was suddenly aware that there was not one book in my apartment. I tried to remember the last one I'd read. Or had pretended to read. *A Tale of Two Cities*, maybe? Actually, I'd never finished it. Muddie had told me the whole story one night while I'd washed out our underwear.

I'd dressed carefully for the evening, drawing my hair back in a ponytail and wearing just a touch of make-up. Plaid skirt, white blouse, flats. Take that, Mrs Greeley.

Hank wore a grey crewneck sweater and grey trousers. He'd tried to wet his hair down with water, but it was already starting to curl. I realized that I was wrong about his eyes and hair; they were the colour of dark honey.

A man didn't so much as rise from the armchair as push himself up with his arms, as though he were too heavy to lift. Yet he was slender, his belly flat in the plaid shirt he had tucked into his trousers. He had Hank's narrow, boyish face, and his eyes were too soft behind black-framed glasses. He shook my hand and looked into my face in a curious way.

"Hank tells me you live alone."

"Well, my dad is up in Providence and can't leave his job, so. . ." I smiled. "Don't worry, I have family friends who look in on me."

"And now you have us."

A vein began to pulse in Mrs Greeley's forehead. "Tomato juice?" she asked, pronouncing it *to-mah-to*. I nodded, although I'd actually never tasted it. It wasn't bad, cold and lemony and thick.

Mr Greeley slid back into the armchair. I wondered if he was sick. There was something in the air here that I didn't understand.

"So, Hank tells me you work," Mr Greeley said.

"At the Lido," I said. "I'm a dancer."

"A dancer! Did you hear that, Nancy?"

"I'm right here, Sam."

"But you don't go to school? Education is so important."

Mrs Greeley got up abruptly and said she had to check the roast.

"I was just in a Broadway play – *That Girl From Scranton!*"

"I haven't heard of that show. We don't get around much any more," Mr Greeley said apologetically.

With a lead-in like that, I couldn't resist. I hummed the tune of "Don't Get Around Much Anymore".

Mr Greeley brightened and sang out the first line. It brought back a world to me, of music on the radio, of dancing with Billy on a Saturday night.

"Please, Dad," Hank said. "You'll crack the glasses." Smiling, he turned to me. "So you sing, too?"

"I'm a better dancer, but sure," I said. "I've been taking voice lessons since I was nine – plus tap, ballroom, ballet, jazz. I want to start acting lessons now that I'm in New York."

Mrs Greeley came back in and sat on the edge of her chair as though she was ready to jump up any second, and it wasn't for the roast. "Perhaps you could sing for us," she said. I could tell – she didn't want me to be good. She wanted to expose me, not show me off. "Something from the show perhaps? *That Girl From. . .*"

"Scranton," I said. "It wasn't very good."

I sang a few lines.

Let's go to the Dappledown Dreamery
Right next door to the cold ice creamery
Don't even stop to admire the scenery. . .

I stopped. "You see? Pretty awful."

"It's sort of catchy," Hank said politely.

"Do you know 'The Way You Look Tonight'?" Mr Greeley asked. "Always loved that song."

"I'll play if you'll sing," Hank said. "C'mon."

Hank sat at the piano and I sat next to him.

I loved the song, too. It was the saddest love song. It was like the person was singing how perfect a moment was even while they knew they were going to lose it. I sang it gently, softly, and when the last note faded, I turned and saw that I'd won over Mr Greeley, at least.

"That was lovely," he said. "Wasn't it, sweetheart?"

"Yes." For the first time, Mrs Greeley smiled at me. "It was."

And the lamps seemed to glow a little more golden, and the room seemed to come closer around us, because suddenly we were all getting along.

Hank swung into a popular tune, "Don't Tell Me".

73

Don't tell me this is just for tonight,
Don't tell me that hearts are meant to be light.
Your dreamy smile, your shelt'ring arms tell me what's
true.
No turning back, no second chance, forever us, forever
you. . .

"It's funny, you remind me of someone," Mrs Greeley said. "I just can't place it."

"Rita Hayworth," Mr Greeley said.

"Oh, Sam, really." Mrs Greeley shook her head. "I'll think of it."

I decided to ask the question I'd come here to ask. "Hank said the apartment has been empty for years," I started.

"Oh, yes," Mrs Greeley said. "Since the war ended. We don't know why. Especially because of the housing shortage, we thought for sure it would be rented. Such a shame; we even asked about it because we knew a family looking for an apartment. One of the other teachers."

"I didn't realize you were teachers."

Mr and Mrs Greeley exchanged a glance.

"Well. Not right now. We, uh. . ."

"Mom and Dad lost their jobs," Hank said. "In the purge."

I had no idea what he was talking about.

"The Board of Education has been investigating teachers for what they call 'subversive activities'. With the

74

help of the FBI," Hank explained. "They targeted Mom and Dad."

"You go to a meeting or a rally ten years ago, and they come after you," Mr Greeley said. "I'm not a Red, Kit. I'm just on the side of the working man. I have the class read *The Grapes of Wrath*, and the next thing I know I'm under investigation. And Mrs Greeley? They go for her next. She's interested in politics, but four hundred years ago. Cromwell is her bailiwick."

I wasn't sure what a bailiwick was, and I only vaguely remembered Cromwell from European History, but I didn't want to look like a dumbbell in front of the Greeleys. "You mean you were fired?"

"I was the one interested in politics before the war," Mr Greeley said. He straightened up and leaned forward, so I knew he didn't mind talking about it. Mrs Greeley, on the other hand, just clutched her glass of tomato juice and shot him a look that told him to shut up. He didn't. "Nancy got called in because she's married to me. She refused to answer about her 'affiliations', they call it. So she got the boot, too." He clapped his hands. "But it's all right, we're looking for work in the private schools. We'll get a job next year. It's just that they're already in the term, so that's why they're not talking to us. We're getting by. Mrs Greeley has a secretarial job, I'm delivering milk and cheese in the mornings, and Hank is lending a hand. We're making honest money."

"Maybe if you two didn't still go on those Teachers

Union picket lines and Ban the Bomb meetings they'd call us back," Mrs Greeley said, holding on to her smile by her teeth. "You know the FBI is watching who's there."

"We've got to stand up for what we believe in, Nan," Mr Greeley said. "They tried to shut us up, but they can't. We're allowed to have political beliefs in this country, or are we going back to your beloved Cromwellian days? Off with our heads, is that it?"

"So, how did you find out about the apartment, Kit?" Mrs Greeley asked me. I could tell she wanted to change the subject, but she'd managed to change it to a subject I didn't want to talk about.

"A family friend," I said.

"Ah, our mysterious landlord, I bet," Mr Greeley said. "We've never met him. We just mail in our cheques to a management company."

They waited politely for me to tell them who the landlord was, but they could wait until the roast burned.

"So it was a couple who lived in the apartment before me?" I asked. Mrs Greeley wasn't the only one who could change the subject.

She suddenly leaned forward. "I know why you seem familiar. How uncanny. You look a little like the woman who used to live in the apartment. We'd just moved in, so I only saw her once or twice before they moved away. A married couple, he was in the army, stationed somewhere down south. He came up on weekends. But they were so quiet."

"Newlyweds," Mr Greeley said. "Kept to themselves. The Wickhams."

"No, it was the name of a hotel – the Warwicks! And of course they had their own private entrance, so we didn't bump into them in the lobby. We only had one conversation. She wasn't very social. But, oh, I remember the last day, I saw her just for a minute, moving out . . . she was so changed. Her husband was dead, she said. How sad, when it was so close to the end of the war. What was her name, Sam?"

"Don't remember. I think I only saw her a couple of times. Never met him. I can't see the resemblance myself."

"Bridget," Mrs Greeley said. "We said we'd keep in touch, but of course you never do, do you. . ." The buzzer on the stove rang, and she popped up. "Be right back. No, sit down, dear."

Now I was a dear. Things were looking up. And now I knew who owned the silver compact. A wife of a soldier, not a mistress of Nate's. That made me feel better about him.

Mr Greeley leaned forward. "Say, Kit, do you know a song from *Carousel*? Nan and I saw that on Broadway."

Hank sat down at the piano, and I slid in next to him. I sang my favourite song from the show, "What's the Use of Wond'rin'?" It's a song that's all about how love can make anybody stupid. That you can fall in love with the completely wrong person and know it, but he's still yours, and you're still his.

77

That night when I got back to my apartment I took out the silver compact and ran my fingers along the initials. Bridget Warwick. She had lived here and drunk her coffee at the kitchen table. She'd squeezed out every minute of time with her husband. They'd met here and loved here, and here is where she probably got the telegram that told her he'd been killed. I wished I could send the compact back to her. He'd given it to her, I knew that; it wasn't something a woman would buy for herself.

Could I do that? I wondered. Could I be that wife, sitting at the table, waiting, always waiting . . . and then getting the terrible news? *We regret to inform you. . .*

I didn't know if I was that brave. Even for love.

Nine

Providence, Rhode Island
March 1945

"Hurry up, Kitty, the taxi's here. Do you have to use the bathroom?" Delia tugged on her gloves without glancing at me. Which was a good thing, because I'd left off my socks. I wanted people to think I was wearing stockings, and hoping that though I was twelve they'd think I was fifteen.

Delia had dressed up, too, in a dress she'd bought when her boss had got her a job in the War Department in Washington, DC, last summer. It was emerald with black satin buttons all the way down the back. She wore a dark green hat with a black veil and fresh new black kid gloves. She'd pulled her red hair back in an elegant French twist. She was even wearing lipstick. This view of my aunt as glamorous was startling, as though Delia had suddenly burst into vibrant song. I was used to seeing her in an assortment of greys, the colours of winter skies. Delia hid her beauty, just like the nuns she visited in Vermont once a month for retreats filled with solitude and prayer. "So I can keep my sanity before the lot of you send me around the bend to the crazy house," she'd tell us, smiling as she headed out with her small suitcase and her train ticket.

She paused at the mirror she'd hung near the front door so "maybe you won't look like tinkers on the way to school if you get a good look at yourselves". Jamie and Muddie and I had long ago outgrown the mattress we'd all slept on in the closet. With Da's overtime and a bit of luck, the increase in the family fortunes coincided with the Duffys moving out of the adjoining apartment to live with their daughter in Pawtucket. We took on their space as well. Since the landlord had thrown up a wall in order to create two out of a full-floor apartment, Da simply knocked it down again. Now Delia had her own room, as did Jamie, and Muddie and I shared the small back bedroom overlooking the yard.

A taxi to the station! I couldn't believe it. I held myself very still in the back seat so Delia wouldn't correct me. It was hard not to ask a question, but I could tell Delia was nervous about missing the train. She kept checking the delicate watch on her wrist. Maybe she, too, was nervous about going to a real Broadway play.

Well, it wasn't on Broadway, not yet. The two of us were going to New Haven for the try-out of a new musical called *Carousel*, and I'd read that there would be a real carousel onstage. Delia had bought the tickets, shocking everyone in the family because she never did anything extravagant

80

and didn't approve of my voice and dance lessons, even though she paid for them. "It's time Kit knows what she's in for," she said. Leave it to Delia to turn a pleasure trip into a warning.

As we sat on the train, I was content to look out the window and not talk. Delia seemed on edge, and when I said I had to go to the bathroom, she snapped, "Oh, for heaven's sake!"

I looked down at my bare legs. I had a scab on one knee, and my calves were dotted with bruises. I realized how silly I was, believing that people would think I was older. Delia's sleek legs crossed and recrossed, her stockings whispering. I could see a man down the aisle looking at her legs, and how Delia's head jerked away, how she managed to convey to that stranger that he was a lout for even stealing a glance. I lifted my chin, too, trying to look as disapproving as she did.

Outside the theatre in New Haven, people were milling under the lights of the marquee, the women all dressed up in mink and high heels. I'd never seen such glamour. I could pick out the ones who had driven up from Manhattan, and they were so perfect I almost lost my breath. I felt very Rhode Island, and was embarrassed that I'd imagined anyone ever saying, "Who is that beautiful red-haired girl in the blue dress?"

Delia moved stiffly through the crowd, the tickets held tight in her gloved hand. "Follow me and don't get lost," she instructed.

We pushed through into the lobby. It was smaller than

81

the glittering palace I'd pictured. My nose filled with perfume and hair spray, a delicious smell.

"Wait, Delia! Can't we—"

"Let's find our seats. We don't want to miss our curtain."

"But it's only a quarter to."

"Shh!"

We were up in the balcony, high up, but it didn't matter. Delia sat the way she always did – straight, her spine not touching the chair. She looked below to where the audience was beginning to file in. I craned my neck, picking out the most elegant dresses.

The lights dimmed and the music began with a swell that felt like a wave against my body. Tears instantly spurted to my eyes and ran down my cheeks. It was a waltz, but like no waltz I'd ever heard.

It was all up there, everything I knew and everything I didn't know yet. Love and lies and cruelty and beauty, and the music that could be like a bruise way deep inside. When the curtain thundered down for intermission, I couldn't speak for a minute.

"What do you think will happen?" I asked Delia. "Why is Billy Bigelow being such a louse when he loved Julie so much?"

"Love isn't enough, I guess," Delia said.

"Sure it is," I said. I couldn't understand a world where it wasn't.

She stood up. "It's not over. Let's go hear what everyone says in the lobby."

I trailed after her, the music still in my head.

"I think the show is a hit," Delia murmured, her gaze darting around the lobby. Her cheeks glowed pink from excitement.

Through the crowd I spotted Nate Benedict. It had been three years since I'd seen him last, but I couldn't mistake his profile with the flattened nose. He stood with that same small woman in a tweed coat with a brooch of red stones. They weren't talking to each other, the woman looking down at her programme while he scanned the lobby. I would have taken him for one of the crowd from Manhattan if I hadn't known him. His gaze moved past us, then snapped back.

Delia touched her hair. "Well, he's seen us. We have to say hello now." She linked her arm with me and brought me forward, almost pushing me. "Hello, Mr Benedict."

"Hello, Miss Corrigan. Angela, you remember Miss Corrigan? My wife," Nate said to us. "And this is Kitty, isn't it? All grown up. Are you enjoying the play?"

"It's so sad," I said. "I thought musicals would be cheerful. Especially one with a carousel in it."

"Yes, you'd think so, wouldn't you?"

I hummed the tune of "If I Loved You", then sang a few lines. I couldn't remember the dates of the Revolutionary War or one scrap of geography, but I could remember a song. "Isn't it romantic how he sings that she'll walk away in the mist, and she'll never know how he feels?"

"But she doesn't walk away," Delia said. "She stays.

That's her mistake." She wasn't under the same spell I was, that was clear.

"I have a headache." Mrs Benedict hadn't even looked at us. "I want to go home now." Without waiting for a word from her husband, she pushed through the people in the lobby.

"Ah," Nate said. "It appears that there will be no second act. Here." He handed me a box of mints.

"But they're yours."

He bent down then, right at my eye level. "I think the lesson of the play is that we can't always have what we want. Maybe it's good that you learned it now."

He moved off through the crowd, out towards the doors to the street.

"What did he mean?" I asked. "And wasn't she rude? She must have felt really sick. Do you think she had to throw up?"

Delia turned abruptly. "Let's get back to our seats. Hurry up now, you don't want to miss the opening number."

I followed, tearing at the top of the box of mints. I felt the sharp taste of peppermint explode in my mouth. We settled back into our seats, not talking, just waiting in suspense for the first notes of the orchestra.

The next act began, just as dark and sad as the first part. I cried again, sopping up my tears with the edge of my cardigan. We'd run out of tissues because Delia was crying, too.

*

We stood on the train platform. The music from the play still vibrated in my body and I tapped out the rhythms of the songs, making my feet move to the ballet. The girl who played Louise Bigelow wasn't that much older than I was. I could dance that part in a few years. I sucked on the last mint, feeling it crumble in my mouth in a satisfying way.

"Is he rich, Mr Benedict?" I asked. "He was wearing a camel hair coat, and I think that pin had rubies in it, the one his wife was wearing."

"Stop asking me questions about him. I hardly know him." Delia looked at her watch. "Where is the train?"

"This was the best day of my life. I'm going to be on Broadway someday. Do you think I could be, Delia?"

Delia looked down the track for the train.

I began to sing the lyrics of "What's the Use of Wond'rin'?" piecing together the parts of the song I could remember. It was the saddest love song I could imagine – something about how love could be false or true, but you had to love him anyway, and that was that.

Delia whirled and slapped me across the face. I was nearly sent to the ground, not so much by the ferocity of it but the surprise. Delia had never struck any of us. This wasn't a spank on the rear to give us a little propulsion to set the table. This was a slap, a grown-up slap of anger and frustration. Tears sprang to my eyes. My cheek felt as though it had burst into flame.

Delia's eyes glittered with what looked like fever.

"Stop your noise," she said. "I've had enough, do you understand? I've had enough."

We were peppered with questions from a sleepy Jamie and Muddie when we got home. Da was asleep, deep into the cushions of the couch. I could hardly talk. Delia went into her room and closed the door.

Late that night I woke and went to the bathroom. The door was shut but not locked. I pushed it open.

Delia sat in the tub, the water up to her waist. Da had left his shaving things on the tub as usual – he liked to shave in the tub. I saw the sharp glitter of the razor. There was a towel on the floor, which surprised me, because Delia was fussy about things like towels.

Steam rose from the water and I saw the pale perfection of her skin flushed from the heat. Her breasts were full and rosy. Her hair was loose and streamed into the water.

That's when I noticed she was crying. She turned her head and looked at me and I saw it was hard for her to focus. She'd been lost in a dream, or a memory, and we stared at each other through the steam.

The water stirred as she lifted a hand, and I thought she would cover herself, but for once she had no shame. She lifted that hand as if to entreat me, or apologize, I still don't know.

I backed up and shut the door.

Ten

New York City
November 1950

Ten o'clock in the morning and the knock was at the door to the street, not the door off the kitchen that led to the lobby. I was barely awake, and I yawned my way to the door. I peeked through and saw Nate looking over his shoulder. He was carrying a load of shopping bags.

I opened the door and he stepped in right away.

"I took the liberty," he said.

"What's this?"

He went into the living room and put down the shopping bags. He began to take out boxes and dump them on the couch and the floor, flipping the lids off and taking some of the items out of the tissue paper quickly as he talked.

"I have a client, someone I've known for years. Last year he sent his daughter off to college with a trunkful of clothes. Only she lived in jeans and sweatshirts and ran off

87

with some poet. Dropped out of Smith." The beautiful clothes were tossed against the cushions and the carpets now, and I could hardly speak, they were so perfect. Skirts and dresses, several pairs of high-heeled pumps, a green cocktail dress, a beautiful camel coat with pearl buttons. "So they go into her room, and they see that she didn't wear one single thing they'd bought for her. You should have seen the parents – they came into my office, practically crying. Begged me to take the clothes – find someone who could use them. If I didn't take them, they were going to throw them away. I was coming down to New York – so I thought of you."

He held out the camel coat. "Try it. I don't know anything about sizes, but it looked like it would fit. I hope it's not out of date."

"They could take the clothes back to the stores."

"They're a year old! They can't take them back. That's the point. Come on – I saw how cold you were in that jacket you have."

The shapeless navy jacket I'd worn for two years already, a schoolgirl's jacket. I gingerly slipped my arms into the thick sleeves of the coat, lined in satin. I'd never felt something so luxurious.

"Nothing but the best for a Smith girl. There you go." He wasn't even looking at me, he was checking his watch, like he'd done his good deed for the day and he was congratulating himself on how he'd managed to fit it in.

The green silk cocktail dress was just my colour. I checked the size on the black suede pumps. Perfect. And the tailored sleeveless black wool dress – it was just like the ones I saw on the other girls, a sophisticated dress, a New York dress. There was even a pair of fawn-coloured slacks and a matching cardigan. New York style, all spread out on my couch. As I stared at a white tailored blouse I realized I didn't just want these clothes, I hungered for them. It was like eating honey from a spoon.

"Have you heard from Billy?"

"He called. He might get leave around Thanksgiving."

His gaze became sharp, focused. "When did he call?"

"The other morning. I didn't tell you because he didn't know when he could get here." I wanted to bite my tongue. I hated the way I sounded, rushing to explain things. Was I supposed to report everything right away?

He nodded and pulled on his gloves. He pointed to another box. "In there are . . . some other things."

I peeked inside the box. I saw bras and panties and girdles and slips, lace-edged, satin, white and black and cream. I blushed and quickly looked away.

Nate was heading towards the foyer. I didn't think he'd seen me looking.

"I have an appointment. You let me know when you hear when Billy's coming. Right?"

"I told you I would."

"One other thing." I noticed now that there was a small suitcase by the door. "I want to leave this here for today.

Someone will pick it up at six o'clock, before you leave for the club."

"But—" I stopped and looked at the suitcase. I wanted to refuse, but I wasn't sure why. And how could I, standing here in my new coat? "All right."

"Enjoy the clothes."

I couldn't wait until he was out the door. Having him here spoiled the pretty apartment, the beautiful clothes.

He paused and looked back at me, his hand on the knob. There was something in his eyes. I was suddenly embarrassed, caught doing something wrong, like a cat lapping milk out of the creamer instead of its own bowl.

"It looks like it's made for you," he said.

I opened my mouth to say something, but he put on his hat and went out.

I hurried to the suitcase and hefted it. I flicked the latch. It was locked.

Was it the clothes? In the next week, New York became everything I wanted, as I lost my fear and learned how to navigate the city streets outside my own neighbourhood. I figured out the subway. I heard about the best dance classes and signed up, and I learned the twisting narrow streets of the Village and that if I sat in a café and asked for coffee it would be the most delicious I'd ever tasted and no one would bother me.

In the dance classes I was up against girls who were just as pretty, just as talented, some taller, some curvier, some more supple, and all of them more stylish. There was a look I didn't have, but the clothes were helping. The girls helped, too; in class we were all just working hard to be better, and after class I swapped stories and tips on how to pad dance shoes and the cheapest places to buy them.

I had to work twice as hard as the others. I had to not rush in but hang back and pick up whatever I could. It was a crash course in how to be a New York girl – how to eat lunch at the Automat, how to avoid snagging your stockings on the subway, how to ignore wolf whistles and catcalls, how to keep yourself close and not give out your smiles to passers-by, how to carve out your privacy and never, ever feel lonely.

I wasn't going to feel lonely. I was clear on that. If on a wet afternoon I started to think of Muddie and Da and Jamie and get teary, I put on my coat and went out. If I thought of Billy, I told myself I would see him and then I'd know if we could be together again. Until then, I wouldn't let missing him stop me from taking what the city held out. I was in the middle of living my dream, and what kind of a fool would I be if I didn't roll around in it like a puppy in fresh grass?

I told myself all these things as I buttoned my camel coat and adjusted my hat in the mirror. I didn't look at my eyes. It would be too hard to keep my cheerfulness going. The truth was, I was used to having a companion. I was a triplet. There was always somebody in line for the

91

bathroom, sure, but there was always somebody to go to the movies with. "Better quarrelling than lonesome," Delia used to tell us, and now I knew what she meant.

Jamie had been by my side since I was born. Nobody had replaced him, not the gigglers at school, not the other dancers at Madame Flo's. We could, just with a look, know exactly what the other was thinking. He could lift one eyebrow at a situation and send me into howls of laughter. We'd gone through every first together, from first teeth to first dance, when he'd been my escort.

I missed him. I knew how much he would love this city. I wanted him here with me to get lost in the crazy streets of the Village, where West Fourth Street could cross West Tenth and no New Yorker even blinked. I'd never gone on a journey before without him. Even falling in love – I'd had Jamie by my side the whole way. He had been Billy's best friend, and mine, too.

If somebody had told me six months ago that I wouldn't be in contact with my brother, I would have laughed at such a notion. But what would Da have done, years ago, if someone had told him that his sister would break his heart and then just disappear?

And so there were the nights, falling into bed exhausted but awake, still with the noise and heat of the club in my head, when I looked at my slippers lined up ready for my feet, my robe at the end of the bed, and it was like I saw my future as an old maid. I told myself I was ridiculous, but I couldn't shake it. I would end up like Aunt Delia.

I don't remember exactly when I noticed him first, because he looked like every other man in a dark overcoat and a hat. Sometimes he was alone, sometimes he was with one other man. They walked down the other side of the street, and sometimes they'd stop in front of the building across the street, underneath the awning.

I was peeking out at them from the lobby door when Hank walked up behind me.

"It's the Feds," he said. "They're there for my parents." He shrugged. "We're used to it – they photograph the teachers' rallies, too."

"So why do you keep going to them?"

"Because my dad has lots of friends in the union," Hank said. "They tried to help him when he got fired. He wouldn't abandon them just because he's scared."

"Your dad is scared?"

"Sure. He just doesn't talk about it." He looked at his feet, then up at me. "You know, I get up really early to help my dad do the deliveries. I could meet you and walk you home sometimes and still be back in time."

"You don't have to do that. I'm fine. And what would your parents say?"

Suddenly, he looked older, not the schoolboy I thought he was. "I don't care what they say. I'm coming."

*

After the show Ted came in to give us pointers. I'd been a Lido Doll for over two weeks now, and I still wasn't used to being in my bra and tights when he came in. I quickly dived behind the wardrobe rack. A couple of the girls – Darla and Mickey, I think – snickered at me. I guess I was more modest than they were. They walked around practically naked without a second thought.

Ted popped out again and Mickey said, "Honey, he's a fairy. He couldn't care less. He's in love with Arthur Frye."

"The actor?" I squeaked. "In all those Westerns?"

She laughed again and patted my shoulder. "There are more things in heaven and earth, Horatio."

"What are you telling the kid, Mickey?" Darla asked as she handed her costume to Sonia. "Who's Horatio? Did Ted break up with Artie? What's the news?"

Mickey rolled her eyes. "Just because I'm a chorus girl, I can't know Shakespeare? I'm an actress."

"Who's talking Shakespeare?"

"I am. That's the point. It's *Hamlet*. Oh, never *mind*. I was telling the kid from Rhode Island that she now lives in Manhattan, USA, and to keep her eyes open. There's lots of ways to live, and she's going to see them all."

"Well, sure." Edna stepped into her pumps. "You see all types. Just the other day on the subway. . ."

Edna went on with her story, and with a raise of arched eyebrows from Mickey, I realized I didn't have to listen.

I slipped into the robe I kept at the club just before Ted

popped his head back in. When he headed for me, I retied it nervously, afraid I'd done something wrong.

"Mr D wants to see you up in the lounge," he murmured.

I looked at him in the mirror and saw my own apprehension. The lounge was upstairs, the private part of the club, where celebrities and the best customers went if they wanted a quiet table away from the crowd, or to keep the party going after hours.

I got my first smile from Ted. "Don't worry, beautiful, you did fine. All you have to do is have a drink – a soft drink. Then you can go home."

Ted moved away, dispensing compliments as he went.

"It's all right, sweetie," Barb said. "Mr D likes to meet the new girls."

Darla frowned. "Did you wear a good dress to work? If you go up to the lounge, you should look like a glamour-puss."

I shook my head.

"Don't worry, we've got a few numbers stashed here for cases like this."

Within a few minutes, I'd squeezed into a flame-coloured brocade cocktail dress.

"Sonia, don't we have matching shoes for these somewhere?" Pat called, searching on the shelves. "Kit, what size are you?"

"Seven," Sonia answered, giving me a pair of matching shoes. "Mr Benedict asked your size just the other day."

"I hope he went to I. Miller," Darla said. She handed me the shoes.

Why had Nate asked my shoe size? And why did he feel so free to talk to Sonia? Was he that much of an insider at the club? I thought uneasily of the clothes and shoes Nate had brought. Had he told me the truth about them?

"Don't look so nervous." Polly grinned at me. Without her make-up on, she looked freckled and young, her hair swept back and tucked behind her ears. "Mr D's not a wolf, he's a family man, so you don't have to worry about that. Just have a club soda. It'll take ten minutes, tops. He'll slip you a ten spot for the cab home, too."

Darla and Mickey and Polly patted and primped me and sent me up the back stairs with a gentle push. They watched like a trio of aunts as I hesitated on the landing, then made shooing motions with their hands until I kept going, up the last flight, down the threadbare green carpet, straight to the lounge.

Cigarette smoke swirled in the dim light. A trio softly played "What Did I Do".

Mr D was across the room at a small table, bald spot shining, one hand waving a cigar held down low in the V of his thick short fingers. There was a dapper man sitting with him, his hair combed straight back, smoking a cigarette. I saw the singer Johnnie Ray sitting with the comedian Jerry Temple. Other famous faces were sprinkled around, people I knew from reading the gossip columns –

96

debutantes and society folks. It was *Manhattan Merry-Go-Round* come to life, and I had a fierce wish that Muddie were here with me. I felt unsteady in the unfamiliar heels and my own nervousness.

A hand grazed my arm, then pressed it. I turned and saw Nate.

"I saw the show tonight," he told me. "You were good."

"Thanks."

"Now there are just a few things I need you to do."

Not again. I had handed off the suitcase a week ago, and Nate had dropped off a package last week that I had to give to a large man with a nose like a sweet potato. I didn't know what had happened to his promise to leave me alone.

"I'm supposed to sit with Mr D—"

"Don't worry about Mr D."

Nate said it with such authority that it took me aback for a moment, and I realized that I didn't know who was really in charge here.

He gestured to my right, at a table well away from the band. I instantly recognized the man sitting there – Dex Hamilton, the columnist. There was a microphone on a stand on his table, and he was talking to the singer Dinah Shore. He ran a radio show right from this room, three nights a week, called *Nightlife After Dark*. Dinah Shore moved away, Mr D nodded at him, and Dex beckoned me.

I pointed to my chest, as if to say, *Who, me?*

Yes, me.

He beckoned more frantically while he spoke into the

microphone, and I quickly moved through the tables. I'd been on the radio plenty of times in Providence, but this was New York, and it was Dex Hamilton, who was almost as big as Walter Winchell when it came to selling papers.

"And now, ladies and gentlemen, here's the newest Lido Doll, Miss Kit Corrigan. Miss Corrigan is five feet five inches of sheer red-headed pulchritude. She just walked in the room and three guests here at the Lido Lounge had to check their blood pressure. Heh. Heh. How are you tonight, Miss Corrigan?"

He had a certain way of talking, somewhere between New Yorkese and trying to sound like a swell. *How're yautawnight, Miss Carrigawn?*

I leaned over the mike. I knew exactly what to say, which was a whole lot of nothing. "I'm just fine, Mr Hamilton."

"And how are you enjoying the Lido?"

"I'm having such a good time. All the girls are so sweet, and I love the routines."

"Keeping the wolves at bay?"

"Oh, that's easy enough," I said. "Most of them don't have teeth."

"Well, hehhehheh. Watch out, gentlemen of New York, Miss Kit Corrigan's got moxie. Ladies and gentlemen, that was the newest Lido Doll, Miss Kit Corrigan, and I see Jerry Temple heading over. . ."

He winked at me, and I gave him a big smile. He'd mentioned my name five times in less than thirty seconds. That was a true professional.

Nate led me away with a hand at my elbow. The man sitting at Mr D's table rose and moved away. He looked familiar, but I couldn't place him.

"Who is that?" I asked Nate as we moved through the crowd.

"Frank Costello," he said.

"The gangster?"

"Well, that's what the papers say."

As Frank Costello passed, he put his hand on Nate's shoulder for a moment and whispered something in his ear. He moved so fluidly that people at the tables probably didn't see it; they thought he was just trying to get around us.

"You know him?" I asked.

"We've met, yes. Come on, Kit. Don't look so shocked. This is New York. All kinds of people come to the Lido. Now you just have to say hello to Mr Dawber. He expects a few minutes."

I looked behind me, but Frank Costello was just walking out the door. The most famous gangster in America didn't look at Dex Hamilton, and Dex pretended to look down at his notes. *If you're a gossip columnist, you don't write about Costello,* I guessed. I'd heard rumours from the girls that the gangster was a partner in the club. I just hadn't believed them. And Nate knew him.

We approached the table, and Mr D halfway raised up and then crashed back down on his chair even as he signalled for another drink. He wasn't interested in me a bit, I could see that right away. He looked around the room, waved at a customer, then twisted his chair to talk to someone at the next table. Nate pulled out a chair for me.

"What will you have?" he asked.

I had to lean in to hear him. "Club soda will be fine." A flashbulb popped, and I recognized Gloria DeHaven at the next table. Across the room, Jimmy Durante lifted his glass to her. Stars. I was in the middle of it. This was exactly what I'd dreamed of back in Providence, lying on my bed with a movie magazine, dreaming over pictures. Why did I just want to go home?

I sipped at the club soda. Mr D wasn't even trying to talk to me. He was completely turned around, talking to someone behind him. I was just here to decorate the table for a few minutes.

I suddenly remembered that Hank had said he might come by to walk me home. I wondered if he'd wait. I wondered if it was too soon to leave.

The band swung into an easy, jazzy version of "It's Been a Long, Long Time", and a few couples were on the tiny dance floor.

"Dance with me," Nate said, leaning over.

"I've been dancing all night," I said. I tried to stall by taking out my compact, the silver one I'd found. I'd gone to the drugstore for fresh powder for it.

To my surprise, Nate took it from my hand. He turned it over. "Pretty."

100

"I found it in the apartment. The girl who lived there before . . . during the war. The Warwicks."

"The mirror's cracked." He snapped it shut but didn't give it back. "I can get it fixed for you."

"No, thanks." I took it from his hand. "I thought I might send it back to her. Did she leave a forwarding address?"

"No. It was the war years. People came and went. How about that dance?" He stood.

I wanted to say no. But he was standing, his hand was out, and I was sitting at the table with my boss. I had to do it.

"Go ahead, doll, Nate is a classy guy," Mr D said, his first words to me since I'd sat down. "Then you can head home and lap up a nice glass of warm milk like a good kitty."

Nate put his hand on the small of my back. His touch was barely there. The back of the dress was low, and if he moved his thumb an inch he'd feel bare skin. But he kept his hand where it was. I didn't think I could stand it if he did. I thought of dancing with Billy, how he'd run his finger along the line of my dress, sometimes insinuating a finger between the fabric and my skin, and rubbing gently.

His voice was close to my ear.

"I like your hair that way. How come you didn't wear the dress I brought you? The black one?"

"I had to borrow a dress from one of the girls."

"I'd like to see you in that black dress."

We were dancing to a song for sweethearts. It had been a hit right after the war, with all the soldiers coming home to their girlfriends and wives. I could see the other couple leaning into each other, the woman's eyes closed as she breathed in the scent of her love. I knew what that was like. *It's been a long, long time, Billy*, I thought, and I had to close my eyes because thinking of him made me feel as though my insides were scooped out of me. I felt hollow, a girl in heels moving to music she didn't feel, dancing with a man she didn't want to dance with.

"You see that man, the one in the grey suit and red tie, at the table next to ours?"

He moved me around so I could look over his shoulder. "Yes."

"Name is Ray Mirto. He's a regular. You should start getting to know the regulars. See the men with him?"

"I see them." They looked all the same to me, like Ray Mirto, men with too much weight on them and red-flushed faces.

His hand tightened on mine. "Pay attention. The guy with his back to you? That's Joe Adonis."

I knew that name; he was almost as notorious as Frank Costello. I looked at Ray Mirto as he lit a cigarette. He was laughing, leaning over to light his companion's cigarette. He put his arms across the back of the booth as if he owned it. I could see that he was talking loudly. One of the men leaned forward as if speaking to him in a low tone, and he waved him off. He looked like he thought he was the life of the party, but he was the only one who thought so.

Mr D had left our table. The waiter had already put

down an ashtray and a fresh drink for Nate. I watched as he unfurled a napkin and quickly polished the table. I worked in nightclubs, I knew that waiters didn't move that fast and mop up a dry table for just anybody. Nate seemed to know everyone, from Mr D to Dex Hamilton to Frank Costello. How could he know who the regulars were if he wasn't one himself?

I felt sick and dizzy, and the noise and the smoke felt as though they were swirling inside my head. I didn't understand any of this. Why had Frank Costello stopped to talk to Nate? He was a Providence lawyer. Why would Frank Costello even know him? What wasn't Nate telling me? Plenty, that was for sure.

What had he said when he came to the apartment? *I was coming to New York – I have a new client here. . .*

Who was his new client? One of the "regulars"? Or Frank Costello?

"I have to go," I said. "It's been a long night."

"I'll see you home."

"No, I like walking." I couldn't wait to get away. I stepped away from him and started across the dance floor. I heard someone call his name, and I took the lapse in his attention to make my way to the door. I ran down the carpeted stairs. The girls had left my camel coat right on the rack by the private door to the street, the one only celebrities and regulars knew about. I threw it on and ran out.

The cold night air hit me hard.

"Kit!"

I turned. Hank was walking towards me. He looked cold, his hands in his pockets.

"You're still here," I said. I was so grateful I could have kissed him.

"I thought I'd missed you." He pointed to the unmarked door. "What's that?"

"The private door to the lounge. I had to go see the boss. I can't believe you're here. You'll fall asleep in class tomorrow."

"I have study hall first period. I can sleep."

We began to walk, and I nudged him with my shoulder. "Hanging around with chorus girls, at your age," I teased. "Young man, you are running wild."

"What are you talking about?" He nudged me back. "I'm with the girl next door."

We swung into step together, our hands in our pockets. The cold air and Hank's presence chased away my apprehension about what had happened in the lounge. We reached the corner. The light was red, and we stopped as a taxi glided by. It was so quiet – quiet enough that I was able to hear the door open behind us. I looked back. Nate was standing in the doorway. He looked one way, then the other. Then he saw me.

He held my gaze and nodded. I couldn't look away. Then the light changed, Hank stepped off the kerb, and I snapped my head away and kept on going.

Eleven

New York City
November 1950

> Dear Kit,
> I don't know what you're doing for Thanksgiving, but Da
> and I would like you to come home. I'll meet you at the
> train.
> Love, Muddie
> PS please come

I held the letter in my hand. Home. If Billy got his furlough,
we could take the train together. The first car, so we could
stand in front and see the future rushing at us. The longing
to see him was growing every moment I was without him.

I read the letter again and put it down on the dresser. I
kept my earrings there, tiny pearls that Billy had bought
me for my birthday last year. Funny, I thought I'd left them
by the lamp, but they were lined up right there.

105

I opened the top drawer. A tumble of lingerie, the things Nate had brought that I couldn't quite bring myself to wear. It seemed too intimate, somehow. Every time I saw them I blushed, wondering if Nate had peeked in the boxes.

Hadn't I left the slip on top? I'd tucked my own underthings to the side, and the black slip had been so pretty I'd folded it on top of the bras and panty girdles that I didn't wear anyway. My own garter belts were tossed in the corner.

I stared down at the tumble of elastic, rayon and silk.

I figured I had to be mistaken. I wasn't a neat person. What made me think I knew exactly how I folded underwear?

Uneasily, I shut the drawer.

Instead of wearing a skirt the next day, I pulled on my old dungarees and sneakers. I looked in the mirror as I brushed my hair, about to twist it into the Lido Doll upsweep.

I like your hair that way.

I left it down. What was so bad about looking seventeen?

I was on Second Avenue, carrying home a grocery sack, when I saw a tall, striking girl walking ahead of me. Something about the swing of her hips was familiar, the lazy way she walked, the gesture of flipping her long, curly hair over a shoulder.

"Daisy?"

She turned. It took her a moment, but then she smiled. "It's the kid from Providence. How are you, Kit?" She strode forward and kissed me on the cheek, and for a moment we greeted each other like long-lost friends, words tumbling over each other, not giving each other a chance to answer – *What are you doing here, Well, I never, How absolutely lovely to run into you.*

We'd been in summer stock together, but she'd been the star ingenue and I'd worked in the box office and been in the chorus. I was surprised at how warmly she greeted me, but I'd also grown used to the fact that I'd joined a family when I'd joined the theatre, and here I was, running into a glamorous cousin.

"I'm just on my way to work," she said, making a face. "My parents cut me off, the dears, so I've got rent to pay. It's not bad – I start after lunch, so I can still make some morning rounds. I just came from the most *horrific* audition. What are you up to?"

"I'm working at the Lido," I said.

"A Lido Doll?" Daisy whistled under her breath. "Nice going. Pretty soon we'll be seeing you in Hollywood. Say, why don't we grab some coffee and have a gossip? I have about twenty minutes. Did you hear Jeff Toland is making a movie with Jennifer Jones? Remember how we all thought his career was over? Including him?" She laughed.

"My place is near here," I said. "I just bought some coffee."

"Perfectly perfect. I'm yours." Daisy followed me back down the avenue. "I'm over on the West Side. I have two room-mates, and one is completely horrific, but she just got engaged, so she's hardly ever there. Hey, do you miss it, though? I mean, the theatre. You were such a great dancer. Isn't the Lido mostly—" And she mimed walking, showing off a leg, and balancing something on her head at the same time. I burst out laughing. It wasn't exactly true, but it made me realize that once I'd learned which way to dip and when to turn, it wasn't exactly challenging.

"Well, I'm still dancing," I said. "Being a Lido girl is every girl's dream, right?"

Daisy snorted. "We get our dreams told to us. Girls. Every day. Life isn't a Palmolive ad. Take my mother. Her dream is me, married, in Connecticut, with a baby on the way. Not mine, though. That's why I'm selling dresses at Bonwit's. The dresses are divine – I just wish I could afford them." She gave my coat a critical look. "If I'm not mistaken, that's one of ours. And from this season, too. Nice goods." I could see the speculation in her eyes.

Hadn't Nate said the clothes were from a year ago? I remembered that he'd asked Sonia my shoe size, and the lie smoothly clicked into place in my mind. He had lied about the clothes; he had bought them himself. But why? So I could look good enough for his son? It gave me an uneasy feeling, which was made even uneasier when Daisy strode past me into the foyer of my apartment and whistled softly.

"Nice," she said. "You're here all alone? Hey, if you ever need a room-mate. . ."

I walked back to the kitchen and started to make coffee. I could feel Daisy's curiosity propel her around the kitchen, as she studied the china and silver. Just last summer I'd arrived in Cape Cod with a cheap suitcase and a wardrobe that I'd dressed up with cheap scarves and bracelets. How could I afford this? I bent over the percolator, blind with shame. I hadn't thought about how it would feel to invite someone over, someone who knew me.

Daisy's parents had cut her off, and she was making her way alone, and she had found a way to pay for an apartment and still go on auditions. Nate had offered me an easy way, and I'd taken it. I'd been so afraid of failure that I'd taken the first hand held out to me. I had no one to blame but myself. I couldn't even blame Nate, even though I wanted to.

I could have said no. I could have found another way.

And the worst part was, I wasn't doing what I'd come to do. I didn't care about Hollywood casting agents. I cared about the stage. I remembered the deep pleasure I got every single time I signed in at the stage door, even for a turkey like *That Girl From Scranton!*

I put a cup of coffee down in front of her. She took a sip and said, "Not bad. Beats drugstore coffee. Listen, as soon as I get a paycheque, I'll spring for lunch at Child's. I've got a friend who's a waitress there – another actress, of course. She puts whipped cream on my coffee. Nice big dollop. We'll go – it's divine."

Whipped cream plopped on a cup of coffee. I remembered the memory then, the first time I'd met Florence. The first time I'd seen Billy. And Delia fighting tears, and Da not knowing where to look. So many things had happened that night, but all I'd been thinking about was the roar of applause I'd got, and how right I'd felt standing on a stage.

"You're right – being a Lido Doll isn't my dream," I told Daisy. "I just got lucky, and there I was, so I took it. But I miss Broadway. I want . . . I want to be an actress." There was a guilty sound to my voice, as if I'd just confessed that I wanted to rob a bank.

Daisy nodded thoughtfully while she blew out a plume of smoke. "You were pretty good last summer when we ran lines. Look, if that's what you want, you've got to study. Go downtown to the Actors Studio and audition. Or find a teacher who will take you on. Just do something. I can get you in to see Stella; she'll take a look at you. Listen, are you still making the rounds?"

"The rehearsals were taking up all my time, and I do three shows a night, and—"

"And you're beat. Sure." Daisy squinted at me, then tilted her head. "Listen, they're casting a new musical. That's the audition I just came from. There's a part for you – a speaking part, just a couple of lines. It's not Shaw, for crissakes, you can absolutely do it. I just read for it, but I'm all wrong, I might as well face it. I can't act sixteen – those days are long gone." She rolled her eyes. "They're looking for a gamine type – young, a little mischievous looking, tomboyish, you know? She's the little sister of the lead. You want the address?"

110

"I don't have any head shots."

"So? That's not a reason not to go. Get some made – you can drop them off later." Daisy quickly scribbled down an address. "It's a rehearsal hall on the West Side. If you leave right now you can make it."

"But I'm not dressed, or made up."

"What are you wearing, dungarees? Perfect. Too bad your hair is so long, but you still look the part. Maybe put it in a ponytail. Don't even put on make-up. Anyway, go. And remember me when you're famous!"

Twelve

Cape Cod, Massachusetts
August 1950

It was the last night of our summer. The cast and crew sat under the trees outside the rooming house, flopped on chairs and blankets in the grass. Those who smoked had lit up cigarettes to drive away the mosquitoes. It was midnight, and still thirty degrees.

I was wearing white shorts and a sleeveless top, a madras shirt that had started the summer with long sleeves that after a week I had cut off to make it easier to work. The cast was expected to pitch in, and I hammered and sawed for the set designer, sewed hems on costumes, and acted as an usher when I didn't have to be onstage.

It was an outfit I wouldn't have dared to wear back home, but I'd learned, this summer, that there was another world out there, where people wore as little as possible, said whatever they thought, and cursed cheerfully at the prospect of sixteen-hour days. Things made sense here

112

because nobody cared – if you were hot, you chopped off your shirtsleeves; if you were tired, you drank a pot of coffee; if your heart was broken, you went out that night and sang the pieces of your heart out onstage. Easy.

I was the baby of the group. Nobody made a pass that summer; nobody offered me drinks or cigarettes. I was here because of Florence Foster. She was the one who'd made the long-distance call, who'd planned the audition, who'd called in favours. "It's time for you to get out of Providence," she'd said, "and get some *real* theatrical experience under your belt."

She could have added *and get away from that boyfriend*, but she didn't have to. Flo didn't approve of Billy. She didn't approve of boyfriends in general, but she'd seen me come to class with reddened eyes and no focus. She'd seen how I'd dress hurriedly, afraid to be late meeting him.

I couldn't have marked how it happened, or when, and I didn't love him less, but there was a pulling and a tearing now to our times together. There was an anger in him that would come out if I couldn't see him, or if I had to work late, or if he saw me talking to a boy at school. He insisted on picking me up at the end of my shift at the Riverbank on Saturday nights, and after my Drama Club meetings. At first I was flattered and grateful, but sometimes I'd want to stay and joke with the waiters about my shift, or gossip with the other actors in the school play. Nobody asked me out for a soda any more, or to run lines. They knew Billy would be coming.

113

When Billy wasn't with me, he was with Jamie. They had a private world of photographs and drawings and talk of light and moments caught in time, truth captured in a frame. I didn't share their language, but I loved to hear their talk wash over me. It was like a lullaby, making me feel safe and lucky that my brother was my boyfriend's best friend.

Jamie and Billy had driven me to the Cape in June. It had been unseasonably chilly, and we'd had our last lunch together bundled up in sweatshirts and then had said our goodbyes. I'd noticed how Billy looked over the other actors and saw how the light shut off in his eyes. But instead of being angry, he looked scared, and that melted my heart.

Jamie had given me a quick hug – he hated goodbyes – and had gone back to the car while I'd kissed Billy goodbye.

"I love you, too," I'd said, and was relieved when it made him smile. "The summer will go before you know it."

"Are you nuts? I'm working for my father, remember? It's going to be the longest summer in history. Especially without you."

I'd walked him back to the car and had gone around to the passenger side to say goodbye to Jamie.

"Take care of him for me," I'd told my brother. Jamie had nodded. Next to Billy's dark handsomeness, Jamie's fairness stood out. During the winters his paleness was odd, his strawberry hair freakish, his freckles standing out against his white skin, but in the summers his hair lightened to a shade close to blond, and his skin turned golden. If you saw the two of them walking down the street, you'd see heads turn at the two sides of a coin, the darkness and then the golden beauty of the two of them.

"Sure thing," he'd told me. "Break a leg. And remember to keep some heads-up pennies around."

At the end of the summer, the beginning of the summer seemed like a different life. Under a full moon I drank my ginger ale and tried not to think about home, where I'd be starting senior year. Because tonight, I was just one of the cast and crew, and there was a movie star in our midst.

Jeffrey Toland had been Spencer Tracy's little brother and Carole Lombard's husband. He'd kissed Bette Davis. He'd been a cowboy, a judge, a gangster, a song-and-dance man, a sailor who died in the Pacific. And now he sat on a wooden Adirondack chair – the best chair, the one that didn't wobble – drinking beer with everybody else. It was the first time he'd joined us. As the star, he didn't room with the rest of us but stayed in a guest cottage on an estate. All that summer he'd left immediately after the show to go to restaurants and parties, driving a blue convertible loaned by another wealthy family that then got to decorate its dinner parties and lobster bakes with his Hollywood presence. When you've seen someone's head blown up to the size of a movie screen, seen him kissing legends – well, it didn't matter that you'd also seen him hungover in an undershirt. He still had glamour.

115

We lived in a rooming house with flimsy screen doors that let in black flies and mosquitoes with the size and accuracy of dive-bombers. There was a faint smell of mildew, spiders in the bathroom, and mice in the kitchen.

It had been the best summer of my life.

I was accepted. It didn't matter that I got the smallest parts or was stuck in the chorus. I got to be onstage, dancing in the musicals. I got to run lines with the ingénue in the early mornings, grabbing a Dixie cup of coffee and complaining with the others about the lack of sleep.

The last show had gone well, and there was a bouncy, boisterous atmosphere that night. Some nights were golden, not a missed cue, not a word wrong, and the audience was in a mood to be amused. Jeff Toland had proved that he was still a star, throwing himself into the songs with the abandon of the twenty-five-year-old he was supposed to be playing.

I had been a part of that energy that night, and it felt like the biggest luxury to indulge my exhaustion and yet not go to bed. There would be no rehearsal tomorrow, no set building, no rushed breakfasts and skipped lunches and quick swims in the ocean. There was only packing up and heading home. Underneath the jokes, there was tension, too. The Korean War had started in June and the young men were worried about being drafted. We were all heading into an uncertain fall.

But a movie star was working hard to make us forget it. Because of Jeff, everything was heightened – we laughed more, we listened harder, we told our best stories, and suddenly the cast forgot moments of jealousy or irritation and complimented each other. Jeff lolled in his chair, a slight, amused smile on his face, telling anecdotes about directors and stars and his early days on Broadway while we crowded close, everyone flushed and beautiful that night from the lights of the candles and the cigarettes.

Suddenly, the chatter fell silent, and Jeff's head dropped back. "Look at that big fat moon," he said. "I love a big fat moon."

We all dutifully tipped our heads back. Someone sang out "Some enchanted evening" in an exaggerated basso, like Ezio Pinza on Broadway.

Jeff Toland looked down and held out his hand to me. I took it and we rose together and began to dance. The singing turned from a clownish operatic parody to a sweet lush melody, as all the voices joined in. Jeff played to the crowd, twirling me out occasionally, showing me off.

He looked into my eyes and winked. I caught his mood and I saw what he wanted me to do, act like lovers. We danced close and dreamy, perfectly in step, exaggerating the romance for the crowd.

When the song ended, he didn't just stop dancing, he unfurled me, then gave me a mock bow as the group burst into applause. I grabbed the cuffs of my shorts and pretended to curtsy, and everyone laughed.

Jeff said, "Ladies and gentlemen, I give you the next Broadway star."

Everyone applauded. It was a joke, but a generous one, and I curtsied again.

This was as magic as real life ever got.

Then I stopped smiling because I saw a dark figure standing by the trunk of the big elm tree – Billy.

He stared at me for just a moment. Then he turned his back and walked away.

I looked for Billy for an hour, by the theatre, by the beach. I didn't sleep much, thinking that he'd come to me. The doors of the rooming house weren't locked; he could walk right in.

I finally fell asleep as the wind picked up, curling around my bare toes in bed and leading me to pull up the cotton cover. For the first time, I could smell the end of summer.

The next morning I waited in my room while I heard doors slamming and taxis pulling up. I had said my goodbyes last night. A sense of dread filled me, and I wondered if I'd see him this morning.

This summer had been one of missing Billy. There was only one phone in the rooming house, and we were rarely there to answer it. Messages were supposed to be written down and put on the table in the front hall, but often people forgot or didn't bother. It was a summer of rushed letters, quick postcards, a few phone calls in which I shouted my "I miss you" while checking my watch. He always managed to call just when I was due down at the theatre.

I packed my one suitcase with my shorts and dresses, silly presents for Da and Jamie and Muddie, everything crammed in so that I had to sit on the suitcase to close it. It was an old one of Da's, the one we'd used so many years ago on our summer tours of county fairs, and one of the latches wouldn't latch. I pinched my finger wrestling it shut.

I carried it down the stairs. When I walked into the kitchen, one of the actresses was still there, a girl with the improbable name of Daisy Meadows. Out of the company, she was the one I watched the closest. She wasn't the prettiest of the actresses but she had an arresting face, startlingly clear blue eyes with dark lashes, and thick black hair that curled in the humidity and couldn't be tamed with a comb. Every performance of hers was slightly different – not enough to throw off her fellow actors, but enough to shade the performance. She lived in New York and studied with Stella Adler, who I now knew was one of the best acting teachers anywhere. Daisy was part of a world I couldn't imagine – late nights in Greenwich Village jazz clubs, hard study with tough teachers, a tribe of actors searching for truth in a gesture.

She greeted me by raising her coffee cup. She was still dressed in her nightgown. "Looks like we're the holdouts," she said. "Everybody left for New York already. I'm taking off in a bit to crash in on my parents. Need a ride, honey? I can drop you in Providence."

"Maybe."

Daisy shrugged her shoulders.

I heard the sound of a car, and I went to the kitchen door and peered out. Billy got out of the car. "I might have a ride."

Daisy took a sip of coffee and watched as Billy stood uncertainly, looking at the house. Dressed in a white shirt and khakis, tanned and lean, he made me catch my breath.

"Catnip," she purred. "Is he an actor?"

"No, he goes to Brown."

"College boy. Lucky you."

I swung open the screen door and stepped out.

"I came to surprise you last night," he said. "I saw you dancing."

"I know. It was Jeff Toland," I said. "You should have stayed. We were just dancing."

"Just dancing. Is that what you call it? I couldn't slip a piece of paper between the two of you."

"We were just putting on a show for the others."

"Some show."

I took a few steps closer. He wasn't angry, I saw, just hurt and confused.

"What's been going on this summer, Kit? Is this why I can't call you, can't come up?"

"You could have come up anytime," I said.

"Why would I, when I couldn't see you? I thought I'd surprise you last night—"

"It was our last night, we had a party—"

"—and I was standing there, watching you, and I thought, this is how it is. I'm right here. She's right there.

And I can't have her, I can't get to her." He shook his head. "Listen, anytime you want me to walk away, I'll go. I can do it. I can walk away."

"I don't! I just want you to trust me." I spread out my arms. "I want you to understand this – the theatre, what I'm doing. It doesn't matter to you!"

"That's not true." He reached into the car and took out an envelope. He handed it to me. "I made you a present."

It was full of photographs of me, duplicates of a shot he'd taken last spring. He'd set up the shot with lights, just like a professional. In it I looked fresh and dreamy-eyed, because I was looking through the lens right at him.

"Head shots," he said. "For you to take around to auditions. I *do* take you seriously."

I looked down at the pictures. They showed a girl who looked like me, just happier.

"One of the things I love about you," he said, "is that you really don't know how beautiful you are."

He took a step towards me, and I was in his arms.

He held me against him. Slowly, our breaths came together. There were nights in his car that I felt this way, so close, heartbeat to heartbeat. "If we could just be together. Really together," he said. "If I could just have all of you. If I could just bury myself inside you."

His words were like an electric shock. I felt something drumming inside me. Our mouths crashed together. Hunger, and then falling. Falling. That's what it felt like as we kissed, and we just held on.

121

I knew what he meant. There was a certain distance between us, and wasn't it because he had to pull away? But something always held me back, Delia's face rising in my mind, and Da's, disappointment and shame, and that was stronger than desire, stronger than need. It wasn't so much what the Church had taught me, but what I'd seen around me in Fox Point: girls pregnant, their lives over, every dream now swirling in the dirty wash water, spiralling down the drain. My mother had died because of babies. That made it easier to be good.

I stepped away, breathing hard, conscious of the windows, of Daisy maybe looking out, or the landlady. "I'll get my suitcase. Let's get out of here."

"I'll get your suitcase." He smiled, still holding me in the circle of his arms. He reached down to nuzzle my neck, and his breath sent me trembling again.

I put a hand on his chest and pushed him lightly. "It's in the kitchen. And I left my sweater in the theatre last night. I'll be back in a second."

I cut through the back yard and down the hill to the theatre, the short walk I'd made all summer, in all stages of exhaustion and exhilaration. I was glad to get away for a few moments, glad to feel my heartbeat settle into a more comfortable rhythm. The stage door was open and a few workers were already there, striking the last set. I waved at them and found my sweater, forgotten in a dressing room.

122

I stood in the wings for a moment. This stage felt like home to me, such a difference from how nervous I'd been when I'd arrived.

I jumped off the stage, walked down the aisle, past the seats, back into the lobby. To my surprise, I saw Jeff Toland there, dressed in a light summer suit and tie.

"Come to say a last goodbye?" he asked.

I held up the sweater. "I left something behind."

"Accidentally on purpose, maybe." He smiled. "I like to say a last goodbye, too." He leaned against the wall, regarding me. "How old are you, eighteen?"

"Almost."

He smiled slightly, the smile that had made Judy Garland and June Allyson fall for him in the movies. "Think you'll stick with it?"

"Yes."

"No matter what?"

"No matter what."

"No matter what the boyfriend says?"

I felt my face redden.

"Yes, I saw him last night. We all did. He was jealous. Welcome to the theatre, baby doll. They always end up jealous."

"No," I said. "He wants me to act, to go to New York. He wants what I want."

"C'mon, I have to go meet my ride. Heading to New York. You?"

"Home. Providence, Rhode Island."

"Providence, Rhode Island," he repeated, as though it were a joke.

He opened the door into the bright morning sun. "Maybe I'll catch you there sometime. I'm in a play this fall and there'll be try-outs in Boston. Come and see me?"

"I'll try."

He leaned over and kissed my cheek. It lasted about half a beat too long – not enough time for me to pull away, but enough time for me to know it was lingering.

"Thanks for the dance, Providence," he said when it was done.

Billy was out front, and he'd seen the kiss. Jeff looked off balance for only a moment. He smiled at Billy, a practised, flashing grin, and waggled his fingers in a wave. Then he ambled away, hands in his pockets.

Billy's face was a mask, set and still.

I tried to smile, and started towards him, knowing the first words out of my mouth would have to be explanation. *I really* did *leave my sweater. I had no idea Jeff would be there.* It all sounded so . . . weak. I knew what it looked like – that I had made up an excuse to say goodbye to Jeff.

"Hey, I—" I started, but he turned away abruptly.

I watched, my mouth still open, as he jumped back in the car and slammed the door. The motor roared to life. He stepped on the gas and I watched him fishtail out of the parking lot. I stood, watching the car disappear down the road, too stunned to cry.

Daisy pulled up as I was still standing there wondering

what to do. My handbag had been in the car, my suitcase, everything except the sweater in my hand.

She tipped her sunglasses down. Even in the middle of my misery, I reminded myself to remember that gesture. She looked so racy and confident.

"Looks like you need a ride after all."

"Thanks." I tossed my sweater in the back seat. Daisy headed down the Cape highway, driving fast and expertly, talking the whole time. I let the talk go on. I was thankful not to think.

We were almost at the bridge when I saw something pink suddenly fly by the window. I turned back and saw the scrap of fabric stuck on a bush. Another white blur – a shirt – flew by.

"Son of a gun," Daisy said. "What's going on?"

Clothes were flying out of the window of a car up ahead. A multicoloured skirt. A pair of blue shorts. A white bra.

They were my clothes. Up ahead, Billy must have been grabbing items from my suitcase and tossing them out the window. I stared as my sleeveless madras shirt got impaled on a bush. A sneaker flew out and bounced on the shoulder.

"Somebody's going to need a new wardrobe," Daisy said.

She hadn't recognized my clothes. I was grateful. I watched it all, the wardrobe I'd saved up for in my job at the luncheonette, the soda I'd wiped up, the rolls I'd sliced, the coffee I'd slopped into cups. Getting up to open the place at six. Soaking in a tub to get the grease out of my hair and off my skin. All those days and nights.

Out the window.

He'd known it, too. He'd known how hard I'd worked.

Now something else was flying by, too. Paper, ripped into pieces.

I knew what they were. My head shots. Little pieces of me, all over the road.

Thirteen

New York City
November 1950

I said goodbye to Daisy at the door of Bonwit's and walked quickly crosstown. I had a plan.

It would start with my hair. I kept remembering how Nate had looked at me, how the Lido Dolls all had to have the same hairstyle, the same teeth, the same smiles. The cans of hair spray, the bobby pins scattered on the counter. All it took for us to get our hair to stay up there – our slippery, springing, disobedient hair.

I'd hardly started working there, and already I wanted to shake up the joint. I wanted control of just one small thing.

I ducked into a barbershop nearby, a place I knew from Shirley, who had endlessly debated whether she should get the short haircut we were beginning to see on the fashionable girls, the ones who wore cropped black trousers and ballet slippers with their fur coats, and sunglasses even in November.

When I walked out, I had a haircut like a boy, just wisps around my face, and the cold wind on the back of my neck felt like freedom.

I slammed through my front door two hours later, pirouetted through the hall, and leaped on to the couch. I bounced three times and then fell on my rear like a kid.

My first callback. And not on a turkey like *That Girl From Scranton!* But for a real show, *A Year of Junes*, with a famous director, an up-and-coming choreographer, and real Broadway stars in the cast.

I'd run almost all the way home. But I'd made sure to stop to buy a postcard of Times Square and a stamp. I'd scrawled *White mink and diamonds!* on the back, and addressed it to the Florence Foster Studio of Dance.

In a few weeks, I could have a part. I could quit the Lido and get away from Nate. I had been there almost three weeks already; I'd have almost three hundred dollars. That was walking-away money. Maybe I could really start again.

With a glance at the clock, I ran for my bedroom. I couldn't show up at work in dungarees. I was pulling on a dress when the phone rang. I ran for it, hoping it was Billy.

"Good, you didn't leave yet."

Nate. I sank to the floor, cradling the receiver against my ear as I pulled on my stockings. "I'm late."

"I want you to do something for me. Just a little thing."

"It's always a little thing."

There was a pause, and I knew I'd annoyed him. "I can't

get to the club tonight. I want you to tell me if Ray Mirto is there. You remember him?"

"The guy in the red tie."

"Just give me a call at midnight. You have a pencil? I'll give you the number."

I wrote down the number. It was a New York exchange, so Nate was in town. "Why do you want to know?"

"No big reason. I just want to know if he's around, that's all. It will help me out. See who he talks to, if you can. If he's drinking."

"What am I, your snitch?"

"Don't be crazy. It's just a favour. Come on, you can't say you don't owe me a few."

No, I couldn't say that. That was the problem with this apartment, with these clothes. With the job. With everything. He had me boxed in, and I hadn't even seen it coming.

"All right," I said, and put down the phone.

"You cut your hair." Ted Roper put his hands on his narrow hips.

"We all think it's darling," Polly said.

Mickey broke in. "Honey, it suits you."

"I'm not talking to you," Ted said to the girls, and they all turned and pretended to powder their faces or reach for a cup of coffee.

He turned back to me. "You're a Lido Doll. You wear an upsweep. That's your look. You don't go cutting your hair without *talking to me*!"

129

"I didn't know," I lied. "It was just an impulse. I'm sorry."

He nodded slowly, staring at me, as though he was trying to figure me out. "You know, I *can* fire you."

"I know," I said. I kept my gaze down.

"Aw, c'mon, Ted," Mickey said. "We're not Fords on an assembly line."

"Yeah," Darla said. "Why can't the kid cut her hair if she wants?"

He put up his hands. "No ganging up on the boss."

I was off the hook.

"So what are you waiting for? Get into your costume," he said. "Full house tonight! They're carrying in the tables to the front, so watch your step, we've got a whole lot less floor out there."

It was a packed house. We could hear the noise as we gathered our skirts and headed for the wings.

Darla fluffed out my skirt for me as we waited for our cue. "So what did he think?"

"What did who think?"

"Mr Benedict. About your hair."

I glanced over my shoulder at her, puzzled. Why should Nate have any say-so about my hair? "He hasn't seen it yet."

The band had swung into our cue, and I heard our introduction from Danny, the announcer – *Ladies and gentlemen, the Lido Dolls go to Mardi Gras!* – and I stepped out into the lights.

130

I knew the routine so well now that it was easy to scan the audience and not miss a step. I didn't see Ray Mirto. The first show was usually full of couples, wives and husbands, young people out on dates, tourists.

It wasn't until the second show that I spotted him at one of the tables that had been added as the crowd grew, right on the dance floor. He was with a woman this time, and another one of the men from the night before.

I would call Nate later, between shows. I would do this favour because I owed him. But I would get to a place where there were no more favours, I vowed, only the ones I wanted to give.

It was easy to say that while I was dancing, while I was joking with the girls over cups of coffee and plates of food, but when midnight came I had to run to the phone, the one in the hallway where the girls passed back and forth during the break. I dialled the number I'd memorized. Nate picked up on the first ring.

"He's here," I said. "With a date and one of those guys from the other night."

"Joe Adonis?"

"No, the giant one."

"Is he drunk?"

"How am I supposed to know?"

"Tell me if he's still there at closing."

"You mean I have to call again tonight?"

"Just a quick one."

I waited and he waited. I didn't want to call again. I

131

didn't want to be on the end of this string, jerked whenever he raised a hand.

"Just do it," he said, and hung up.

I was still feeling shaky when I hit the street at three a.m. I'd made the call and told Nate that Ray Mirto was heading up to the lounge. I felt dirty, like I was some kind of spy. I *was* a spy, but it was for a side I didn't believe in, in a war I didn't understand.

Hank was waiting outside the back door. I was never so relieved to see anyone in my life. Hank with his open face, his open life. He wasn't buried in secrets. He wasn't tied up in lies. I didn't deserve his friendship, but I wanted it. I wanted somebody to look at me like he did, like I was good.

"You look kind of shook," he said. "Everything OK?"

"Fine. Just a long night." I swung into step next to him.

We didn't say anything for a few minutes. "You know," Hank said, "when I was a kid and I had a lousy day and didn't want to talk or anything, my mom had this routine. I'd have to come up with one thing – just one thing that had made me happy that day. Like, I had pudding with lunch. Or I rattled a stick along a gate on the way home from school. Anything, no matter how little."

We took a few more steps. "Actually, something good did happen to me today," I said. "I got a callback."

"Great! You see?"

We walked a few more steps. "What's a callback?" Hank asked, and we laughed a little.

132

"I went on an audition, and I made the cut. I'm one of three girls up for a part in a new musical. A small part. But it's good! It's called *A Year of Junes*. I get one whole song, and a dance with the lead. And this choreographer, it's his first show, his name is Tom Cullen – but he's been doing work in Hollywood, and he's the next Jack Cole, that's what everyone says." As I told Hank the news, I started to get excited again.

"Jack Cole."

"He's a famous choreographer. But this guy today – you can't imagine how he makes me move – it's a whole different extension. You should see what I had to do with my hands! Like this." I bent my wrists, thrust out a hip, and did a slow slide step. "Hardest audition, I had to *changement, changement, aire plié. . .*" I burst out laughing at Hank's expression.

"Yeah, I do that every morning when I brush my teeth," Hank said. "And you cut your hair, too. I like it. It suits you."

"Thanks."

We were crossing Third Avenue, and a train roared overhead. Hank waited until it was gone.

"OK, we need to celebrate."

"But I didn't get the part yet."

"Callbacks deserve celebration, don't they? Let's go ice-skating at Rockefeller Centre on Monday – after school. You have time, don't you?"

"Sure. But I don't have skates. And . . . I can't skate."

"Don't they have ice in Rhode Island?"

"Sure." But we never had money for skates.

"You can pick it up in two seconds. And you can borrow my mom's skates, or we can rent a pair. Say yes," Hank urged. "You need a day off, don't you?"

A day off from everything. The breeze quickened, and for the first time, I smelled snow in the air. It was almost Thanksgiving, and Thanksgiving meant Billy. All of that was ahead, but right now I could take a few hours and learn to skate.

"Yes," I said.

Fourteen

New York City
November 1950

On Monday afternoon I met Hank in the lobby and we took the stairs down to the basement of the building. I stepped into a big room with a painted concrete floor. I followed him past the washing machines and into another room of storage areas separated by chain-link fences. Each apartment had its own space.

Hank went to the storage unit for 2A. He fitted a key into a padlock on one of the doors and pushed it open. Inside were cardboard boxes, a bicycle, and an overturned chair with stuffing popping out of the seat. The skates were balanced on top of a cardboard box.

"This is where we come when they drop the Bomb, I guess," he said. "We're supposed to duck and cover with the baby carriages and the bicycles."

"Hey, don't forget ice skates and catcher's mitts."

He picked up skates. "Will these fit?"

He waited while I tried them on. I wouldn't call Hank's mother and me a perfect fit, but her skates would do.

We took the crosstown bus to Rockefeller Centre. Hank bought tickets and we laced up our skates. Hank took off quickly, and I stepped cautiously out on the ice. It looked so easy, but as soon as my feet hit the ice they slid out from underneath me and I fell backwards with a whoop.

Hank circled and skated back to me. "Oh. You really don't know."

"You think I was lying?" I shook my head, laughing.

He held out his gloved hand, and I placed mine in it. "Come on, I'll hold you up."

We made a slow circuit of the rink. After a few turns I understood the rhythm of the motion, how to push off, how to glide instead of taking staccato steps. I let go of Hank's hand.

We went round and round, not talking, smiling at everything and nothing – the little girl in the plaid coat, the older couple holding hands in their thick gloves. The music was playing, and people were laughing, and it seemed as though that golden Greek god posing so magnificently behind us was the still centre of a quickly spinning world.

"I hope you get the part," Hank said. "You were right – I *am* falling asleep in science class."

I laughed, and I heard it ring out into the cold air, a crack of happiness. I felt at that moment that things were just about to change. I'd get the part, I'd find another place to live. I would be free of all debts.

I tilted my head back as we skated, looking at all the people lining the railing looking down at us, no doubt wishing they were skating, too.

A soldier leaned against the railing. He had a camera in front of his face and he was aiming it at the rink. It looked like he was aiming it at me.

The toe of my skate locked in the ice, pitching me forward. Hank saved me from falling. When I looked back up at the railing, the soldier was gone. Could it have been Billy? That would be crazy – how could he find me in the middle of Manhattan?

"Tired?" Hank asked, and I nodded. "It's not too late; we could get a hot chocolate."

But I wasn't feeling carefree any more. My mind couldn't hold the blue sky, the sound of the blades against the ice, the pleasure of my body moving in a new way. My heart had seized up like an engine, just because I'd glimpsed, for one second, someone who looked like Billy. "I can't. This has been lovely, Hank, really, but – I really have to go."

We skated off the rink, bumping on to the rubber matting. Hank awkwardly made his way on his skates inside to retrieve our shoes, and I sank on to a bench. I tore off my gloves with my teeth and went to work on my laces.

"Need some help?"

I looked up and there he was. All my breath went out in a rush. He seemed so much older in his uniform, with his new short haircut.

"How did you find me? When did you get here?" I tried

to stand, awkwardly, with one skate unlaced, and I had to grab both of his hands to stay upright. Skin against skin, the hard feel of his cold fingers, the look of his mouth – it all sent a charge through my body, and it was all I could do not to throw my arms around him. I wanted to – why didn't I?

His face changed a bit. I saw how he'd hoped that I would, but he wouldn't push me. We were somewhere between sweethearts and friends now. "I went by your place, and you weren't home, so I waited for a while. I saw your upstairs neighbour and she told me where to find you. You cut your hair."

"I just did it. You don't like it."

"Your beautiful hair. I almost didn't recognize you."

"It's still me," I said.

"Kit, I have your shoes."

Hank. I had forgotten Hank.

I twisted, almost losing my balance again. Billy dropped one hand and put his arm around me to steady me, then kept it there.

In all my imagined meetings with Billy, I had never imagined being this unprepared.

"Billy, this is my neighbour, Hank. Hank, this is Billy. Someone from home." I babbled out the introduction. I didn't say boyfriend because he wasn't any more. I wasn't sure what he was.

"Glad to meet you," Hank said.

"I think I can handle it from here," Billy replied, taking my shoes from Hank. "Nice meeting you."

138

His voice was cordial but I could see how flattened Hank was.

"Billy," I said. "Hank and I came together. We can all walk back together."

"Sure, let's do that," Billy said. He knelt down to take off my skates. He lifted out my foot and cradled it in his lap. Hank stared down at Billy's hand on my foot.

"No, I – I have someplace to go first," Hank said. "An errand. I forgot. I'll see you later, Kit." Hank took his mother's skates and swiftly knotted them together and slung them over his other shoulder. "Bye." He turned abruptly and threaded through the crowd, the skates bumping hard against his back.

"Sorry about that," Billy said. "He seems like a nice kid, but after all, I've travelled on a bus for a million hours to spend time with you."

When I stood up, my steps were uncertain, as though I were wearing lifts in my shoes. I could feel the air between the soles of my feet and the ground. It was like something important had altered, like gravity, or the air itself.

Fifteen

The apartment was dim and chilly. I hadn't pulled the shades open yet in the living room. I quickly crossed to them, and the even grey light of late afternoon flooded in.

Billy stood in the doorway to the living room, his cap in his hands. He turned it over and over while he looked around.

This was it, the moment I'd dreamed of, and I couldn't seem to move. He was looking at *our* apartment, the one we'd live in together, only I couldn't tell him that. I couldn't tell him that this could be our future, if only we could say the right words, get back what we had.

All I knew, standing there, looking across the room at his uncertain face, was that I still loved him. It had been crazy to think that I didn't. I had run here to New York not just because I was furious at my father. I had run here because I couldn't imagine being in Providence without Billy.

Billy's tie was crooked, and I wanted to straighten it. All those things I could do once, I couldn't do now. That simple gesture, of straightening his tie, looking up at him, and he would look down and kiss me. Did I have a right to those familiar gestures?

He cleared his throat. "It's nice. I didn't realize you could get such nice places in New York."

"I make a pretty good salary at the Lido," I said. We were talking like strangers. In my head, a counter was whirring. Counting up the lies. "It's not the Riverbank."

At the mention of my old job, he blushed, and I realized that I'd made a mistake. I shouldn't have brought up something that would remind us of that night. I quickly tossed my coat on the couch. "Should I make coffee?"

"You drink coffee now? You never drank coffee."

"I'm a New Yorker now," I said. "At least, I'm trying to be. Everybody drinks coffee, not tea. And you can get a bag of chestnuts for lunch and just walk in the park. I'm trying to get up the nerve to go into the jazz clubs in the Village. Maybe we could do that? While you're here. How long are you here?"

The question escaped before I knew it. Because what I was really asking was, *When do I have to start dreading when you'll go?*

"I have two weeks," he said. "But I guess I have to go see my parents. I haven't really been in touch."

I crossed to him and took his cap. Our fingers tangled and he held on.

"Kit. You don't know how good it is to see you."

"What happens after two weeks?" This was the answer that would hurt, that would take my breath away. "Are you being shipped out?"

"I don't know. Probably. They don't tell you anything in the army. Some of us will be picked out for more training. I'm trying to get into the Signal Corps . . . maybe work with photography somehow. But it doesn't seem like it will happen."

"That would be great."

"I'd still be going to Korea. But at least I'd be doing something. Not just . . . shooting people I don't know."

I wanted to ask him if he was afraid, but I couldn't. I'd talked for hours and hours to Billy, lying on the grass in a park, at a beach, in a car with rain drumming on the roof. We talked about everything. But now there were places so tender we couldn't go near them. Things that were just too hard to say. I had no right to ask him the questions he wouldn't want to answer, no right to go to those secret places and hope I could make them better.

Could we still make things better for each other? Or was that gone?

"Why did you do it?" I whispered. Our fingers were still touching. "Why did you enlist?"

He pulled his fingers away. "I didn't see another way to go. I was boxed in. I'd lost you. I thought I was going to be arrested for what I did to Toland. Jamie and I drove around for hours. Then we got a little drunk. Suddenly, we decided that the army was the answer for both of us. I still don't know why."

"Have you heard from Jamie?"

He shook his head. "He hasn't written. I think we both want to forget that night." He looked down and away, his hands dangling. "The question is, can you? You said you were afraid of me. That was the worst thing I ever heard. The worst thing I could imagine."

He looked so stricken, so lost, that tears came to my eyes. "I'm not afraid of you."

"I didn't mean to hurt him. I couldn't see, I was so mad. And the funny thing is, I can't even remember why. I was so afraid. I don't know why I'm always so afraid of losing you."

"You were so angry at me."

"I'm never angry at you. I'm just angry. The awful thing is that people get in the way."

"You keep saying I can help you, but I can't, Billy. I've tried."

He nodded. "You know something strange? The army is helping. I mean, basic is awful, you're exhausted and you get yelled at all the time and you don't know what you're doing, but you can't get mad. You can't really step out of the lines, you know what I mean?"

"My father said that the army would make a man out of Jamie. It made me furious."

He took a step away and walked to the window. His profile was sharp against the light. "I know, it seems like a stupid thing to say, like the army can just make you into something new, something better. But sometimes it can be true." He turned around again. "I'm in basic with all kinds of fellows, from places I never thought about. I'm about to go over an ocean. The world is just bigger than I knew. Maybe I can see further." He ran his hands through his hair. "I don't know what I'm saying. There's places I can be, ways I can be that I never thought about. If I make it through alive."

I crossed to him quickly and put my hand over his mouth. "Don't say *if*. Don't ever say *if*. Say a prayer, right now."

I prayed silently. *Dear God, please let him live. Please. We'll do it all over again, we'll do it right. Don't ignore me, God. Amen.*

He ran his palms over my short hair, over and over, and then cradled my head against his chest. "From the first minute I saw you, it was you. It will always be you."

The cloth of his uniform was rough and unfamiliar. I felt his heartbeat speed up against my cheek. I was conscious of everything – the vague street noise from outside, the ticking clock, my own breathing.

We were alone, truly alone, maybe for the first time. There were no parents, no friends, no brother, no sister. Just us.

He must have had the thought at the same time. His hands moved over my back and down to my waist. I pressed against him.

He pulled away slightly. "Let me just look at you."

"I don't have much time. I have to get to work in an hour."

"You're not going to work tonight?"

"I have to. You know that. I didn't know you were coming—"

"What time do you get off?"

"If I can leave right after the last show, I can get out by three."

"Three a.m.?" Billy's arms dropped from around my waist.

"Three shows a night, seven days a week. This is New York – people stay up until four and five in the morning. Where are you staying?"

"At a buddy's in Brooklyn."

There was a short silence. I guess I should have offered him the couch. But that seemed just too much temptation for both of us.

"You should call home."

"I know. But my mother will want me to take the next train up. I'm not ready yet. I'll go up on Thanksgiving, I guess. The thing is, it's awful to say, but I don't miss home. Everybody knowing my business, calling after me, 'Billy, where are ya going?' 'Billy, stop in, I got something for your mother!' I couldn't go five feet in that place without somebody stopping me from doing what I wanted. I'm sick of it."

"So is the army so much better?" I asked, trying to joke.

"No," he admitted. "It's different. One thing about the army, it sure isn't personal."

I remembered what Flo Foster had said about Billy. *That boy has something chasing him*. I still didn't know what she meant. Maybe it was home.

"We're here *now*, Kit. Now is what we've got. Look" – he grabbed my hand – "I know I have to win you back. I know that night is like . . . a stain between us. If it scared you, it scared me, too. You have no idea how much. But we can get it all back. I'll make it happen. I'll make it all happen again, for the first time. We can start again, can't we?"

"I don't know."

He drew back, puzzled. "Then why did you write to me?"

I stared back at him, realizing that I had no idea what to say. Answers become such complicated things when you have a lie between you and the person you love.

He kissed me gently, and there was the answer we needed. Billy had always had the softest mouth. It had always been able to unfold something closed inside me.

"Remember?" he asked. "I do. I remember every perfect day. How we met. The beach at Narragansett. Just driving around with Jamie. We had it absolutely perfect. Remember?"

I did. I remembered every moment. But what, out of all those memories, should I land on? Lying on the coarse sand, tasting the salt of the ocean on his mouth? Dancing in a white dress on a deck on the beach? Sharing autumn

146

pears while we walked, not paying attention to streets and sidewalks? Because when I thought of that, my heart rose with joy, but at the same time, other pictures came, of a fist smashing into a face on a dark rainy night. Of clothes flying through the air, catching on a breeze, caught on scrub on a two-lane road.

If I could just concentrate on the beginning. If I could just get it clear.

Sixteen

Providence, Rhode Island
September 1949

I'd just started junior year of high school, but I already knew that this year would be the same as the others – a half-distracted glance at my books at night before bed, a stab at homework. If I made myself listen in class, I didn't have to work much outside of it to pull a C average. Da didn't talk to us about college; if we managed to graduate from high school, that was achievement enough for him. He didn't know that Muddie went to Thayer Street on weekends, pretending to be a Pembroke girl. Pembroke was the sister school to Brown, and Muddie wore kilts and cardigans and brushed her hair until it shone, hoping some Brown freshman would ask her what courses she was taking. Then she would spend the afternoon drinking a soda with him and lying. She'd learned the names of professors and courses, and she'd groan about classes and studies until it was time to go down the hill and shop for dinner.

Da also didn't know that Jamie had quit the basketball team and was staying late in the art room, drawing with Mr Hulce. He didn't know that Jamie checked out art books from the library and hid them under his bed.

As for me, I always ducked out of study hall in order to practise my dance routines in the gym. As long as we were safe, looked presentable, and were home by nine, Da left us alone.

For a long time, Da had escaped the Irish curse – the whiskey bottle was only for Saturday nights and guests. But since both Delia and Elena had gone, he'd begun to wander down to Wickenden Street in the evenings for company, and that meant drink. He'd arrive home late and have trouble taking off his shoes. We didn't know what to do about it, so we didn't say a word about it, even to each other. He was never mean; he was either sleepy or silly, wrapping my sweater around his head and pretending it was a turban and he was Bing Crosby, or getting sentimental and crying at dinner just from looking around the table. Once I caught him standing in the doorway of Delia's old room, staring, weaving, and crying.

It was Jamie who had the job of fetching him on the nights he couldn't stop. Jamie, who slung an arm around him and helped him home, took off his shoes, wiped his face with a cloth, got him strong tea in the morning. One night the phone rang and I heard Jamie speaking softly, and then the front door closing. Within the hour, he was back, and I heard him putting Da to bed. In another minute he came to my room and sat on the edge of my bed. Muddie was asleep, so he whispered his hello.

"Is Da OK?" I asked.

"He took all his clothes off in Murphy's Bar," Jamie said.

"All of them?" I began to laugh – I couldn't help it – and Jamie joined in.

"He was naked as the day he was born, standing there on Wickenden. Somebody called the police, but we're lucky, because it was Johnny Tatum who came. You know, Da plays cards with him sometimes? So Johnny says, 'Mac, go inside and put something on.' And so Da disappears back into the bar and comes out again – wearing somebody's tie."

I laughed again, imagining the scene. Jamie flopped back on the pillow, facing the ceiling. "You should have seen it, Kit. All the bar was there, laughing and clapping and whistling, and Johnny Tatum had to laugh, too." He shook his head. "He's lucky he wasn't arrested."

"What can we do? He's bound and determined to humiliate us. At least he's a crowd-pleaser. What would make him do such a thing, get so blind drunk like that?"

"The thing is," Jamie said, "I heard the news earlier. Elena got married today."

With Delia gone, we were poor again, truly poor where we had to worry about rent and food. Da brought home a salary from the American Screw factory but it wasn't enough, so we all had after-school and weekend jobs. I

150

found it was easier to wear my leotards to school underneath the blouses I couldn't be bothered to iron. Sometimes I'd even borrow something of Jamie's, or hold up my skirts with one of his ties. Girls whispered behind my back. Boys thought I was fast and asked me on dates, and I always said no. After a while they left me alone, too.

I walked home each night to save on car fare. That evening, I was coming from my voice lesson. I wanted to think about the radio show I was doing on Saturday and go over the song "It's Magic" in my head. I had a new teacher now, and I'd learned I was a contralto. Just today she'd told me to stop imitating Doris Day and find my own style. "Listen to the words, not just the notes!" she kept saying, raising her hands from the piano keys. I thought I *had* been listening. I knew I wasn't getting it.

I carried a bag with the first of the fall pears, brought home for dessert, because I'd probably missed dinner. Muddie would have kept something warm for me. She had taken over the cooking duties since we'd hit high school. She had given up on making the dishes from Elena we'd loved, and was making stews and fried potatoes and chicken. If it wasn't as good as Elena's cooking, at least it wasn't as bad as Da's.

I passed the gates of Brown and headed east. The university was expanding with the swell of new students and was knocking down buildings for dormitories, one after the other, making their way across College Hill and pressing into Fox Point. The factories were closing and moving outside the city, where land was cheap. Highways were being built, old roads widened for the cars that were being manufactured again. Squeezed from all sides, Fox Point was falling back into poverty, missing out on the postwar boom. Neighbours were moving out, going after the jobs. Da had heard talk that they might pave over the river, just so cars could cross more easily. A river turned into a highway. Da had swum in that river when he was a boy. And before him, people had fished in it. People had sailed away to Africa right from the harbour. Providence was turning its back on its heart.

I could hear the calls of the college boys as they tossed a football back and forth on the lawn of a fraternity house. That never changed – fresh crops of boys with haircuts and good shoes.

Suddenly, an object sailed into my peripheral vision and I almost dropped my bag of pears as I just managed to catch the football. Years of street games had given me good reflexes. The whoop across the street congratulated me, and I fired the ball back to one of the four boys on the lawn.

"Did you see those hands, Jack?"

"Exceptionally fine."

"Did you know angels played football?"

"I didn't know angels had red hair."

To my dismay, they were now heading towards me, tossing the football easily back and forth as they walked.

I started walking quickly down the hill, but of course

they followed me. I realized that it was getting late, that it was chilly, that everybody had gone in to dinner or to study. Power Street, the border of College Hill and Fox Point, was still blocks away.

"Why, oh why, doesn't our team have such an arm? Such a face, such a walk, such a—"

"Move aside, boy. Methinks the comely coed mistakes your raillery for true wit."

Coed? They thought I was a Pembroke girl. If only I'd been Muddie, I would've been pleased as anything.

"What light on yon window breaks? Is that a smile?"

"We almost had windows breaking, if she hadn't caught your pass."

A guffaw, a certain jockeying of position around me. One of them threw the football and another dropped it. I still hadn't looked at their faces.

"Angels don't smile, they glow." This voice was lower, and closer to me – too close, in fact. I could smell grass and perspiration. "Come on, bright angel, don't break our hearts. Speak."

The four of them had surrounded me now, with one walking backwards, facing me. They were just boys, dressed in the kinds of clothes that these kinds of boys wore, pressed chinos, loafers, crewneck sweaters with knotted ties underneath. Trying to impress me with their talk, showing off their fine educations with silly quotes from Shakespeare. I couldn't tell one from the other, and they were in my way. I tried to walk around the one in front, but he only laughed.

153

I stopped. "Listen, you have a swell line, but it's not for me. I have to get somewhere."

"Fair damsel, Providence is a dark and frightening land."

"Find some other distressed damsel, all right?" I gave them a quick smile as I tried to brush past, trying to be a good sport. Mistake.

"Hey, not so fast. We're just trying to make friends."

"Yeah, what's the rush?" The voice was low and insinuating, and the boy made a show of looking at my legs.

No, they hadn't mistaken me for a Pembroke girl. I knew that now. I was wearing what I usually wore to dance class, black tights and leotard under a skirt and cardigan, my bare feet in scuffed shoes. My hair was in a bun loosened from class, stray ends spilling out, waving around my face. I didn't have the brushed perfection of a Pembroke girl.

One of the boys nudged the other one aside. "Hey, dad, the girl isn't interested." He took my arm. "She's looking for real class. Come on, beautiful, why so standoffish?"

We had stopped next to an empty lot, a construction site for a new building for the university. Suddenly, they were all around me in a circle, blocking me in. For the first time, I felt afraid. Their faces blurred into one face with the same expression. I tried to push my way through, but they stood shoulder to shoulder.

"Just let me go," I said. My voice shook a little.

"But we're just getting acquainted. We're just being friendly."

"Gentlemen."

I saw another boy appear through the gloom.

"I think this young lady is trying to go about her business," he said. "Why don't you do the same?"

"Who do you think you are?" One of the boys turned halfway to the new boy, then turned back in contempt.

The other boy stood easily, his hands at his sides. "I think she'd like you to go."

Something about him was familiar. Black hair, thick and uncombed, a little longer than the other boys wore theirs. A white shirt, open at the throat, with no necktie. Dark, dark eyes . . . and then I knew, even though I hadn't seen him in four years.

"Hello, Billy."

He nodded at me briefly. I wasn't sure if he knew who I was.

"You know this character? Billy Macaroni?"

Billy didn't react. Instead, he smiled at me, and I smiled back. I knew he remembered me then. His gaze shifted to the boys and it turned hard. His hands hung loosely at his sides, but suddenly the atmosphere tightened, as though he'd made a fist.

"Time for a drink, boys," one of the boys said, and they ambled away, careful not to hurry.

I let out a breath and turned back to Billy. "Thanks for that," I said.

"You're welcome."

"I could have taken them, though."

He laughed, then stood uncertainly for a moment, his hands in his pockets. "Maybe I should walk you . . . just in case."

I dug into the bag and held out a pear towards him. "I didn't know you went to Brown."

He took it but didn't bite into it. "I'm a sophomore. I'm on the boxing team. That's why they took off."

"You just made a few enemies."

"That's all right – they wouldn't be my friends anyway. I'm a townie, and I'm Italian," he said, biting into the pear. "And they know who my father is. Billy Macaroni – they don't even bother saying it behind my back. The way they look at me – or, I mean, the way they don't look – it's like their glances slide off. Like I'm a mirror, and if they don't see themselves, they don't see anything."

"I thought I'd be invisible, too."

"You? That could never happen."

To cover my embarrassment, I bent down and picked up the forgotten football. I hefted it in one hand and then hurled it, hard and straight, toward the construction site – a clear, spinning pass into the darkness.

"How about that?" he murmured. "The girl's got an arm."

"I can climb trees, too."

"I remember." He took a bite. "I remember that day I met you. I liked you because you liked my pictures. You said, 'If I could do that, I'd do it all the time.' Before that" – he shrugged – "you were my enemy."

156

"Little old me?" I said it flirtatiously, but there was a seriousness behind his eyes. "What do you mean?"

His gaze went blank for a minute. Then he grinned. "You were a girl. Believe me, I've changed."

"That wasn't the first time we met, you know," I said. "The first time was on the Fourth of July. I was wearing red, white and blue. And eating ice cream. I was with my aunt and my dad."

"I don't remember that," he said.

"I was nine. Skinny as a beanpole. All knees and elbows."

"I bet you were a knockout."

We began to walk down the hill, eating our fragrant pears and talking. All the while I was wondering how to keep walking for ever, circling around College Hill, never getting to the narrowing streets and bumpy sidewalks of Fox Point.

When he touched my elbow as we crossed the street, I felt a shimmy down through every nerve. I knew I'd found it, and I didn't even know its name. I felt it in my body, the way my bones were suddenly held together by air, not muscle. What would happen next, I didn't know, but I knew it would have to happen. I would make it happen. I was a motherless child, and I knew that the deepest of tragedies was simple: to love, and not to be loved in return.

I knew I needed an ally, and there was really only one candidate.

157

A couple of days later, when I needed him most, I tried to rope him in.

Jamie lay sprawled on the couch, legs up on the arm. I sat down next to him and peered over his shoulder. "I want to make a deal."

"Not now, pup. I'm studying."

"Since when?"

"Easier that way."

"Easier how?"

"People leave you alone when you're smart. You should try it."

I nudged him. "Hey, you might know trigonometry, but can you keep an eighth note triple count with your feet?"

"The question is, why would I want to?"

"Look, are you working on Sunday?"

"No."

"Well, I have a date, and I need you to come along. My friend has a car. You can bring a girl."

"I don't have a girl."

"Oh, for crying out loud, Jamie, help me out. So I can say a gang is going."

"Why don't you ask Muddie?"

"Because I don't think I can stand her asking, 'And how are you enjoying your studies?' all afternoon long."

He snorted. "And why," he asked, "can't you just tell Da that you have a date?"

"Because he's in college, and Da won't let me date a college man. And because . . . because he's Billy Benedict."

158

Jamie looked at me over his book. "The kid with the camera? Nate Benedict's son?"

I nodded. "Oh, Jamie, come on – if you'd just come out with us, it won't look like a date, it will look like we're all friends."

"And I'll be a third wheel."

"Not a third wheel! We'll have fun. We'll have a picnic or something. He said we'd go to Roger Williams Park. You need to get out anyway. You're starting to study all the time, just like Muddie. He's picking me up Sunday morning. Come on, you want to." I smiled at him.

"Please note that smiles like that don't work on brothers. But all right."

Jamie jumped into the back seat and I slid into the front. Billy looked surprised, but not annoyed. That scored a point, right there.

"I asked my brother to come," I said. "I hope you don't mind. It's just that—"

"You don't trust me. Good. I'm completely untrustworthy." His grin lit up his face. "Hi – Jamie, right? Another one who can climb trees."

"Right."

"Let's go. My mother packed a basket." He took off and instead of heading to the park, he kept on going. He wore a blue shirt, the cuffs rolled up. I watched his hands on the steering wheel. Even his hands were beautiful.

"I thought we were going for a picnic," Jamie said.

"It's such a great day, how about the beach?" Billy asked.

"Sure," I said. "We never go."

"I have a favourite spot. We used to go there when I was a kid, before. . ."

"Before what?"

He shrugged. "I still go on weekends when I can."

Probably with a girl, I thought, and my heart felt squeezed with a new emotion – jealousy. But here I was in the front seat next to him. Today, I was the girl.

We swung the hamper between us as we walked to the beach. The air was chilly but the sun was warm. The water was a deep navy frothed with white. We spread out a blanket and sat watching the waves.

Jamie settled in with a sandwich. "So, are you going to be a lawyer like your old man?"

"He thinks so."

"What do you think?" I asked.

"Well, I know I don't want to be in his business. What about you?" he asked Jamie.

Jamie laughed. "College is not in the plan. It's the Irish form of advancement – you don't dare do better than those before you. Our dad never made anything of himself. Course, he expects the same of us. Maybe I'll join the army. Or the air force. Fly away." He tossed a piece of bread to the gulls. "Better than factory work."

"You sure about that? What if we go to war again?"

160

"That'll never happen. We'll just do rescue missions now, like the Berlin Airlift."

I'd seen Jamie looking at those pictures in *Life* magazine, Germans looking up at the sky, at the planes, waiting for the food and medicine to drop. I could see him wanting to be that pilot, looking down at upturned faces, knowing he was saving them. It was Jamie who could transform a gloomy afternoon, or end a squabble with a joke. He was always saving us, why not do the same for strangers?

Jamie dug into the hamper for a napkin and came up with a camera. "Hey, this yours? Sweet."

"You're still taking pictures?" I asked.

"When I can." His hands were sure and easy as he took the camera. "I'd like to do it for a living, but my father thinks it's crazy." He aimed the camera out at the ocean. "But wouldn't it be swell, travelling around taking pictures for magazines? Robert Capa, Cartier-Bresson – that's what I'd like to do. Capture moments in time. Truth. Not what people say, not even what they do . . . but how they stand, and the look in their eyes they can't hide."

I had no idea what he was talking about, but I saw that he had come alive. He rose on his knees and took a few fast shots of me, then a few of Jamie. He aimed at the sea and the sky.

I looked up at him, on his knees against the blue sky, the wind whipping his hair, and it was like he was electric, a sparking wire. He sent out a charge, and I felt it vibrate inside me. All I wanted to do was touch him.

It was twilight as Billy made the turn on to Hope Street. He pulled up at the corner. We'd stayed at the shore as long as we could, until cold and hunger drove us back to the car. We'd eaten all the sandwiches and run through the surf and screamed at the shock of the cold water. We'd walked and looked for shells and tossed a football. We hadn't talked of anything much. But none of us had wanted the day to end.

On the way home, "It's Magic" came on the radio and I sang along. I wasn't embarrassed. Billy looked over at me from time to time while he drove, a big, delighted grin on his face. Now I understood it. I understood magic.

Billy cut the engine and we sat at the corner of Hope and Transit. The light was almost gone and the tree branches looked black. The wind had knocked a carpet of gold leaves on to the ground.

I knew it was time to say thank you for a lovely time, but the usual phrases seemed so small compared to the day. Putting words to it would cheapen it. I knew Jamie didn't want to speak, either.

Billy got out of the car to open my door. I stepped out as Jamie opened the back door, and the three of us stood for a moment, not moving. Suddenly, Billy flung his arms around both of us. "Mark it on your calendar," he said. "One perfect day."

At that moment Da appeared out of the gloaming. His expression of greeting froze, then hardened.

"Good evening to you," he said. "Is that Billy Benedict there?"

"Hello, Mr Corrigan. I didn't think you'd recognize me."

"Sure I do. You're the image of your father. Kit, Jamie, time to come in now. Muddie will have supper on the table." I was startled by the coolness in his tone.

"Time for me to be getting home, too," Billy said.

I wanted the goodbye to last longer, but that was it. The song was done. Magic was over. Time to turn the record over and listen to the B side – Doris singing "Put 'Em in a Box, Tie 'Em with a Ribbon".

Da stood there as Jamie and I watched Billy's taillights disappear up Hope Street. All the air went out of the day.

"I didn't know you two were friends with Billy Benedict," Da said. "Since when?"

"Since today," Jamie said.

Da's gaze turned to me. "And you, miss?"

"What's wrong with Billy?"

"I don't know Billy. I know his father."

"We just went to the beach. It's not like you ever took us anywhere unless there was a profit in it." I flung out the words, not knowing that I meant them until they were out.

He took a breath and stared down at the sidewalk. Then he looked up. "I've seen enough of beaches. I've probably seen every pebble of sand in four hundred miles of coastline. Nate Benedict and I drove them together back in

163

the twenties. We were both working for Danny Walsh. I learned how to drive a getaway car at sixteen."

I suddenly remembered that night so long ago, after the hurricane, when Nate had sat at our table. "Delia, too?"

"Once or twice, even Delia. She drove the covering car a few times – that's what we called the second car that would block the Feds or the police from following. Good to use a woman – she would pretend to break down and block the road. Listen, in those days, you tripped over bootleggers in Rhode Island. For me and Delia, it was a job, a way to get by so that they wouldn't catch up to us, separate us, and send us to orphanages. It was Delia who saw I needed to stop or I'd wind up in one of the Irish gangs for good. She saw the way the wind was blowing, that we'd repeal Prohibition and then I'd only have one skill, how to outrun someone who's chasing you. The crash had happened, and she couldn't find me work. So she brought home a girl instead. I knew Maggie would never marry a man in the rackets, so I quit. But Nate didn't, did he? Danny Walsh disappears in thirty-three, the Italians take over, and Nate gets himself an education. Then he has to pay back what he owes, and that means working for them. Now look at him. He's just as bad as they are."

"He's not a gangster," I said.

"He's in it up to his neck, just the same," Da said. He looked tired. "So why should I be happy to see Nate's son with his arms around my children?"

"But Billy isn't in it," I said. "He's not his father."

"I know, he got into the university, I heard." But Da said

164

this as if it didn't matter. "Just now, walking towards you like that . . . it was like seeing myself and Delia and Nate when we all met. Down at Buttonwoods Cove, it was."

Jamie and I exchanged a surprised glance. Billy had taken us there today.

"She swam out to meet the boat in the pitch-black – we never went if there was a full moon. She was fearless back then. She hauled herself up the boat, her braid over her shoulder, and she wrung it out. And Nate looked at her like she was a selkie. A creature from the sea, not quite human . . . well, we were in each other's pockets for a while. And nothing good came of it."

"What do you mean?"

"If your aunt were here, she'd say, 'Stick to your own.'" Da looked over at the house, as if wishing Delia was on the front stoop to back him up.

But what if Billy is "my own"? I wanted to say. "That's the Irish in you talking," I said instead. "Things aren't like that any more."

"I hope I've taught you one thing anyway – that saying a thing doesn't make it so." Da sighed. "Well, now. I'm an ignorant man, but I can see down a road. You can't stop something that's got to go on. I can't stop this any more than I can stop the moon from rising." Da looked at me, and he shook his head. I saw that something had happened without my noticing – he looked older. Grey at his temples, lines at the corners of his eyes. "I just want you to know, it will break my heart to see it. That's all."

Seventeen

New York City
November 1950

I was in his arms, against the kitchen wall, every inch of me against him. Billy's hands were on my hair, my face. His mouth was soft and yielding, hard and so warm. Searching, searching for everything I had to give. Like he wanted to get to the very core of me.

One kiss had led to another and another and we couldn't stop. It had been too long without each other. The kettle screamed and we ignored it. Finally, I broke away and turned off the burner and we walked, still kissing, to the living room, where we fell on the couch.

He was mine again, and he was leaving, going off to war. I'd never expected this; I had lived through a war and looked at other girls crying in train stations and bus stations and I'd only seen the romance of it, the luxury of so many tears. I hadn't realized that inside all those girls

166

was the terrible knowing that who they loved was going away and might not come back.

For a minute the former tenant flashed into my mind, Bridget Warwick, waiting in a quiet apartment, believing her husband would come back, and hearing the bell ring one day and a man with a telegram on the other side of the door.

"I just want to hold you," he said. "I want to remember this." He drew back and looked at my face. And then he yawned.

I laughed, and he laughed, too.

"Am I boring you?" I asked, and we both laughed again. Billy slid off the couch and leaned his head back against it.

"I'm sorry, I'm just so tired. . . It was a long bus ride to get here."

I patted the couch cushion. "Come on back up here."

We lay on the couch together, my head on his shoulder. He played with my hand. "This is nice."

"Nice," I agreed.

"It's kind of like our dream, isn't it?" he said.

"It is our dream," I said, and the stab of guilt I felt made me feel queasy. It was a dream orchestrated by his father, the web that Billy had dropped into without knowing it was a baited trap.

I heard his breathing slow, and his hand slipped out of mine. Carefully, slowly, I drew back to look at him. His eyelashes on his cheek, his lips slightly parted, he looked peaceful and young.

167

He said he was changed. And I felt it, I felt the change. His kisses had been sweet and loving. He hadn't pushed or pressed. Something was missing, and I could put my finger right on it. It was desperation.

All I felt was warmth and sweetness, and I fell back against his shoulder. He stirred and rested his head on top of mine. Then I thought of Nate, and I stiffened. Billy was here, and I should call his father. That had been our agreement. But how could I, with Billy right here? I couldn't, not yet. I needed to hold this sweetness, my spoonful of honey. For just one more day.

I lay there stiffly now, afraid to move, afraid to wake him up, afraid to curl into him. Nate had come between us. What if Billy came to the club tonight, and his father was there? What if someone told him that Nate was there often, that Nate and I knew each other, that we'd spoken, that we'd even had a dance together? What would Billy say, how would he feel? Discovery felt so close now. I hadn't done anything wrong, not really. I'd accepted a loan of a place to stay. Was that so wrong? I went over and over the decision. I was trying to protect Billy, that's all.

Obviously, I hadn't thought this through. Had Nate?

I looked at the clock. It was time to go, but I didn't want to wake Billy. I slipped off the couch and hurried to dress. I put on my make-up, knowing that I wouldn't get to the club on time. When I came back into the living room, Billy was sitting up, his face soft and sleepy. I wanted to hurl myself into his lap, but I just stopped and smiled.

"You look so . . . sophisticated," he said. "Like a movie star."

"Stage make-up. Look, you're exhausted. Why don't you go to Brooklyn, and come over tomorrow morning."

He stood and stretched. "No, I'll come with you to the club. I want to see the show."

I hesitated. What if Nate was there? "Are you sure? You can catch it another night. There's not much to see, anyway. I'm just another girl in the line."

"You're never just another girl." He stood and tucked in his shirt. "Come on, get your coat. I don't want you to be late. They might blame me."

I slipped into my camel coat. We walked out together, arm in arm. Like a real married couple, so much in love they needed to touch, even if it was fabric against fabric. Sleeve against sleeve.

Monday nights were usually slow, but the club was crowded that night. I glimpsed Billy during the shows, sitting in a small table against the wall. He sat through two shows, and then signalled me at the start of the third that he'd be back.

We were all beat when we finally made it to the dressing room. We dragged ourselves into our clothes.

I figured Billy would be outside the front entrance, waiting. I would be like the other girls, sweeping out to see my beau. Suddenly, I remembered Hank. Would he show up tonight? I doubted it, after the scene at the rink.

I would call him tomorrow, make sure things were OK with us.

I walked into the club. The lights were still low, and the waiters were trying to get the last stragglers out. I walked across the dance floor and saw a sudden shaft of light touch my sleeve. I turned back and saw Nate silhouetted in the doorway that led from backstage to the door of the private lounge.

My heart fell. I'd been on the lookout for him tonight, and had been relieved when I hadn't seen him. I figured he was back in Providence.

He signalled to me, and I had no choice but to walk over.

"Mirto just went upstairs to the lounge," he said. "Could you run up there and sit with him for a few minutes? Just chat him up. I have to—"

"No," I said, and I could see he wasn't happy I'd interrupted. "I can't. I already changed, and I'm going home."

I saw the flare of anger in his eyes. "What makes you think you get to say no?"

My breath caught. We were alone in the hallway. He had said the words so calmly, but I felt the menace, the threat.

"Don't be a dumb kid and kick down a ladder," he said. "Understand? I'm telling you, it's just a few minutes, sit with a guy and make him happy."

I was afraid to say no. I said it anyway. "No."

His eyes narrowed, but before he could say anything we

heard footsteps on the dance floor. We both turned our heads and saw Billy. When he saw who I was talking to he stopped walking.

"Billy." Nate breathed his name almost like he was afraid.

Billy walked towards us, a slight, puzzled frown on his face. "Hey, Pop. What are you doing here? I thought some guy was trying to muscle in on my girl."

Nate gave me a sharp look. "I didn't know you were in town."

"I just got in today. I didn't know you went in for nightclubs." Billy looked from me to his father. He was watchful, careful. I knew that look. He didn't like to be surprised.

"I've seen your father here a couple of times," I said.

"I have a client in New York now, so I come down pretty often," Nate said casually. "It's good to see you. You look well."

"I'm all right." Billy looked uncomfortable under Nate's gaze. He wasn't giving him anything.

"Would you kids like to get a late supper? I could take you to Reuben's. We can sit, have something to eat, talk."

"No, thanks," Billy told him.

"Coffee, then." Nate shot me a look that said, *Help me out here*.

"Billy, why don't you go," I said. "I'm completely dead. I'll see you in the morning."

"Maybe tomorrow," Billy said to his father. It was like,

171

now that he was wearing a uniform, he was able to say no, and Nate had to take it. "I was just going to walk Kit home, then head to Brooklyn to stay with my buddy."

"Let me give you cab fare—"

"No, Pop!" Billy's voice was sharp.

As he took my arm to lead me out, I saw Nate's face, clenched and furious. I just didn't know who he was mad at more.

172

Eighteen

New York City
November 1950
We walked out the front entrance. Billy held my hand, but his mind wasn't on me. He was walking fast, and I had to double-time to keep up. We slipped through the stragglers at the entrance. Billy waved away a cab. His hand tightened on mine as we darted across Third Avenue. It wasn't until we were on a quiet crosstown street that he spoke.

"What the hell is he doing here? I figured he was in Providence."

"I've seen him a few times," I admitted. "I think he likes to check up on me, make sure I'm OK."

"I guess he thinks you're still my girl," Billy said. "I never told him we broke up."

I held up our entwined hands. "See how that worked out?"

I was relieved that he smiled, but it faded right away. "I wasn't ready to see him," he said.

173

I squeezed his hand. "So, what did you think of the show?"

"I thought it was swell. And I couldn't take my eyes off you. I was trying to figure if it was because you're my girl or not. And I decided that it's not. There's always a girl everybody notices. You're that girl."

"That's sweet," I said. "But I'm sure you think that because I'm your girl."

"No, I mean it," Billy said earnestly. "I can really see it now, Kit. You're in this big New York production, with the right costumes and the right dances, and you can really shine. You belong here. I'm really proud of you." He stopped and put his hands on my shoulders so I could look into his face. "Really proud."

He was being genuine, I could see it. His approval meant more than anybody's. More than anything. I wanted to tell him about the callback right then, see the excitement in his eyes. But what if he slipped and told his father? Nate might tell the owner of the club.

Another secret to keep. Would I ever be able to get to the place where everything was open between us?

He tipped my chin up with his finger. "What is it? You looked so happy, and then so sad."

"There's so many things to say," I said. "And there isn't any time to say them. I'm afraid of what's going to happen."

He leaned over and kissed me. "I promise you. I'll be back. The thing is – I started giving a damn again."

I leaned into the kiss, and the world dropped away. We

174

only stopped because someone harrumphed behind us, a man walking a dog.

"Carry on, soldier," he said as he passed us.

We slowed our steps, letting the man and his spaniel get ahead of us. Someone was buying a newspaper and an orange at the place that stayed open all night. What people don't know about New York is that someone is always awake. I hadn't realized how comforting that was. You give up your home when you move to Manhattan, but you get something else – a feeling that you're right smack in the world.

"I can see you here, making your way in Manhattan," Billy said. "I just wish I could be here with you."

"You will be."

"Onstage, you look so beautiful, so . . . mature. Like a doll, like a beautiful living doll."

"I'm not a doll. I'm just me. I'm just a dancer."

"No, I mean, guys will be after you. You could fall in love with someone else. No, don't look at me that way, I'm not being jealous. It's just a fact. Men chase after girls like you, Kit, and now that you're dancing in this big nightclub, you think it won't happen?"

"It doesn't matter if they chase if I don't get caught. Anyway, I don't want to do this for ever. I want to go back to the theatre."

"It's not easy, having a girl who's a dancer. It's not going to be easy when I'm halfway around the world. Because what you want to know is that your girl is the same as when you left her. Waiting."

I stopped walking. "Are you asking me if I'll wait for you? You know I will."

"I'm asking you to marry me before I go."

This time it was real. It wasn't a dream for a hazy future. I wasn't a schoolgirl, and the future was as real as the steel and stone surrounding us. I was conscious of how big the moment was, how easy it would be to say the wrong thing. Because squealing "Yes!" and jumping into his arms wasn't something I could do. Everything between us had taken that option away.

"Or else I'll just go," he said. "Because it's going to be worse for me, not knowing."

"Is this a proposal or a threat?" I asked, trying to keep my voice light. This wasn't the way I imagined Billy's proposal would go.

"No, no, not a threat. It's just that if I'm not sure of you, it will drive me crazy. I'll be waiting for letters, I'll be reading between every line. . ." He shook his head. "Maybe other guys can go off to war like that. I can't. I want my future to start before I leave."

The funny thing was, Nate had been right. Billy did need a dream.

He took my hands. "I know I'm not saying this right. I should have a big fat diamond ring to put on your finger. But we can do it right. We can go down to Maryland – you don't need to wait for the licence, and you can get married at seventeen. We can have a honeymoon."

"Billy, I don't know. . ."

176

"Do you love me?"

"Of course I do." The cold wind roared off the river, making my eyes tear.

"You said yes once before."

"I did not."

"Well." His eyes twinkled. "You *wanted* to. I just didn't let you."

"That is not how I remember that conversation," I said, smiling. I fell against him, my cheek against his chest.

"You're shivering," he said. "It's so cold. Come on."

We kept on walking, quickly now, his arm around me. We approached the building and stopped in front of my door. "Come in," I said. "We can talk inside."

He leaned back and looked up at the sky as if looking for something to help him. "There is nothing I want to do more than come inside."

"Then come inside." I slipped my arms around him.

He shook his head. "I think it's a really bad idea." Gently, he reached behind and took my hands. "Look. We have time. Not a lot, but enough. I'm going to go back to Brooklyn, and you're going to go to bed. And tomorrow, we'll talk. We'll talk it all out. We can go over all the reasons getting married is a bad idea, if you want. We'll walk and we'll talk and we'll figure it out together. But if I come inside tonight . . . we won't talk, I guarantee you."

"Are you sure? It's an awfully long way to Brooklyn." Now that he said he was going, I didn't want him to. I didn't want to say goodbye one more time than I had to.

"I'm sure." He brushed his lips against my cheek. "Sure enough for both of us. Look, it's four in the morning. Get some sleep. I'll call you around eleven."

Reluctantly, I left him and went inside. I closed the door and leaned against it. My mind whirled, and I could still feel the touch of his hands.

Married at seventeen? I had never wanted that. I'd seen too many girls go off in their white gowns and bouquets, some of them glowing, some of them miserable and pregnant. I'd seen them at twenty-two with two or three kids hanging on their skirts. I'd seen them disillusioned at thirty, not in love, not even satisfied, just trapped.

No, I had never wanted that.

But there was another way, wasn't there? To marry your true love, and start your life? How easy it would make it to turn down dates if I had a gold ring on my finger. I could concentrate on dancing, on acting, and know I had Billy in a safe, protected place in my heart.

I walked slowly into the apartment, turning on the lights one by one, until the whole place blazed. This place could be mine, then. Really mine. I would be Mrs Kathleen Benedict, living in the family apartment. I would have a right to be here. And here, I would sit at my own table and write letters to Billy. Another wife of a soldier sitting at the kitchen table. *Come home, darling. I'm waiting for you.* But the difference would be this: our story would have a happy ending. He would come home.

Nineteen

Providence, Rhode Island
September 1950

After Billy threw my belongings on to the Mid-Cape Highway, I swore we were through, and it didn't seem like he'd put up much of an argument. Still, he lived in my head. We had terrific conversations in which I explained how his jealousy had driven us apart. Jamie slipped out of the house with a guilty expression on weekends, and I knew he was going to see Billy. They had spent a lot of time together over the summer, and just because Billy and I weren't speaking didn't mean that they had to stop.

I caught Jamie alone after school one day. "So how is he?" I asked.

"He's OK."

"You know, I didn't want to hurt him. It's just he gets so jealous for no reason."

Jamie crossed past me to get to the kitchen. "You don't know what to do for him."

"What do you mean? What should I be doing?" Insulted, I trailed after him. Jamie and I had our squabbles, but this felt like a real criticism, and it stung. Jamie knew me better than anyone, even Billy. "Let him think he owns me?"

"He's not like that." He took the milk bottle out of the fridge and put it down. "You don't know how hard he's trying. Would you just think about it for a minute? His mother should be in the bughouse, but everyone pretends she's OK. And his father . . . you know about the Kefauver Committee hearings, right?"

"Sure I do." I didn't read the paper much, but you couldn't walk down the street without knowing about the mob hearings – there were headlines every day in the paper, and everybody was talking about it. Senator Kefauver was going after organized crime, and he had scheduled hearings all over the country. Kansas City, Chicago – they put the hearings on television, and even though hardly anyone had a set, people piled into bars to watch it. Everybody knew they'd be coming to New York and Kefauver would be going after the big mobsters like Joe Adonis and Frank Costello.

Jamie sighed when he saw I didn't get it. "They're saying the hearings might come to Boston, and if they come to Boston, that means Providence, and Nate could get a subpoena. Nobody's saying anything, but who knows how things will shake out?"

Da's words came back to me, about how Nate was in it up to his neck.

"So maybe it's better that you broke up with him," Jamie said. "He's got a lot on his mind."

"Whose side are you on?" I asked my brother. "He threw my whole wardrobe to the seagulls!"

"I'm on the side of true love," Jamie said. He smiled, but his eyes looked sad. "However it falls."

I'd been back to school for only a week when I found Billy waiting at the tree where we used to meet. He swung into step beside me and we didn't say a word. Silently, he handed me a pear.

If he thought a reference to our first real meeting would undo me, he had another thing coming. I took a bite, and it was sour. I threw the rest to the squirrels.

We walked without talking. Finally, as we passed Prospect Terrace, he gently took my elbow and steered me to the railing. We were high above the city, and we could see the river glinting below and the dome of the statehouse. On the other side of the railing, Roger Williams looked out at the city, tilting back and raising one stone hand in a regal hello. We'd learned it all in school, how he'd founded Rhode Island on the principle of religious liberty. *Everybody should have their own God and get along*, said Roger. It was a nice story, but I was still waiting to see how it was all going to work out. Billy and I shared the same religion, but that didn't mean our worlds were the same. Fox Point was a long way from Federal Hill.

Billy reached out his hand, and after a moment I put

181

mine in his. To refuse him was more than I could do. We laced our fingers together.

"I sat down with my father last night," he told me. "He says he's going into wills and trusts. It's going to take a while, but he promised that by the time I graduate from law school, he'll get rid of the clients he has and he'll have new ones before we hang out the Benedict and Benedict sign. This time, I actually believe him."

"That's good."

"I told him no."

I turned, startled, to look into his face.

"I told him no, once and for all no. I'm going to New York after I graduate and I'm going to become a photographer."

"What did he say?"

"He offered me a deal." Billy's mouth twisted. "He's so good at deals. He said, 'Go to law school first, and after you graduate, I'll stake you for a year. If you can't make it you have to come home. But I won't help you otherwise.' And I said, 'No, I don't need your help.' It was not a pleasant conversation. I don't know, it's like he's got to do his life over, like he's making penance or something. If I say no, it's like I'm damning him to hell."

"That's ridiculous," I assured him, the look on his face breaking my heart. I knew what it was like to struggle against your own father, but Da was nothing compared to Nate. "Besides," I said, "there's always purgatory."

He let out a reluctant laugh, then took me in his arms.

182

"This is why I need you," he murmured. "I need you to make me laugh."

We kissed, and I rested my head against his chest. The next words were muffled, but I heard them.

"I also told him that I'm going to marry you."

I pulled back to look at him. "Don't you think you should ask me first?"

"I know better than that. You'd just say no."

"This is one heck of a proposal," I said. "You don't even ask the girl, and then you answer for her."

He grinned. "In less than a year, you'll be eighteen and I'll have graduated. We could get married in June and move to New York. We've got all year to save up. I'll get a job—"

"Billy—"

"No, listen. The whole world could explode tomorrow. Did you read *Life* magazine? It's not a question of *if* the Russians will drop the Bomb. It's *when*. So what are we waiting for? We've got to get going on our lives."

"So we should elope because the Russians are going to blow us up anyway?"

"We could get an apartment, someplace close enough so that you can walk to the theatre and your dance classes—"

"A year is so far away."

"Can you imagine us in New York? We'd conquer it! We'd get everything we want out of it. And we'd get away! Don't you want that, too?"

"You know I do. Or at least I did." I knew I had to say it. "I can't have you exploding on me again. I couldn't take that."

183

"I'm sorry. I know how wrong I was. It's like, I get angry and I just can't see anything. Jamie will tell you – I've been kicking myself about it ever since. I just couldn't stand seeing you with him. I thought . . . well, I thought the wrong thing. I know that now. I understand that. It will never happen again."

"Never again?"

"Never, ever again. Never, ever, ever."

"You've got to trust me, Billy."

"I do. That's the crazy thing. In my heart, I do. I can do anything if you're with me. If we're married. You don't have to say anything, this isn't a proposal. No, don't say a word. I just wanted you to see it like I do."

Our bodies crashed together and we hung on. The last smell of summer was in his hair. Over his shoulder, past the rooftops of Providence, I could see our future. The apartment, the jobs, the way we'd discover the city and not let it frighten us, because we were together. We would lie together in our own bed, in our own home, and make our own lives.

"We can do it," he said. "One more year."

That embrace, right there, on the top of the hill? So tight, so urgent, so necessary. That was how love felt. That's what safe was.

Twenty

New York City
November 1950

The headline screamed up at me from a neighbour's morning paper when I bent down for the bottle of milk outside my door.

GANGLAND SLAYING AT LIDO
Ray "The Coat" Mirto Shot to Death on Dance Floor in
After-Hours Hit
Cops Say Mob War Likely

My stomach dropped, and I couldn't catch my breath. I didn't believe the headline at first. But the photograph said it all – a man slumped in a chair on the dance floor of the Lido. The man Nate had asked me to spy on.

My heart went triple time, and I pressed one hand to it. I tried to swallow. Quickly, I snatched the paper from my neighbour's mat, grabbed my milk and slipped back inside.

I winced at the sound of the door slam. I felt faint, and I sank down into the chair.

I smoothed the newspaper out on the kitchen table. I tried to read the article, the type jumping in front of my eyes. My hands pressed against my heart as if I could stop its thumping.

Ray Mirto, "reputed crime boss in Frank Costello's operation", had been shot sometime last night, right in the club. I looked again at the gruesome photograph of the dead man. A thin sliver of light illuminated one outflung hand. His white shirt was stained black with blood.

I want you to tell me if Ray Mirto is there.

All that interest in Ray Mirto and when he was at the club, how long he stayed. Nate had asked me to sit at his table last night! To keep him there?

Was Nate involved in the murder?

Because if he was, I was, too.

I ran to the sink and splashed cold water on my face. I grabbed the faucet and hung on, trying to think. What should I do? I had reported back about a man who turned up dead.

When the phone rang, I nearly jumped out of my skin. I ran for it.

"Hello, Kit, it's Ted Roper."

I sank down on the carpet, holding the receiver hard against my ear. What did Ted Roper know?

"Did you see the paper?" he asked.

I swallowed. "Yeah." My voice came out hoarse and barely there.

"I'm calling all the girls, just to reassure them. The club is safe. The cops were all over it this morning, but we're set to open tonight, like usual. And you know they caught the guy."

I sat up straight. "They caught the killer?"

"It'll be in the next edition. Come on, you're kidding me, you didn't know?"

"Why would I know?"

"It's all over the radio, kiddo. I guess Mirto was skimming off the top, the lunkhead, and Costello ordered the hit. Some button man from the organization."

"What?"

"You know, a hired killer. The guy's got a good lawyer, though. C'mon, you really don't know?" Ted paused. "Benedict's the lawyer."

"Nate Benedict?" I couldn't believe what I was hearing.

"There'll be reporters at the club tonight. If I were you, I'd come in early and get out fast. It won't be long before they start kicking up some dirt on your boyfriend."

On Billy? But how would reporters know about Billy?

"Listen, it sells papers. Don't worry about it. Keep your head down and your powder dry, right?"

"This is all so awful," I said.

"Sell, sell, sell, doll. That's New York."

Francis Maretti Arrested and Charged
Providence Lawyer Nate "No Witnesses"
Benedict to Defend

Reputed hit man Frankie "No Bones" Maretti got a
surprise this morning when he picked up a bag of
doughnuts for his usual breakfast in Fort Lee, New
Jersey. Police surrounded Maretti and slapped on
the cuffs. Protesting his innocence, Maretti was led
away, even while he insisted he'd already paid for
his Boston creams.

The phone sat on the table, black and squat. I dressed and
sat there, staring at it, waiting for Billy to call. What would
I say? I couldn't tell him that his father had asked me to
keep tabs on a guy who'd been murdered. Then the whole
story would come out, how I was living in Nate's
apartment. *Billy must never know*, I thought suddenly, with
horror. Before, I'd figured that we could tell him eventually.
But he wouldn't understand. He would never understand.
He thought I'd made my own way in New York, that I was
that strong. But I wasn't.

I wasn't strong at all.

I had to talk to Nate. I had to see him face to face and
ask him about Ray Mirto. I didn't know if he'd tell me the
truth or not, but before I talked to Billy, I had to talk to his
father. I had to know if I was in the clear.

188

I was waiting for the ring of the phone, but it still startled me. I picked it up after two rings and said hello.

Billy's voice was low and deep, still husky from sleep. "Good morning, beautiful."

He didn't know. He hadn't seen the papers yet.

Relief made me sag back against the couch cushions. "Good morning."

"Did you sleep well? I did. Like a log."

"Me, too."

"So what time should I swing by? I'm going to grab some coffee here, and—"

I was suddenly scared to see him. "Would it be OK if . . . if we didn't meet until later?" I asked. "I need some time to think. Can I meet you at the club tonight?"

I could tell by his hesitation that he was hurt. "Sure. Of course. I don't want to push you."

"It's just easier to think if you're not in front of me. Or touching me."

He laughed softly. "Tom here was at me to meet his buddies. Why don't I do that today, and I'll see you tonight. Would it be pushing to say I love you?"

"No. It would be nice."

"Then I love you, too."

"I love you, too," I said, and hung up.

I needed to clear my head, and I needed to get away from the phone. I pulled on some clothes and my old navy coat. I slipped outside and started for the corner. A walk in the park with a bag of chestnuts. I'd been wanting to do that for weeks.

I don't know where he'd been, but suddenly he was walking next to me, a man in a dark suit, his hat pulled low.

"Where are you off to?"

I walked quicker, but he kept up easily.

"Listen, Kit, can you take a tip from somebody?"

"Who are you? How do you know my name?" I stopped and faced him. He had weary grey eyes and a big nose.

"You're just a kid," he said, looking at me with a glance that seemed to add me up like a cash register. "How'd you get mixed up in this? If you want to talk. . ." He handed me a card.

I almost threw it in his face, but I caught the initials. FBI.

"I'm not going to inform on anybody," I said.

"Just keep the card," he said.

I was too afraid not to. I turned and walked back to the apartment, and he let me go. I went in the lobby door. Hank was there, just sitting in the gold chair by the mailboxes.

"Are they out there?" he asked.

"Yeah," I said. "One of them just tried to talk to me. I didn't tell him anything. I can't believe they're hounding your parents like that." I looked at Hank. "Are you OK?" He looked even jumpier than I did.

The question seemed to take a long time to settle. "Can

190

I go out your window, in the back?" Hank asked. "I know it's a weird question, but they could be out there, and I don't want them to see me."

"Sure," I said. "But how will you. . ."

"My friend Iggy lives in the building behind this one. I know they leave their back door open."

Hank followed me into my kitchen. He went to the window and opened it.

"Are you going to tell me what's wrong?" I asked. "Is it your parents? Did something happen?"

"I have to go see my mother at work."

"Can I walk with you a little bit? I've got to get out of the house for a while. Did you see the papers this morning? Somebody was killed at the club last night, and I'm spooked."

He turned for just an instant, but I couldn't read his expression. "I saw the papers." Then he turned back and was out the window in a flash. I jumped out and trailed after him over the cracked pavement of the garden to the far wall. He hoisted himself up and I scrambled after him. We jumped down into a nicer yard. Here I could see more clearly the back of a town house. There were curtains at every window, pushed back to let in the light.

Hank knocked on the door, and when there was no answer, he pushed it open. "Mrs Kessler? Hello?" There was still no answer, so he walked in. "Iggy's at school. His mother works on the third floor; she knows I come in and out."

He walked down the centre hall. I could see rooms as we passed, rooms with couches and rugs and polished tables with silver vases on them filled with flowers.

"These guys have dough," I said.

"His father is a lawyer. Who knows, we might need him someday." Hank gave a hollow laugh.

"Hank, what's the mystery? Are your parents in more trouble?"

He didn't answer. He opened the front door and peered around. He walked out, and I followed, the heavy door shutting behind us. I followed him all the way to Second Avenue without speaking.

"Billy – is he your boyfriend?" he asked.

Boyfriend, fiancé, or love I had to part with. Because if I said no to marriage, he would ship out and it would be over. No letters, no dreaming, no waiting. Suddenly, I felt empty, thinking of that.

"Honestly, I don't know what he is now."

We didn't say anything for a few crosstown blocks. I guess the talk about Billy dampened the conversation, and Hank seemed lost in his troubles. A little girl was walking in front of us, carrying three balloons. Yellow, blue and red. They bobbed in the wind over her shoulder. I tried to catch Hank's eye, but he was walking fast, eyes straight ahead.

"In my family, balloons are magic," I said.

He cocked an eyebrow at me.

"Really," I said. "Once, we—"

Suddenly, a siren went off. People on the sidewalks

192

stopped in their tracks. A traffic cop up ahead held up a white-gloved hand, and all the traffic stopped on Lexington Avenue.

"What's going on?" I asked as a woman grabbed her child and hurried away.

"It's the air-raid drill," Hank said. "We're only a block from the subway. Come on."

"Air raid?" I asked, struggling to keep up with his long stride.

"Didn't you see it in the paper last week?"

"I only read the gossip columns and the headlines."

"Today is A-day. You know, in case Russia drops the Bomb on us. We've got to prepare. Duck and cover, remember?" Hank said the words with a sour twist.

People were getting out of their cars, pulling over and abandoning them right on the street. The man with the little girl and the balloons picked her up when she began to cry.

It was eerie. I knew it was a phony drill, but I could still feel the apprehension in the air. People were walking faster, some almost running to the office buildings that had yellow-and-black FALLOUT SHELTER signs. Nobody spoke, and without the roar of traffic the city was quiet. You could hear footsteps on Lexington Avenue. It felt like the world was actually ending.

"It's all stupid," Hank muttered. "If there was a real bomb, we could go underground, but when we'd come up, we'd be dead from radiation in a couple of weeks anyway."

193

"That's comforting, thanks."

"Sorry. I hear about it at dinner. Who wants to talk about Hiroshima while you're eating roast chicken? Not me."

There were a couple of men in white helmets directing us towards the subway stairs. We joined the people waiting to go down. All we could hear was the shuffle of footsteps, like everyone in Manhattan was doing the soft shoe.

We followed a crowd of people into the subway station. Most people just stood around, and Hank and I found a place to lean against the wall. There were so many people pressed close, and I felt a sudden flutter of panic. I'd seen pictures of people doing this in London, during the Blitz, while the bombs rained down. Now we only needed one Bomb, so powerful it had a capital B. And it could destroy a whole city. Everything gone in one bright flash.

"You look scared," Hank said. "It's only supposed to last ten minutes. Don't worry."

I had no idea how to do that. Not worry. There was way too much to worry about.

I squeezed my eyes shut. A body in a chair, arms flung out, like the end of the very last dance. A dark pool of blood on the floor. The eager photographer, angling for the shot. The police, asking questions. Who knew the guy, what was he doing there, who talked to him, who knew him.

Everything gone, in one bright flash.

Twenty-one

Providence, Rhode Island
May 1937

It was Muddie who saw them first. Three balloons, floating on the breeze, heading straight for us.

She reached out her arms. "Look – it's our present!"

Jamie and I followed her, all of us racing to be first to catch the waving strings. It was our fourth birthday, so of course the balloons had to be for us.

Muddie clutched the string of her blue balloon. She wound it tightly around her index finger. "It's our present," she repeated. Her eyes shone. "From heaven. It's from her."

"Don't be a dope," Jamie said. "She's dead."

"She's an angel," Muddie insisted. "Da says so. And she sent them!" She stamped her foot.

I tipped my head back and looked up at my red balloon. Behind the balloon, blue sky. And heaven, up where I couldn't see. Was my mother looking down, right then, right into my face?

We never did find out where the balloons came from. Balloons did not fly around the neighbourhood of Fox Point. It was made up of the working poor, and in the Depression, that changed to the occasionally working poor and those desperately hanging on to the little they had. The Irish shared the neighbourhood with the Portuguese from the Azores and Cape Verde, all of them drawn to the work on the docks, despite the fact that it was disappearing and heading into the factories instead.

In Fox Point the air smelled like the river. Visitors were ushered to the kitchen, not a parlour, where *manchupa* simmered on a stove, fragrant with garlic and the parts of the pig the swells on College Hill would not eat. In the back yards, tomato plants and grapevines competed with shrines to the Virgin Mary for attention. You could buy a New Deal lunch for fifteen cents on South Main. If you had fifteen cents.

We saved the balloons until they were just scraps of rubber trailing on grimy strings that we worried like rosary beads. Even years later, after I knew the balloons hadn't dropped from heaven but had probably floated down from up the hill, from a birthday party where children got presents and cake and ice cream, even then, I couldn't shake the feeling that I was watched over by someone unseen. Someone greater than God. I'd burn in hell for thinking such a thing. But that would probably happen anyway.

Someone I'd killed on the very day I was born.

*

Da always told the story the same way.

They didn't have money for the doctor, you see. They didn't know it was triplets – the midwife thought twins. After ten hours of labour, Da saw the fear in the midwife's eyes and ran down the street at three in the morning and pounded on Jack Leary's door. Jack was a good man, and he had a car. He drove them to the Lying-In Hospital with Maggie groaning in the back seat. Even then, Da said, she was too polite to scream. The woman had the manners of a duchess.

They took her away from him and he started to pray, even though he'd walked out of St Joseph's when his parents died and had never gone back. God would have to find him where he lived, Da always said, because why should he have to go to His house all the time? *He seems like a bit of a loafer, if you ask me,* Da would end, with a glance at his sister, Delia, and a wink at us. Delia would press her lips together and shake her head and say God *did* live in our house, He was watching all the time, in every room. One time Jamie asked, *Is He in the crapper, too?* And Delia had to get up and leave the room she was so mad, because Da had laughed along with us.

That night when Da heard the first scream, he couldn't stand it any longer and pushed back the nurse who was saying – and here Da would imitate a high, bossy soprano – *Mis-ter Corrigan, get back where you belong!* And he had shouted, *I belong with my wife!* and burst in.

And then tears would roll down his cheeks. *I saw her pretty feet first,* he would say. *Her pretty white feet. The room*

197

was full of blood. A river of it. And the butcher of a doctor was still working on her, but I saw her soul rise to the angels, saw it clear as day, and felt her breath on my cheek as she passed. She blessed you, each one as she went, she did. You were blessed by an angel.

And Da would touch our heads, one by one, in order of our birth.

She was naming you all as she went by, because I heard the names like a bell. Margaret, James, Kathleen.

Your mother is an angel, he would say, tears still rolling down his face. *She forgave me, too, for not going to the doctor right away. I saw her smile at me. She forgave Kitty for not wanting to come out and join her brother and sister. Even then, our Kit had to make an entrance.*

You are all blessed, he'd said.

And I thought – *blessed with what?* Cursed was more like it. For being the last one out, from swimming away from the doctor's forceps with a will of my own. Did I want to stay near my mother's flickering heartbeat? The curse was clear in the way Jamie and Muddie turned to me with a look of awe – because I had killed our mother.

And so my birth was Irish to the core – guilt and suffering, attended by a ghost, scored with celestial bells and the whispered blessings of angels.

It was only the next day that the commerce began.

Since their parents died, he and Delia had always scraped by, dropping out of school and finding work when they could.

At least, that was the story they told. Not the whole story – that came later. Just a few sad facts sprinkled in for a bit of waterworks from the audience, and the rest jokes and exaggerations. Da was never afraid to talk about the past, but he had locked in his stories on bar stools and at kitchen tables over the years, and he stuck to them. He knew every beat and every pause.

And so there he was, a widower with three babies to raise. Delia had moved out of their small apartment to give the couple privacy, taking a room nearby. The day of Maggie's funeral, she moved back in. They'd saved up for Delia to attend a secretarial course, so she had a good job at the artificial flower factory, in the front office, not at the machines. A good salary, but not for a family of five.

That first night while the babies slept, Da and Delia sat in the kitchen and discussed their options. They were two people used to calamity and it didn't scare them. There was no question that Delia had to keep working. There were no jobs now, in the worst year of the Depression. How would Da cope with the babies, with feeding and diaper pins and baths? How could they afford blankets, and soap, and milk, and medicine? That's when Da got the idea.

The day he left the hospital, three nurses following him out with the babies in their arms, a taxi drove him home for free. Turned out the driver gave tips to a newspaperman at the *Journal*, and in no time at all there was Da on the front page, holding the babies in his arms. Within an hour, a delivery of free formula from the local drugstore arrived at his door.

Wasn't the world apt to cry at the sight of motherless babies? Three at once?

Da didn't have much, but the man knew what to do with a story.

THE CORRIGAN THREE SLEEP THROUGH
THE NIGHT IN SLEEP-TITE CRIBS

WHEN IT COMES TO EVAPORATED MILK,
THE CORRIGAN THREE LOVE THEIR PET!

THE CORRIGAN THREE SAY "YUM!" FOR
DEAL'S COD LIVER OIL!

LISTEN TO THE CORRIGAN KIDDIES:
"DADDY BUYS SLEEK-O-TYRES FOR A
SMOOOOOTH RIDE!"

So we became the Corrigan Three, and within a few months we were famous in Providence and Boston and, after a newsreel team came to film us, around the entire United States of America. When we were babies and toddlers, companies would pay for our endorsements – the endorsements of tiny things who spit up for a living – but later, as the Depression ground on and the public moved on to a fascination with flagpole sitting and dance marathons, Da was reduced to accepting things in trade. Rarely did the trade involve something we could use. Suddenly, the apartment would fill up with cartons of bicycle tyres or laxatives while we opened a can of beans for dinner. But Da would take the tyres, or the laxatives, and go around the neighbourhood, trading them for a bit of butter, or second-hand shoes.

All of Providence knew us, the red-headed Corrigan triplets. Every Easter we were invited to the egg roll at the statehouse, and as soon as we could walk, we marched in as many Fourth of July parades as Da could cram in, driving from one small town to another. Our pictures were taken on Santa's lap every year.

We were famous for being famous. For a while.

All families peg their kids – the smart one, the slugger, the mischief maker. Imagine a whole country pegging you as one thing. Da decided early on that we needed personalities. Muddie was the shy one (Muddie, trained to make a show of peeping out from between Da's legs), Jamie was the charmer (trained to bow and say "how do you do" from the age of three), and I was the ham, the sassy one who stole the show.

During the summers, Da traded in every favour in order to borrow Jack Leary's DeSoto and take us on tours of state fairs as far west as Iowa, where we learned how to sing "Galway Bay", repair a blown tyre, and pee in a can.

It was a grand gypsy life, we thought. We slept on the ground, wrapped in blankets, or in the car as Da drove from one fair to another. Occasionally, he was able to book us into a theatre, where we would open for the movies, singing "I Faw Down an' Go Boom". We lived on cheese sandwiches and the food at the fairs – candy apples and funnel cakes, pickles and pies. We rehearsed in the car, singing as loud as we could as the hot air slapped our sticky hair against our cheeks.

In those hot summers, full of flies and white skies, corn and pigs, I learned what America was – people looking up from their work and trouble and hoping someone would tell them a story, sell them a dream. And I saw what it was like to be looked at, and came to like it.

Prosperity was just around the corner. So people said. At first I thought it meant that if Da could just walk another few blocks, he'd get a job, because the streets in Providence had names like Benefit and Benevolent, so why not Prosperity? But there was no Prosperity Street, and there were no jobs, even on a street called Hope. Delia's salary was cut, and endorsements dried up. We were growing fast, and it was hard to look cute in a dress made out of an old faded pillowcase, even for me and Muddie. Shirley Temple was the child everyone wanted to see, with glossy curls and the fresh plump cheeks of someone who had a chicken in her pot and warm water to wash with.

In the winters, we spent all of our time in the kitchen, the biggest room at the front of the apartment, where the coal stove gave out a thin, inadequate heat. A bonus was that we were away from the thin walls of the rear bedroom, behind which the Duffys in the next apartment argued every Saturday night when Duffy came home drunk.

Delia had the bedroom, Da slept on the couch, and Muddie, Jamie and I slept on a mattress in the hall closet, all tangled together, pushing each other and arguing about who got spit on the pillow. *Aren't you the luckiest of children,* Da said, *who get to sleep in a cave like wolf cubs, instead of in a regular room with a door?*

And weren't we lucky to hang on to that home when we saw other families losing theirs and disappearing in the middle of the night?

We were five years old the day Delia was fired, and we saw her cry for the first time, as fiercely as she did everything else. She prided herself on being a secretary, on her clean fingernails and her grey dresses and her pretty scarves. She was a professional.

We had never seen Da and Delia scared before.

Jamie stood up. "It's time for the lucky pennies," he announced.

It was a ritual we saved for only our most dire circumstances, and this was the worst one yet.

Da and Delia stood. They emptied all the coins from their pockets and Delia's purse. Delia went to get the spare change she kept wrapped in a handkerchief for church. Jamie looked at the pile on the table. He took each coin and went around our apartment, placing them heads up on window sills and door frames.

Then he put his hands on Delia's knees. "All we have to do now," he said, looking straight into her face, "is wait for the luck."

"Darling boy," she said, putting both hands on his cheeks.

That was Jamie. Darling boy.

At night we'd face each other, lying down in the darkness, and we'd press our cheeks against one another so that we could be eye to eye. Our eyes would be black and deep, and yet we'd wait to see the reflection of a point of light, the diamond that shone in our eyes. Then we'd shout the word straight in each other's ears: *Diiiiiaaaamond!* Trying to blast each other's eardrums and laughing fit to bust. I don't know who thought of the game – it wasn't a game, really, more like a ritual, a hunt to find the light in the darkness. There were diamonds in our eyes and all our coins were heads up. Everything would be all right.

Delia folded her dresses and the blouses and carefully placed them in the bottom drawer. She looked for work, coming home tired and thinner every day, insisting that she preferred her bread without butter and her tea plain, so that we'd still have bread with butter and sugar for our treat. She tried to take in washing, but others had got there before her. Finally, she found a job cleaning offices at night.

"That's what our mam did when she came over, on her knees mopping floors," Da said. "There's Irish progress for you."

Delia didn't laugh. She tied a turban around her bright

hair and went off after tea, leaving us to Da's cooking. A pot on the stove with some kind of thin stew he called slumgullion. When one of us was hungry we'd take a bowl and slop some in, and that was dinner.

I've heard people say about their childhoods during the hard times, *We didn't know we were poor*, and do you know what? They're lying.

Twenty-two

New York City
November 1950

I told some of the story to Hank as we stood there in the subway, leaning against the wall, and he listened so intently to my whispers that I felt the grip of nerves ease and the time pass. As we climbed the stairs back up to the light, it felt like a miracle to see the sun and everybody going back to the cars and the buses, taking up their lives on an ordinary day.

An ordinary day for them. Not me.

He kept asking more questions and I kept remembering because it was easier than thinking, and soon we were standing outside his mother's office and we'd walked twenty blocks.

"So you're a triplet," he said. "I can't imagine two more of you."

"Oh, we're as different as night and day. We don't even look alike."

"So when did you meet Billy, then?"

"That's another story, a longer one. I met his father first, Nate Benedict."

Hank's face changed. "Nate Benedict? The lawyer?"

I nodded. "He knew my father back in the twenties."

"And . . . you know him now?"

Hank was suddenly looking at me as though I were someone he didn't recognize.

"He comes to the club sometimes," I said. "It's not a big deal." Even as I said it, I realized how hollow the words sounded. Even if Hank knew nothing about how I was tangled up with Nate, he knew from the morning paper that Nate was defending a murderer. "Listen—" I started.

Hank looked up at the clock hanging over the entrance to the office building. "I'm late," he said. "My mother will be worried. I'm never late. Listen, I've got to go. Thanks for the walk."

"It's OK," I said, even though it was miles past OK. He had turned away so fast, and now he was almost running. He had to get away, as though just knowing Nate Benedict was enough to taint me.

It was a good thing Billy never read the papers, because when he called that afternoon, there was no mention of what had happened at the Lido. Instead, he asked me if I wanted to join him and his army buddies for an afternoon on the town.

"They're taking me to – where are you taking me? – oh,

207

Coney Island, because Tom says I have to have a hot dog at Nathan's or I didn't see New York. So I guess that means you do, too."

"It's sounds swell, but—"

His voice pitched lower. "Look, I'm going crazy, thinking about you. You don't have to come to Brooklyn. I'll ditch the guys and come to you. I miss you."

I heard hoots of laughter and some voice yelled, "Get out the violins, Tommy boy!"

"I miss you, too," I said. "But it's only a couple of hours until I have to get to the club. You'd spend all that time on the subway. I'll see you tonight."

He didn't like it, but he said he'd see me at the club. He'd come to the last show so he could walk me home.

I wanted to tell him everything. But "everything" was so much. So I hung up, and after I did, I wished I'd spilled it out over the phone, every last secret, and just let it fall.

He'd know tonight, anyway. So at least I could give him a carefree afternoon on the boardwalk, one last good time with his pals, with hot dogs and roller coasters and the Parachute Jump.

I hadn't expected to see Hank again that day, but he knocked at the kitchen door later that afternoon. I was starting to get ready for work, and I had to throw on a robe when I answered the door.

He held up a piece of paper. "I got your note."

"I didn't—"

I heard a knock at the other door, a quick, sharp rap,

208

and then the sound of the door opening. I could have sworn that I'd locked it. I ran towards the front of the apartment, Hank behind me.

Nate swept off his hat. "Hello, Hank."

Hank froze. "I guess I'll be going, Kit—"

"In a minute," Nate interrupted. "Kit, why don't you make us some coffee?" His voice was low and polite, but Hank looked nervously towards the kitchen, as if he wanted to dash that way and out the other door.

"What's going on?" I asked. My hand drifted to my robe, holding it tightly closed. This felt like an invasion. Nate had walked in as if he owned the place. Which he did. Like he had every right to be here. Which he didn't.

My words got swallowed into the tension in the air. It was like I wasn't even there. Nate just held Hank's gaze.

"I'm Nate Benedict, Hank," Nate said.

"I know. I saw your picture in the paper."

"And I'm your landlord. I own this building. Isn't that right, Kit?"

I nodded. Hank gave me a swift, surprised glance.

"I bought it before the war, as an investment. I'm the one who's been giving your parents a break on the rent. I know they got a raw deal, losing their jobs because they're Reds."

"They're not Reds."

"Doesn't matter, does it? You see, I don't like it when people get pushed around. That's why I became a lawyer, no matter what the papers say. Kit, go make some coffee," he said, and this time the tone in his voice made me move

209

towards the kitchen. I just didn't want things to get worse than they were.

I ran the water and filled the pot, measured the coffee and dumped it in, but I didn't plug in the percolator. I moved back towards the living room to listen.

"You're going to Yale, right? Scholarship and everything, smart kid, you have a future, no question about it. This is just a rough patch in the road. I'm sure you'll get through it. The thing is, I can help. Believe it or not, I take an interest in my tenants."

"I don't need any help."

"Just hear me out."

I could recognize something hard behind the pleasantness in Nate's voice, like he'd knocked Hank's shoulder, the way kids do before they fight. And I could tell by Hank's voice that he was scared. I couldn't leave him alone like that. I walked back into the room.

"Coffee ready?" Nate asked.

"Not yet."

"I have to get home," Hank blurted. He went by me without seeing me, blundering into the kitchen. I heard him fumbling with the knob.

Nate followed him quickly. "Hank, wait. One more thing." He slipped an arm around him and talked quietly to him. I couldn't hear a word unless I got right on top of them.

I'd seen this before.

That night at the Riverbank, Jeff Toland holding the napkin-wrapped ice to his swollen face, listening as Nate

210

put a gentle arm around his shoulders. That quiet voice in his ear, telling him what was going to happen. I knew that now. Jeff had listened, and he'd gone off to Hollywood, and his career had been saved by a contract. Was that what Nate had promised him that night?

When Nate released him, Hank opened the door so fast he slammed it into his forehead. Then he rushed out, shutting it behind him.

Leaving me alone with Nate.

"What was that all about?" I asked.

Nate lit a cigarette and blew out the smoke. "He's a good kid. I'm just trying to help out."

I started to get an ashtray and stopped. I wasn't going to wait on him.

"Did you just walk in the door before?" I asked.

"I knocked, but you didn't hear. It wasn't locked."

"Funny, I thought it was. I have to get dressed."

"You have time."

"No, I have to do my make-up and my hair and everything—"

"Kit, it's only five-thirty. You've got an hour. You heard what happened at the Lido last night." He opened the cupboard and took out a saucer. He tapped his ash on to it.

"I can read the papers like everybody else."

"Yeah, well, Tuesday is a slow news day. They need headlines."

Tuesday. It was Tuesday. How could this impossible, terrible day . . . be a Tuesday?

211

And then it hit me.

It was the day of my callback audition. And I was already an hour late.

"I have to go. I have an appointment—"

"Kit, sit down."

Never in my life had I wanted someone to leave so badly. He tapped his ash on to the saucer. He didn't drop his eyes. "You have the apartment, the clothes, the job. You have *my son*. You think all that comes without a price?"

I could feel the fear rise up against my throat, and I swallowed, reaching for my nerve. "What's the price?"

He smiled. "Five minutes. Is that so bad?"

I didn't sit, but I put my hands on the back of the chair. My palms were wet, and my hands slipped. "So talk."

"You look nervous. Don't be. I know, the murder in the club was upsetting."

"A bad meal is upsetting. A murder isn't pot roast."

"The thing is, this isn't about us – I mean, what I asked you to do. It's a war we're not a part of."

"You made me a part of it!"

Nate's amiable expression faded. "Don't ever say that again. You're not a part of it. I'm not a part of it. I'm defending the guy. That's a straightforward deal. But I wasn't involved in the hit."

"You were there that night, I was there, you asked me to keep tabs on him—"

"I told you." Nate's voice was low, and that made it even worse, the menace in it. "Don't say that again. Forget I asked, forget what you said, forget his face, forget it all. You're a girl dancing in a club. That's all. Just do your job. Anybody asks questions, you don't know anything, you don't know Ray Mirto from a hole in the wall. Do you understand?"

I didn't say anything, I just clutched the chair.

"Do you understand?"

I nodded in one sharp jerk. "I understand."

He took another drag of his cigarette. "Now, about Billy. Where is he?"

"He's with some army buddies. They're seeing the sights."

"When are you going to see him again?"

"Tonight. At the club."

He blew out a long plume of smoke, then stubbed out the cigarette. "All right. I'll see him there. Is there anything I should know?"

I stared at him through the smoke. Anything he should know? Like, I might become his daughter-in-law? Like, his profession made his son sick?

"No," I said.

I trailed behind him as he picked up his hat and walked towards the front door. "Just do your job," he said. "Smile, show your legs. Just don't take a wrong step, Kit. That's all."

The director and the choreographer were still in a huddle when I arrived at the rehearsal hall more than an hour late.

They sat against the mirrored wall on two metal chairs in close conversation, but they looked up when I arrived. I caught a glimpse of myself in the mirror, pink and out of breath.

"I'm sorry, I had an emergency. . ."

"That's too bad." The director turned a shoulder away. "Auditions are closed."

"But I—"

"This is the theatre, Miss Corrigan," he said icily. "There is only one emergency, and that is if you're unconscious, in the hospital, with amnesia."

"That's funny," I said, "because that's exactly what happened."

The director didn't laugh. But the choreographer, Tom Cullen, grinned. He had pale grey eyes in a slim, long face, and they brightened as he gave me a sharp glance, squinting at me through cigarette smoke. I shrugged as if to say, *It was worth a shot*.

"Wisecracks still don't get you a try-out," the director said. "They get your ass kicked out the door. Good afternoon, Miss Nobody."

The sting of the remark hit me like a slap. I bit my lip and turned around. I made my way down the dingy hall and leaned against the wall near the elevator. I couldn't believe I had blown my chance at a big break. I'd thought about the murder at the club, I'd thought about Nate, I'd thought about Billy. All day I'd thought about everything but the most crucial appointment of my life.

214

"If it makes you feel better," Tom Cullen said behind me, "we'd already decided Janine Taylor would get the part."

I quickly swiped at my tears before turning around. "That's supposed to make me feel better?"

"Kid, I've looked at your résumé. You've been in the chorus of one stinkpot show. And now you're a Lido girl, hoop dee doo. You're a good strong dancer – that's why I wanted to see you again. You've got a voice and a look. You were close but not close enough, and that's something. Just keep plugging away. How long have you been in New York, six months?"

"Not even."

"It shows. Never talk back to a director, especially Hobart Dean. He's old school, baby. He wasn't nice, but he was right. So learn your lesson. Show up. That's the easy part, or it should be." His eyes were kind in his long, mournful face. "Look, kiddo, it's not a question of whether you want it, it's a question of how much."

I rolled my head against the wall. "I know that."

"Then act like it." The elevator door opened. "Going down?"

"I sure hope not."

The elevator doors closed on his smile.

Twenty-three

New York City
November 1950
None of us knew what to expect that night, but even Ted Roper was surprised that a murder didn't drive away crowds – it brought them in. A table covered the spot where Ray Mirto had died, but it didn't stop anyone from looking for the bloodstains.

I got through the three shows dancing like a puppet, like somebody else was moving my arms and legs, pulling the corners of my mouth up over my teeth. I searched the club for Billy and Nate, but I didn't see either of them. Nothing was good any more – not the lights or the applause or the cheers, or even feeling at the centre of everything. The centre suddenly felt like a bad place to be. I was exposed, and everyone was looking.

And tonight, Billy would want his answer.

"I'm beating it out of here as soon as I'm offstage tonight, let me tell you," Pat announced.

"You said it. My mother flipped her wig when she saw the headline," Mickey said. "My dad's coming to walk me home."

"My husband said this is it, I've got to quit," Edna said.

Darla leaned forward, powdering her face. "I heard there's a witness."

That stopped all of us. "Who?" Mickey asked. "Someone from the club?"

"Nobody knows," Darla said. "I just heard the rumour from one of the waiters, that's all."

Nobody looked at me. They all looked at each other, or in the mirror, and I could swear that Mickey kicked Darla on purpose.

Ted stuck his head in the door. "Thanks, kids. Tough night. Everybody uses the lounge door when you leave tonight. We got some vultures outside the main entrance."

I wrapped my coat around me and followed the others out. Everybody hurried through the crowd outside. Nobody wanted to talk to a reporter. We could see them, hanging near the front entrance, their eyes moving, trying to pick out people to interview.

Billy was leaning against the building, waiting, not moving a muscle despite the cold. I hurried towards him. As soon as I got close I could tell that he'd seen the papers at last.

"Everybody's entitled to a good defence, right?" he said.

"Sure. It's the American way."

I could feel the waves of tension coming from him, the

217

way he held my hand, dropped it, picked it up again. The way he stretched his neck.

"He'll never get out now," he said. "I didn't realize – we had a blowout tonight. I saw him as I was coming into the Lido. We couldn't talk here, so we went out someplace for dinner. I shouldn't have talked to him at all. He's in with Frank Costello now? How is that getting out? Wills and trusts – my God!"

I didn't know what to say. My brain was buzzing. How much did he know?

We walked quickly, our breath like smoke in the cold air. "He says he owes them," Billy said. "Him and his favours. Do you know, he actually said it was because he pulled in so many favours to get me out of that Jeff Toland jam? I didn't ask for his help!"

But I had. I opened my mouth, but Billy kept talking.

"He runs his life on debts. I never thought I'd say this, but I can't wait to ship out. Korea isn't even far enough. I'd go to the moon if I could."

"Maybe it's true. Maybe it's his last job."

"I was still with the guys, we were walking on the street when I saw the headline. We all saw it. One of the guys bought a paper. We saw the name Benedict. They just looked at me. I said I didn't know him." Billy turned to me, his eyes anguished. "I said I didn't even know my own father, Kit!"

We stopped on the sidewalk outside my door. I reached for his arm. "Come in for a while," I told him. "You need some coffee before you head to Brooklyn."

218

Inside, when I put out my hand to turn on the light, he stopped me. We stood in the dark hall, just breathing for a moment.

"Can we be together tonight?" Billy asked.

"Billy, I don't know. . ."

"I won't . . . push for anything. But can we just . . . sleep in the same bed? We don't have to do anything. I want to be near you. I don't want to be alone. Can I stay?"

Tomorrow morning I had planned to call Daisy and see if her horrific room-mate was moving out to get married. I'd have to confess that I'd missed my callback, risk looking like a lightweight, but it would be worth it if I could have a place to stay, even if I had to sleep on a couch again. Tomorrow I would take the first step to being free.

But tonight Billy looked so beaten down, so full of anger and sadness. It could be our last chance to be alone.

"Yes. Of course."

I made hot chocolate and we listened to the radio, turned down low, Billy in his trousers and T-shirt, me in my robe and slippers, like nothing was wrong at all. When our cups were empty, I put them in the sink and went to the bathroom to brush my teeth. I opened a new toothbrush for him and left it on the sink. Then I went to bed, took off my robe and slipped under the covers. The sheets were cold and I curved into myself, hands between my knees, and waited. I closed my eyes when I heard him leave the bathroom. He switched off the light and got under the covers. He lay on his back, and I could feel the tension in his body without even touching him.

I moved closer and he shuddered as I tucked myself underneath his arm. Slowly, warmth crept in. He moved until he was circling me. He was wrapped around me now. My ear was pressed against his heart. Every inch of me was against every inch of him. Even our bare feet were touching.

I wondered what would happen, what he would do, and how this moment that we'd waited for would move into another moment of closeness, and another. His lips brushed my hair.

"Goodnight, sweetheart," he said.

The endearment was lovely and soft.

"Goodnight."

"I think I can sleep," he murmured. "I think I can finally sleep."

I closed my eyes and saw the blackness of the blood in the newspaper photograph. The stain spread on the floor. The man's outflung hand and the thin beam of light.

That night I held Billy while he twitched and moaned, deep in his dreams. I slipped in and out of sleep, as Billy thrashed in his sleep. Everywhere I moved on the mattress, he would move, too, following me even though he was dreaming. I'd thought that sleeping with Billy would be the most peaceful way to rest, but it was as though we had taken all the darkness into the bed with us and were each trying to make it through to morning.

*

When I woke, he was still sleeping. The sun made a stripe along the bed and just brushed his cheekbone. I looked down at him. The army haircut made his features look sharper. The perfection of the way his nostrils curved and his lips met made me believe in God more than church did.

He woke slowly, stretching first, then opening his eyes. When he saw me so close, leaning on my elbow looking at him, he looked startled, and he came awake immediately.

Then he smiled. "Wait until I tell the guys I slept next to a beautiful girl and all I did was sleep. I'll never hear the end of it."

"Breakfast. I'm starving, aren't you? I have eggs, I have bread, I have jam, everything." I slipped out of bed and quickly put on my robe, knotting it tightly. "Can you get the milk?"

"Sure." He smiled lazily at me, making no move to get up. "Hey, this is what I want to wake up to every morning."

"Get up, lazybones. We need to talk about Thanksgiving. If you're going home, if I am . . . we can take the train together. We can tell our parents what we're doing."

"What are we doing?"

"If you'll get the milk, I'll tell you."

Suddenly, I knew. I knew it absolutely, and I knew it was right. I couldn't let Billy ship out and not be his wife. I would tell him everything. I had forgiven him for things, and he would forgive me, too.

I'd tell him over eggs and coffee. It wasn't moonlight and roses, but it was our kind of romance, and it would be perfect.

I padded down to the kitchen and got out the eggs. I put the bread into the slots of the toaster. Measured out the coffee. I heard his footsteps, heard the door open behind me, then close. I broke the eggs into a bowl and whipped them with a fork.

"Where's that milk?" I called.

Billy didn't answer.

"Billy?" I turned and he was looking down at the paper, barefoot in his army pants and T-shirt, the milk bottle tucked under one arm. I was so happy that I did a little shimmy, just like Lauren Bacall does at the end of that movie where she knows Bogart loves her and they're going to get off the island, escape the Nazis, and be together.

He didn't smile. The milk bottle slipped out from underneath his arm and crashed to the floor.

"Don't move," I said. "The glass—"

He walked towards me, right over the glass. He flipped the paper so that I could read the headline. He shoved it up against my face and at first I couldn't focus.

NATE'S MOLL IS LIDO DOLL

On the front page was a photograph of me and Nate dancing. The photographer had snapped the picture just as Nate had leaned closer to talk to me. It looked as though we were staring into each other's eyes, but I knew I was pushing against his chest, wanting distance between us.

The night in the lounge, the flashbulb popping . . . I thought they were taking pictures of the stars.

Dread dropped in my stomach, a cold, cold stone. "Billy, you can't think that I—"

"It says he pays for this apartment."

"Let's sit down and talk. Billy, your foot! You're bleeding."

"It says he pays for you!" He suddenly punched through the paper, making me cry out and jump back. "Is it true? This is his '*love nest*'?" He spat out the words with contempt.

"No!"

"How do you afford it, then? Was I so stupid? That you'd make that much as a chorus girl? Enough for your fancy clothes and this place?"

"Just listen. . ."

"I'm listening!"

"He does pay for it, but—"

His face was clenched, every muscle tense. "Is this why you keep putting me off?"

"I'm not! I was going to tell you this morning, I want to get married—"

"What did you do yesterday? Did you see him? Is that why you couldn't see me? Did you see him? *Did you?*"

I couldn't answer. I couldn't lie. "Billy, just listen. If we could just sit down—"

He walked past me towards the bedroom, leaving bloody footprints behind. I followed him, grabbing a dish towel for his foot.

When I reached the bedroom, he'd pulled on his shirt and was reaching for his socks.

"Let me help you," I said, crying now, the dread moving up to my throat, choking my words. I couldn't seem to catch a breath. "Please, let me help you."

I went towards him with the towel, but he jerked away. He pulled on his sock and I saw blood staining it, spreading outwards in a bloom of dark red.

"This apartment – it's for you and me," I explained, the words tumbling out as fast as I could push them. "He came to see me, he said if you had something to come back to, it would keep you safe. He said he wasn't against our marriage any more. I'm not his . . . moll, or whatever they're saying. How could you believe that? You said you'd trust me, Billy!"

He thrust his arms into his shirt. Suddenly, he jackknifed forward, his head in his hands. He pressed his hands against his temples. His shoulders shook. He let out a wrenching sob, and the sound was the most terrible thing I'd ever heard.

Alarmed, I touched him gently. "Billy—"

He twisted away and kicked out at me. "Keep your hands off me!" he screamed. His mouth was pulled out of shape, his eyes wet with tears.

I backed against the wall. "Please," I whispered.

His fingers shook as he jammed his foot into his boot.

I fell to my knees. "You have to believe me."

"*Believe you?*" With an outstretched arm, he swept my cosmetics off the bureau, my lipstick and rouge and powder. The silver compact skidded across the rug. He stood for a moment, weaving, looking down at the lipstick and the compact, the powder spilled on the floor. "My God," he said. "I've been so blind."

"No! If you'll just listen—"

He kicked the compact out of his way and crashed out of the room and I fell trying to get up, tripping on the sash of my robe, trying to catch him, trying to make him understand. I ran after him to the front door just as he flung it open.

"My life is full of lies," he said. "Isn't it crazy how it happens? Just when I think it's over, it starts again. One after another after another. Lies. And deaths. And *love nests.* Do you think you're the first to shack up? Maybe you should ask your Aunt Delia. Hell, maybe I should ask her. That's the start of it, isn't it? Is that what he wants here, a second chance?"

"I don't know what you're talking about," I said. "What does Delia have to do with this? You have to listen to me!"

"No! I'm tired of listening. To you. To my father. I can't listen any more. Can't you see, you're destroying me! *You're all destroying me.*"

"No," I said. "We love you. We both just wanted to give you something to come back to."

"I don't want love any more," he said. "Love is nothing. From now on, I just want truth. I want all this to stop, do you hear me? I have to stop it. Starting now."

All I could do was whisper his name. "Billy. . ."

The door shut behind him as he stumbled out.

Twenty-four

New York City
November 1950
I sat huddled in my robe.

I imagined the whole city opening doors, picking up the paper, reading that I was a gangster's moll.

How had it happened, how had I got here, what else could I have done?

I knew this: there were things I could have done. Life gives you plenty of chances to be stupid, and I'd taken every single one of them.

Now I knew why Mickey had kicked Darla, why the girls wouldn't look at me, why Darla had asked that night if Nate approved of my hair. All along, they'd thought I was Nate's girlfriend. Sonia had given him my shoe size. Ted had seen me because word had come from Nate Benedict, one of Frank Costello's mouthpieces, that I was to be given a chance. He'd been expecting a no-talent nothing that day. And what had he said on the phone yesterday? *It won't be*

long before they start kicking up some dirt on your boyfriend.
He hadn't meant Billy – he'd meant Nate.

And now the news would spread from the club to the entire city. Daisy would read that headline, the girls from the chorus of *That Girl From Scranton!*; Shirley and her mother would have the best morning of their lives today with gossip like this.

It was no wonder Billy didn't believe me. You're fed something by a paper, you swallow it whole.

Whenever I thought of Billy trying to tie his shoe, blinded by tears, I felt as though my body would simply fold up on itself and disappear. I wrapped my arms around my legs and rocked back and forth, trying to think. Trying not to feel.

I couldn't sit still. I mopped up the milk and the blood and the glass. I roamed the apartment, avoiding the bedroom with the mussed sheets. I would write him a letter. I would make Nate explain. I would take the train to Providence and wait outside his house. I would see him somehow, I would explain it all. This time in words he would be able to hear.

When the phone rang I was tempted to ignore it, but I hoped it would be Billy. I picked it up and listened.

"Hello? Kit?"

"Ted?"

"How are you?"

"Perfectly swell."

"Well, don't let the papers get you down, kid. Listen, the

reason I'm calling is . . . you don't have to come to the club today."

"Ted, I'm fine. I don't want to miss work."

"Well, the thing is, I have to let you go. Mr D's orders, I'm afraid. The club doesn't need this kind of publicity right now."

"But I'm not Nate Benedict's girlfriend!"

There was a short silence.

"The papers got it all wrong," I said. "He's my boyfriend's father. I knew him in Rhode Island."

"Honey, it doesn't matter one way or another. It's in the papers. It's publicity, good for you, but it's wrong for us. Never mind the cops, we're square with that, but now the Feds are breathing down Mr D's neck, and so . . . look, kid, it's better this way. You can hole up for a while. If you need a reference, you call me. You have a future, Kit. It's just not at the Lido. I'm sorry."

He hung up hastily. I knew he didn't believe me.

Why should anybody believe me?

I *was* mixed up with Nate. I *was* living off him. This apartment wasn't mine. I hadn't bought these clothes. Of course it looked bad. It *was* bad.

I picked up the paper again. I hadn't been able to do more than scan the article. There was another photograph of me, the one a photographer had taken the night I'd spoken to Dex Hamilton on the radio.

Who was that girl? That eager smile, the lipstick and powder, the bombshell in the tight dress?

They were comparing me to Virginia Hill, the mistress of Bugsy Siegel, the gangster who'd been shot a few years ago. The Flamingo, they called her. They hadn't come up with a nickname for me yet, but I had no doubt that they would.

I'd always wanted to be famous.

Lucky Delia wasn't around. She'd always told me that being famous was an occupation for fools.

Delia. I'd put out of my head what Billy had said about Delia.

Do you think you're the first to shack up? Maybe you should ask your Aunt Delia.

What did he mean? Delia? My prim and proper aunt?

I looked over at the mirror, hung in an awkward place just to reflect a splinter of the blue-grey river. A reminder of home to someone who had seen a river every day, who breathed marsh and damp and salt, all running into a tidal bay towards the vast ocean.

And suddenly I could see her, I could see Delia placing that mirror just so. I could see her tapping in the nail, hanging the mirror, stepping back to adjust it. Staring at it when she felt herself lost in a place that seemed too big and yet too stuffed with people to have room for one more soul. Just as I had.

Could it be possible? The knowledge was like a rush of air inside my body, and it lifted me to my feet.

Is that what he wants here, a second chance?

Here. Here, in this apartment? Did Billy mean that Nate and Delia . . . but they hardly knew each other!

230

Good evening, Miss Corrigan.

Hello, Mr Benedict.

I shook my head slowly, trying to fit the pieces together. Nate and Delia? Delia, with the rosary beads slung on the bedpost. Delia, with her disapproval of kisses that lasted too long in movies. Delia, who pressed her lips together at a dirty joke.

Delia and Nate?

What had Da said . . . that the three of them had been in each other's pockets when they were young. They met that night, Delia swimming out to meet the boat, tossing her braid over her shoulder and wringing it out, and Nate looking at her like she was a selkie. At Buttonwoods Cove, he'd said. I'd thought it was funny that we'd been at the very same beach that day. Because Billy remembered it from his childhood.

I stood up as the realization pierced me. The beach was in Warwick.

I walked slowly back to the bedroom. I ignored the rumpled sheets, the blanket trailing on the floor, the memory of Billy in that bed. Instead, I knelt and looked for the silver compact that he'd kicked.

They'd taken the name of the place where they'd first laid eyes on each other, where, no doubt, they'd fallen in love. The Warwicks. Of course. And when Billy had looked down at the compact . . . how had he known?

I traced my finger over the whirls of the letter B. And suddenly memory flashed, uncertain and hazy, and I grabbed it. Me, twelve years old, leaning against my father's side as he sat at a table, staring down at a legal document. I couldn't decipher the language, but I saw the names, bold and black.

BRIDGET ROSE CORRIGAN
JAMES GARVEY CORRIGAN

Bridget was Delia's birth name. She never used it; she'd used her nickname since she'd been born. I hadn't even known her name until I'd seen it that day.

The Warwicks had lived here that last summer of the war, Hank's mother had said, and before that, he'd only come on weekends. She was a quiet tenant. . .

Hadn't Billy told me that his father had begun to have clients in New York? Had spent time there during the war? And Delia had told us that she was working in Washington the summer of '44. For the war effort, she'd said.

And the weekends! All those weekends she'd told us she was going to a convent! She'd taken the train to New York.

Billy was right. Not about me. But about them.

The truth thudded into my brain. How could I have been so stupid? Because Delia had been so smart. Delia, who'd turned down every invitation from a man. Delia, in her prim, tight bun. Delia, going to morning Mass on Mondays. Doing her penance, no doubt. Doing battle against the world with nothing but God and a hairbrush.

232

I sank back on my heels as memory followed memory. That evening in the lobby of the theatre, the trip to see *Carousel* . . . Angela hadn't had a headache. She *knew* Delia was her husband's mistress. No wonder Angela had hated me.

Delia's tears, her anger, the slap . . . was it all about her own heart's agony?

And that very night . . . I'd seen Delia, in the bathtub, crying, her body white and rose, her breasts bobbing on the water, her red-gold hair like glittering seaweed on her shoulders. I'd turned away because I'd been embarrassed – Delia's naked body was so beautiful, so womanly. So I'd turned away and forgotten what I'd seen.

Turning away. Wasn't that what we did in my family?

I like your hair that way.

I'd like to see you in that black dress.

The way Nate looked at me, the way he'd held me when we danced . . . and the clothes! Dressing me the way he'd dressed her, most likely. He'd recognized the compact, of course. He hadn't wanted to fix it, he'd wanted to take it. Maybe that's why I'd felt he'd been here, maybe that's what he was looking for.

Everything made sense, except for one thing.

Why had Delia disappeared?

Twenty-five

Providence, Rhode Island
September 1938

The first time I saw Nate Benedict was after the hurricane of '38, which Muddie, Jamie and I spent in the bathtub, waiting for the roof to blow off. Nobody knew the storm was coming – people went on church picnics, they went to work, the children went to school – and when the rain and wind came, it was so ferocious that it didn't take long before everyone in Rhode Island knew they were in trouble. Some of them didn't know it until their houses were sailing away with them inside.

The rain was bad but Delia went to work anyway, because if she missed a day, she'd miss a paycheque. She left early so she wouldn't be late. She was trapped downtown. In a burst of surprising piety, Da told us to pray. No phones were working, we'd lost electricity, and there was no going out of doors with trees slinging by in the wind. We were sure we were going to die, and it terrified and thrilled us.

People did die in the hurricane in Rhode Island, hundreds of them, drowned in their cars, struck by trees, swept straight out to sea, but after the skies cleared, Fox Point cheered up, for the hurricane meant jobs. Anyone who could hold a shovel had immediate work if he wanted it. It was tough going, cleaning out muck and dragging downed trees, and Da came home exhausted and slept in his clothes.

I was the only one who heard the quiet knocking that night, a week after the hurricane. I was lying awake, warming my feet against Jamie's back as he slept at the bottom of the mattress.

Was that it, was that the start of it, the change in the family, a movement of knuckles on a door?

I stuck my head out of the closet and watched as Da greeted the stranger in a murmur. Da's hair was matted with dust and stuck up in back, and he was in a white undershirt and work trousers, his feet clownish in thick wool socks. A man stepped through the door, dressed in a grey suit spotted with rain. Men in suits didn't come to our door, and I crept out to get a closer look.

They talked about the storm, of course, because everyone was still talking about it. I heard Da chuckle as he hurriedly tucked in his shirt. He quickly ushered the guest into the kitchen, past the shabby furniture, the blanket falling off the couch, and his boots caked with dirt sitting on a newspaper by the door.

I followed the murmurs and skidded next to the wall to

listen. The whiskey bottle taken down from high in the cupboard, the chime of glasses – a rare event, so the man must be important. I wanted to hear his hurricane story; maybe he'd seen a drowned body, something to tell Jamie and Muddie tomorrow to make them jealous. Jamie and Muddie could read already, but I wasn't much for books, since letters seemed to shimmer all around on a page. Stories, though – those I could remember.

He said he was downtown, that he'd seen Delia there. How the water had risen so fast that people were swept away. It rose above the reception desk in the Biltmore Hotel. He and Delia had battled their way to an office building and he had the key to an office, he knew someone, so they climbed all the way to the top and spent the night there. Down in the street the water surged up to six feet. I wanted details, the more gruesome the better. I perked up when he described people climbing out of the trolley and sitting on the roof, then getting knocked off into the water. He saw a mink coat float by and he thought it was a bear.

I pressed closer, but the topic changed just as it was getting interesting. I thought that only happened when children were around to overhear.

Da said that Delia was out, that she worked until late at night, most nights.

"Remember her that night down at Narragansett?" the guest said. "We talked her into driving the covering car—"

"—and she drove so fast she rammed our bumper!" Da slapped his leg.

The two men chuckled softly together. It was the first time I realized that they were friends. Before then, it had just seemed odd and jerky. I yawned. It was exciting to see a stranger, but I started to think of my warm bed. Then I heard the word that made me pay attention.

Job.

The man had heard about a job. Maybe Delia would be interested? A secretary for a firm he knew downtown.

The dresses could come back, and the stockings! Delia would be pretty again. She'd turned pale and scrawny, her lips bloodless and her moods foul.

I hadn't stirred a hair, but Da suddenly sensed me.

He said, without turning, "Go to bed back there."

The stranger rose and peeked around the doorway. He smiled, and I saw how handsome he was. He took two steps and swung me up in his arms. "And which one are you? Muddie or Kitty?"

"I'm Kitty," I told him, insulted to have been taken for Muddie, who was shorter than I was.

"How do you do. I'm Mr Benedict." He took me back to the kitchen and settled into the chair. He smelled like rain and cigarettes, a nice smell. I didn't mind being on his lap. I swung my legs, excited to be in the kitchen with the men.

"So you'll tell her, Jimmy?" he asked Da.

"I'll tell her, Benny."

They started to make those noises that meant the visit

was over, a cough, a decisive slap as the whiskey glass hit the table.

I trailed after the men to the door. When the man named Benny opened it, the fresh smell of rain on pavement invaded the apartment, as well as something else, the smell of dead leaves from the coming autumn.

Da stared at the door after it closed, not moving except to tell me to get back to bed.

But he didn't seem that interested in my obeying him, so when he sat on the couch and sagged back against the cushions, I scooted up next to him. I knew he was too tired to fuss at me. It was rare that I got my father to myself, and I knew better than to pester him.

We sat in the darkness, hearing the rain against the windowpane. I could smell the faint sweet smell of whiskey on Da's breath and feel the warmth of the stranger, see his hands on the glass, the hands of a man who did not work with dirt and grease for a living, the fingers clean, with no cracked or blackened nails. He'd brought us a job from that world, the world that my aunt had known and slipped away from. I fell asleep dreaming of a doll for Christmas.

I woke up to the door opening again, and Delia stepped in, shaking the drops from her umbrella. "What a night, not fit for man nor beast." She always said that when it rained.

She leaned her umbrella against the wall so that it would drip on to the newspaper Da had spread out, took off her coat and hung it up, told me to go right to bed and went to

238

the kitchen for her tea. Da still hadn't said anything but hello. So it was me who sprang towards her, to say that a man had come, a handsome man in a suit, and that he had a job for her, that she wouldn't have to be a cleaning lady any more.

Delia put her hand on my shoulder and I felt the weight of it, like she was tired from work and needed support to stand. She looked across the living room at Da.

"Who was it, then, this man?"

"Mr Benedict," I said, proud to have remembered the name.

She said something about it being good news, but she'd sounded more excited about the rain.

I knew how Delia had prayed for things to get better. Hadn't I seen her just last night, kneeling by her bed, her long red-gold hair braided, her white hands pressed together, her lips moving in her march of Hail Marys?

"It's a job!" I sang. "A job, a job, a job!" As if saying it like that would get her to pay attention.

"I didn't say I would take it," Delia said, but she wasn't talking to me. She was looking right at Da, and there was defensiveness in her tone and fear in her eyes.

Of course Delia took the job. She got out her grey dresses and pressed them, washed out her sweaters, brushed her hair and twisted it back in a hard knot like a two-day-old roll you had to dunk in your tea to soften. She worked for two businessmen who shared her, Mr Loge and Mr

Rosemont, and their names were almost as sacred as Jesus in our house, for we all knew how close we'd come to the kind of poverty that meant empty bellies and no heat.

The next summer, we were on our own, because Da now had a job at the American Screw factory. He worked out a deal with our neighbour Mrs Duffy – in return for his working in the garden on weekends, she'd feed us lunch and keep an eye on us. But Mrs Duffy wasn't much for keeping an eye on anyone except her husband, who was up to no good, she assured us, and had to be watched every minute.

We met Elena because we hated the Duffys and we were up to our necks in waxed paper. Da had finagled a radio ad in which we sang, "We love Howland's because it's three times as good!" and instead of payment, Howland sent over two cartons of waxed paper, which Da kicked across the room because that lousy chiseller had promised cash.

So when Jamie suggested we take the waxed paper and hold it across the Duffys' back window at eight-thirty a.m., the time Mr Duffy reliably relieved himself of the pints he'd had the night before at Murphy's Bar on Wickenden Street, Muddie and I thought it a swell idea. It was only when Duffy slowly realized that the arc that should be hitting the grass outside was instead splattering on his bare feet that we considered that we had neglected to plan our route of escape.

We ran as Duffy hit the back stairs and landed on Muddie's jacks with his bare feet. We hooted with laughter as he screamed and chased us across the yard, though we got a little nervous when he threw Mrs Duffy's prized Virgin Mary statue at us as we scaled the wall in three seconds flat. Now Mrs Duffy was screaming, too, and we were on foreign soil – the Baptiste driveway. Mrs Duffy hated the Baptistes, too, because they were from Cape Verde and "black as the ace of spades", she'd say, which wasn't true – first of all, they were dark brown, and second of all, it was puzzling, because every other house in Fox Point belonged to a Portuguese family. ("That doesn't mean I have to like it," she said, slicing a sandwich in half with a large knife, her meanness lending the slice an extra, deadly precision.) When we told Da about this, he had sighed and said that people climbing a ladder had a tendency to piss downwards.

The windows were open and we could hear the radio playing "The Dipsy Doodle". Someone was singing along.

The window was raised higher. Elena beckoned to us with her hairbrush. We didn't know her well, hardly enough even to say hello to, but she was called "the pretty sister" out of the three, and we all agreed with that. "What are you waiting for?" she whispered. "Get in here."

One by one we wriggled up and in, Elena hauling us by the back of our shorts. We hit the floor and stayed there.

A moment later we heard Duffy's puffing breath and the slap of his fat bare feet. He asked for us, and we watched, impressed, as Elena sweetly lied and sent him away down Hope Street.

She put her hands on her hips. "The famous Corrigan Three," she said. She was mocking us and we knew it, but we didn't care. "I think you could use some looking after."

She came over that night, when Da was furious and still berating us with a fork raised in the air as he turned the sausages.

"Hooligans, that's what I'm raising! What am I to do now with the lot of you?" He used the fork like a baton, orchestrating his irritation. "Who's going to watch over you now?"

The knock didn't stop his tirade. Glad of the diversion, the three of us tumbled towards the door. Elena breezed right past us, wearing a flowered summer dress and sandals. She went straight to the kitchen.

"Hello, Corrigan," she said to Da. "May I come in?"

Da stood in the kitchen, astonished, as she walked in. He nodded politely at her. And waited patiently while the sausages sizzled. "Did my children do something else?" he asked. "Break a window?"

Elena laughed. "The thing is, it's clear you need a hand with them."

"Ah, true. They roam the neighbourhood like a pack of dogs, so I'm buying them leashes tomorrow."

"Instead," Elena said, crossing the kitchen and taking the fork from his hand, "you should hire me. I see them outside, getting into trouble. They need a hand."

"I don't have much to offer in the way of payment."

242

She turned the sausages. "I don't need much, just a bit of money to help with things at home."

We watched how easily she moved from turning the sausages to slicing bread with quick, competent strokes, then spread the slices with butter. She flipped a sausage out of the pan and tucked it into the bread, folding it over and handing it to Jamie without even looking at him. "If you cook these with wine and a little garlic they'd be even better," she said. "My father makes wine. I can bring over a drop or two to cook with."

Da looked at her as though she were speaking Japanese. "I'm a plain man, and plain cooking is enough for me."

"Well, I won't be cooking your dinner, will I? I'm cooking for the children." She swiped at the stove with a rag. "You'll have to clean this place. I don't mind wiping up, but this is just plain dirty."

Jamie ate the sausage, his jaw working as he watched. I saw he was already in love, but I didn't mind, for I was, too. Elena turned and handed out sandwiches packed with sausage to me and Muddie. Da looked at the empty pan and the lack of his own dinner. We giggled. Elena rinsed and dried her hands.

"If you could come at seven in the morning and get their breakfast, too?" Da began. "One dollar for the day."

"I'll be here at ten of. And a dollar and a quarter."

243

Twenty-six

Of course it was a terrible thing to say, but war did make everything jump all of a sudden. As a sole provider for three children, with flat feet to boot, Da was exempt, but threw himself into the war effort, which consisted of teaching us three-part harmony for "Boogie Woogie Bugle Boy" and turning us into a novelty act for radio. He got a better job in one of the now-booming factories, making parachutes.

Soon Providence would be all noise and jive, with servicemen on the buses and cramming the trains. The bars would roar all night to accommodate their thirst. Brown University would hold commencement three times a year, pushing the men out towards service. Everyone would have a purpose, and somewhere to go.

But July was early in the war, and we grabbed on to patriotism because every day in the paper the war news

244

was bleak. For Fourth of July, the local theatre was putting on a pageant, and it would be my first big solo show. At nine, I was the youngest performer. Part of the proceeds were going to war relief, and it would be a sold-out crowd. I had been rehearsing for weeks for the ensemble dance number to "You're a Grand Old Flag" and the finale. And I had a solo, right after the opening number – just me on a stage, singing "Get Happy". *Forget your troubles*, I had to sing to an audience full of people saying goodbye to sons, brothers, husbands. I was going to chase their blues away.

I was only nine, so I was sure I could do this.

When my feet hit the boards and I began to sing, I realized that I didn't belong on that mattress in the closet, or at the tiny apartment on Hope and Transit, or in a classroom, or anywhere but where I was. I heard the crack of the applause and it hit me solid in the chest. I knew that everything, everything had changed. This was where I belonged.

Afterwards, there was a crush of people in the lobby – teachers, parents, families, some of the fathers and brothers already in uniform. It was a sight we all were getting used to. It was no longer a surprise to see that Mary McGee's dad was now in the navy, or that Mr Sankey, the gym teacher, was home on leave after basic training. The senior classes of the high schools had drained of boys in a rush to sign up.

Through the crush of parents and relatives and neighbours backstage, I saw Da. Behind him was Delia in

245

the grey dress she'd worn to work, looking sombre in the midst of all the bright summer dresses. Jamie and Muddie lagged behind. Da was, as usual, crying.

He swept me up and hugged me hard. "You were the best up there, and everybody says so!"

"Shhh, Jimmy, have a little grace," Delia said, looking around. "There's other parents here with their own kids."

"Well, they know she was the best, nothing wrong with it." Da slipped an arm around my shoulders.

"You didn't stink up the joint," Jamie told me. He reached into his pocket and took out a ball. Smoothly, Delia took it and put it in her handbag.

"I thought for sure you were going to mess up at the end," Muddie said. "I was holding my breath!"

A plump woman dressed in a purple dress and a hat with a bird on it swooped down on us. "You," she said. She bent over and looked me in the eye. "You like to dance, don't you?"

I nodded, trying not to stare at the stuffed bird.

"I saw your name in the programme. Kathleen Corrigan."

The woman's eyes were as small and bright brown as the bird on her hat. Her mouth was as tiny as a gumdrop.

"A bit too Irish," she said.

"I beg your pardon," said Delia.

"We call her Kitty," Da said.

"Kit Corrigan," the woman said. "There you go – that's your stage name. You're her parents."

The woman turned questions into statements.

"I'm her father, and this is her aunt," Da said.

"Your daughter," she said, pointing at Da, "has a gift. When she's onstage with the other dancers, nobody looks at anybody else."

Da beamed. "That's just what I was saying. She's a star."

"No." The woman held up a finger. "She could be a dancer. With training. With *my* training. I'm Florence Foster. I've danced with the most prestigious troupes in the United States and Europe. I've danced on Broadway."

"Did you now!" Da said. "Did you hear that, Kitty?"

"We have to be going." Delia pressed her lips together. I could see how she disapproved of Mrs Foster's hat, of her bright red lips, of the fat that strained her buttons. She didn't look like a dancer.

Then Mrs Foster angled her body towards Da and waved her hand, and I saw the movement and the gesture as a single, fluid thing, not the aimless wave of a regular person. "I take some promising students, not many, for dance classes," she continued. "My students go on to ballet troupes in Boston, New York – into show business, if that's what they want. They become *dancers*."

She said the word *dancers* like it was a title, something special, like *Doctor* or *Judge*.

"We really must be going," Delia said again, and she took my hand.

"We're going out for ice cream," Da said joyously. "Why don't you join us, Mrs Foster?"

Delia threw him a look that could slice paper into ribbons. "I'm sure Mrs Foster has her own plans."

"I usually do," Florence Foster said with a cool glance at Delia. "Here is my card."

Da took it, looked at it and placed it in his pocket. "We'll be speaking to you, then. Sure you won't come for a sundae? Ice cream at Wolfe's?"

This was a wonder. Wolfe's was a downtown restaurant. On the rare occasion we went for ice cream, we went to the drugstore on South Main.

"You enjoy yourselves," Mrs Foster said. "Call me next week – my classes fill up fast."

"Wolfe's? Really, Da?" We all clamoured for an answer, hanging on to his arms, and him laughing, pretending to be alarmed.

He half ushered, half danced us to the restaurant, Delia having to walk in double time in her sensible heels. It was like a fine spring night with the warmth of summer, and the streets were crowded with other families hurrying to shops or restaurants, and servicemen still getting used to the deference their uniforms brought them.

We bounced in our chairs, planning how many scoops and how many toppings, for Da was in a mood to splurge, that was clear. Sundaes arrived, along with Delia's coffee.

A family brushed by in the crowd, and the man stopped.

It was Nate Benedict, dressed in a light-coloured suit with an open shirt. The woman wore a dark print dress and matching hat. She looked at us for a moment, then turned away. She put her arm around the boy standing with them, a boy with dark hair and eyes and a lean, handsome face like his dad's, minus the squashed nose. "We'll meet you up front, Nate," she said.

Before he turned away the boy looked straight at me, and I hoped he noticed my satin costume, red, white and blue.

"Hello, Corrigans," Nate said. "Good to see you, Mac. Miss Corrigan."

"Benny! Oh, I mean, Nate." Da stood and extended his hand. "We're celebrating the performance of our girl Kitty. She was over at the holiday show at the Carlton – you remember Kitty. . ."

Nate looked down at me. "The one who can't sleep." He reached out his hand, and I felt Delia flinch for a second as he rested it on top of my head. "We saw the show. You were wonderful." His compliment made me glow. *Wonderful*. Such an important word, a grown-up word.

"She was the best one on the stage, let me tell you."

"I agree. Enjoy your ice cream." Nate walked towards the entrance, putting on his hat. He joined the woman and the boy and they left, pushing through the doors to Westminster Street.

"Can you imagine, that teacher singling Kitty out like that," Da said, scooping off his cherry and holding it up.

Jamie, Muddie and I all grabbed for it, but Muddie was fastest.

"Now don't tell me that you're thinking of those lessons," Delia said tightly. She smoothed her paper napkin into little creases. "You're going to fill poor Kitty's head with dreams."

"What's wrong with dreams?"

"They don't come true, that's what. Life isn't a picture show."

"But she singled Kitty out!"

"She singled *you* out, more's likely, as the softest touch in Providence. She should be singing in church, lifting her voice to God, not on a stage. You want your daughter to parade herself on a stage?"

"Please, I'm begging you, Delia, don't bring Jesus into this one. I know he wasn't a song-and-dance man, but he *did* believe in pleasure. What about the wedding at Cana? Plenty of wine for everybody!"

"Oh, when you start quoting the Bible to me, I know I'm being conned." Delia drew her cardigan closer about her shoulders. "Don't go casting me as some puritan. I like singing and dancing as much as anyone. I'm not a Baptist. But have you noticed Kitty's grades? She should be concentrating on her studies."

"She has her heart set." Da said this as if it settled the matter, even though, of course, it didn't. He never had the last word.

"Listen to you, *her heart set*. As though getting your

250

heart set on something meant you should have it." Delia wiped at her mouth with her napkin, scraping it across her lips.

There was a silence. I didn't know why Delia was so angry. I just knew I wanted those lessons more than I'd ever wanted anything.

"I could go on Saturdays," I said.

"And who would bring you downtown?"

"A trolley would bring her, Dee," Da said.

"She's nine years old – she can't ride a trolley by herself. Man, what are you thinking? With all these sailors and strangers around now? I know you're raising these children like a pack of wild animals—"

"Dee." Da sighed, exasperated. He scooped up a bit of whipped cream and held it in front of her. "For once in your life, let someone else have something sweet without finding a way to spoil it. You're turning into the sourest old maid." He plopped the dollop of cream in her coffee.

Delia stared down at her cup. Slowly, a tear ran down her cheek. The four of us stared at her, spoons aloft. Nobody said a word. The tears dropped one by one on to Delia's paper napkin.

Finally, unable to bear the waiting, Muddie ate another spoonful of ice cream. We all dug back into our sundaes, careful not to bang the spoon against the metal dish. Da gazed at his plate, at his lap, at the signs advertising cherry floats and ham and cheese sandwiches for ten cents, anywhere but at Delia.

251

"You're not an old maid," I said finally. "You're. . ." I searched for the perfect word. "Wonderful."

Underneath the table, she squeezed my hand.

Her students called her Madame Flo, but she was about as formal as a Sherman tank. She was a hammer on my forehead, counting beats. I had to learn about beats until they were part of my bones and I could stop thinking about them and just move. I had thought dancing was only about steps and music. I didn't realize that rhythm could be so complicated.

When I started, suddenly nothing, it seemed, was right about my body. My feet didn't have enough turnout. My shoulders – down! My chin – lift it! She became my life after school and on Saturdays, and I learned what discipline was. No longer could I flop around on couches and hunch over stoops. I learned how to stand as well as dance. I practised tap on our bathroom tiles until Muddie and Jamie pounded on the door, begging me to stop, and Da laughed behind his newspaper.

Through Mr Loge, Delia got a war job in Washington, DC, in the summer of '44 and we didn't see her until September. Elena came on Saturday nights to cook us dinner before Jamie, Muddie and I headed out to the movies. She even cooked for Da now, laughing at his attempts to chop onions and pushing him out of the kitchen. "You're making me weep just watching you, Corrigan," she said. It seemed a terrible time to be happy, while the world was falling apart. But we were.

As boys we'd known from the neighbourhood or husbands and fathers were killed and gold stars began to appear in windows, we huddled on the living room floor over the newspapers, knowing our secret, that we didn't care about heroes, that we got to keep our dad.

Twenty-seven

Providence, Rhode Island
March 1945

That last weekend – the weekend after *Carousel* – Elena came and cooked us chicken and rice. She looked pretty in a flowered dress and heels.

"You have a boyfriend," Muddie guessed.

"Elena's in love!" I said, and was surprised to see a flush on Elena's neck. "Shut up, you two," Jamie said. "Don't be girls."

We did what we kids did every Saturday night – ate our dinner and headed to the Boys Club for free movies. That night, halfway through the cowboy serial, the projector broke. Everybody groaned. We waited, but finally we heard the bad news. We had to go home.

The three of us sat on the kerb outside, spinning out the evening, reluctant to go in.

We heard heels tapping on Hope Street, and in a moment we saw Delia appear out of the gloom. We were surprised to see her. She had left for the convent on Friday.

"What are you doing home?" Jamie asked.

"I'm home, that's all. Why are you sitting out here, you three? It's your bedtime, isn't it?"

"We stay up late on Saturdays," Muddie said.

I didn't say anything. I still had not recovered from the slap Delia had given me the week before, and I was punishing her with silence. It was infuriating that she didn't seem to notice. But tonight she seemed nervous. I noticed lines at the sides of her mouth for the first time, brackets around the curve of her lips.

"You can't sit out here. Come on, then." Delia started up the stairs, and we followed. She pushed open the front door and stood for a moment. The house was dark and quiet.

"Maybe he's asleep already," I whispered.

Suddenly, we heard a groan.

"He's sick!" Muddie cried.

We all crowded through the doorway to the living room. Delia was first, and we heard her "Mother of God!" and quickly we tried to squirm around her but she suddenly spun around and pushed us back towards the front door.

"Get outside."

I had a confused impression of Da in a slow motion roll, turning his head, his mouth open. Elena was on the couch in a funny position, her dress up to her thighs, gleaming in the darkness. Was she sick? Why was Da bent over her that way?

"Out!" Delia shouted at us.

But of course we didn't go out. We hovered just outside the door, which was still open a crack. We heard every word.

"Delia, for God's sake, turn around. We're decent."

"How dare you fornicate in your own home with your children outside!"

"They were at the movies!"

"Mother of God, Jimmy . . . this sin, right in your home, with the children—"

"Delia, could you please try not to drag God into this, I beg you. Or His mother."

"I'd better be going, Mac." Elena's voice was soft.

"Yes, indeed," Delia said. "You'd better go, and not come back."

"Delia. Dee. I love her. We're in love."

The silence lasted for a full minute.

When Delia spoke, it was in a voice short of breath. "You can't be serious. You can't be in love with a black woman."

We stared at each other, wide-eyed. Da in love with Elena? How had this gone on, underneath our noses? We all loved her, sure, but—

Delia laughed. It chilled us and we huddled closer.

"What do you think is going to happen to the two of you? Use your head! For once, Jimmy, look ahead. You never took a step on your own, I know that – never took a job that somebody didn't walk over to offer you, never passed up an opportunity as long as it tapped on your shoulder. You never stretched for anything in your life!

256

Don't you think I knew what I was doing when I put Maggie in front of you? She was the first pretty girl who was too nice to say no to you, so you decided you loved her. And now, this one – how like you it is, to fall for someone who's right next door. You've taken every easy chance, why not this one?"

"That's enough. Did you hear what I said? I love her."

"Love! It happens to you, so what? It happens to everybody. It's what you do with it that matters! You can live it or you can put it away, and you can pray to Jesus to help you either way."

"It's not that simple, you can't make it that simple. Love is a gift."

"Oh, don't be such a child! How long do I have to take care of you and your children? You lived off them and you've lived off me. You've never stood on your feet—"

"Dee, don't go on, I'm begging you. This isn't you. What's happened to you?"

"You killed your wife by not wanting to pay a doctor, by waiting so long—"

"*Delia!*" He shouted the word. It had been going on for some time, but now we realized that underneath the shouting, Elena was crying.

"I gave up my life for this family," Delia said. "I've been mother to these children, and I walk in and see you like this. . . I don't care if you go to hell, Jimmy, but I won't let your children fall into sin!"

"Sin! You're standing there talking to me about sin?"

Muddie put her hands over her ears. She could never bear a cross word, our Muddie. Jamie and I looked at each other, our mouths open and working like fish out of water. We didn't live in a world where grown-ups said the worst things they could to each other. We lived in a house where there were undertows, things we didn't understand, and jokes and stories passing for truth.

"At least I'm not afraid to walk into God's house!"

"Get out! Get out of my house!"

"I pay for this house, too! This is my house as much as yours, and they're my children as much as yours, no matter what the law says. And if the law knew about what you do in front of your children—"

"Get out. Get out right now."

"I'm leaving, but I'm coming back, Jimmy. I'm coming back for the children."

All the air seemed to leave the front stoop. I stared at Jamie. Muddie's face was screwed up tight, her eyes closed, tears dripping into her collar.

Now Da's voice was low and dangerous. "Don't threaten me with that. They're my children. They've never been yours. They never will be."

It was so quiet. Even Elena's sobs could no longer be heard. When we opened the door Da and Delia were standing opposite each other, enemies.

When the social worker came, we were playing poker. The kitchen smelled of burning. Muddie had made breakfast.

258

She'd tried to make Elena's fried dough, but what emerged from the pan were hard, bitter lumps instead of the airy sweet confections we were used to. Elena had gone, moving to Woonsocket to live with one of her sisters. We never got a chance to say goodbye. Da went grimly to work and came grimly home.

The social worker was a woman with tight curls and big yellow teeth that she kept flashing at us in an imitation of a smile. We stared at them, fascinated, half expecting them to leap out of her mouth and chatter on a table, just like in a cartoon. We told her how perfect a father Da was, but all we saw was teeth and we knew they would chomp us into bits no matter what we said. We were suddenly aware of Da's old trousers hanging from the towel rack in the kitchen, of my tap shoes sitting in the dish rack. The normal cheerful jumble of the household looked suddenly suspect in our eyes, too.

By the time Da came home from work and opened the door, the house was tidied up, everything put away. He closed the door and stood looking at a clean house.

"What's wrong?"

We told him about the social worker and he sat at the table, his head in his hands.

"She asked us if we ever saw you kiss Elena," I said. "We said no."

"She asked us where our Bible was and we pretended that we couldn't find it," Jamie said.

"Do we have a Bible, Da?" Muddie asked.

"We did the best we could," I said.

"I'm sure you did, my girl."

"You could talk to that woman," Muddie said. "You could explain things and tell her what a good father you are."

"What's the use?" Da said. "They're against us."

I asked the question we were all dying to ask. "Can't you talk to Delia, Da? Can't you make it up with her? Where is she, where did she go?"

"I don't know, maybe she's with those nuns of hers." Suddenly, he grabbed all of us, reaching to gather us in. "I could never talk to Delia," he said. "I can't start now."

In playground battles, the tactics are vicious and the play dirty. You can insult your opponent's mother or his looks or his abilities with a ball and bat. You can make him cry. But if that person shows up at your door the next day, offers you an orange, and says, "Wanna play?" you go.

So we thought the fight would just go away. Then one day a letter came telling Da to show up for a court hearing before a judge.

That night I saw the light in the kitchen and I went out to see, hoping it was Delia come home. It was only Da, smoking a cigarette at the kitchen table. He held out one arm and I walked into it, and he pressed me against his side. We didn't hug much in our family, and I leaned in, studying the way his dark hair curled against his ear. He stared down at the table and I saw the document on it, with names bold and black – official names that were foreign to me, like they didn't belong to Da and Delia – and the words *CUSTODY* and *HEARING*.

Fear entered me then, a fear so big I didn't think my body could contain it. Da was afraid of the courts, afraid of the officials, and he had already decided all was lost. I knew then, for the first time, that Delia was going to win.

Twenty-eight

New York City
November 1950

When the phone rang, I ran for it and then stood over it, hesitating. In my deluded brain the ring sounded like Billy's. That's how much I needed to talk to him.

I picked it up and just listened.

"Kit? Are you there?" It was Nate. "The newspaper, did you see it?"

"I saw it," I said.

"Do you know if. . ."

"He saw it." Suddenly, I wanted to hurt him the way he'd hurt me and Billy. I wanted him to know what he'd done to us. "He spent the night here. He saw the headline. He left. He's gone. He's gone for good."

"Didn't you explain that—"

"He wouldn't listen. He hates me. He hates you."

"Now, wait a minute, I can—"

"No, you can't. You've lost him. Don't you get it? All the

lies you've told him? Why would he believe you now? He'll never believe you."

The silence was so long over the buzz of the phone. I could hear him breathing, absorbing what I said, then dismissing it.

"This will be fixed."

"It can't be fixed! You've *lost*!"

"He'll cool off and listen to reason. Give him a day or two. Just don't talk to reporters tonight at the club—"

"I got fired today."

"Well, that might not be so bad. You can disappear for a while and people will forget. The Providence papers haven't picked it up yet, so you won't have to worry about that."

I closed my eyes and leaned against the wall. I felt weak. I hadn't even thought this through. I'd been cringing, thinking of strangers in New York. What about people who knew me? What about Da? Of course the Providence and Boston papers would pick this up. Nate was news. And the Providence papers would jump on it. Reporters there would remember the Corrigan Three. Shame flooded me, brought heat to my face.

"It's Thanksgiving tomorrow," Nate said. "Billy could be on his way to Providence."

"I don't think so," I said.

"He won't disappoint his mother. Are you coming up?"

I shook my head, then said, "No." Thanksgiving was for families. I couldn't face Da and Muddie once this came out.

263

"I think that's best. I can't imagine what Mac would say. He doesn't have what you'd call an open mind, does he?"

The words stung. But I was alert suddenly, jolted to the bone. There was something in Nate's voice. . .

He hates Da. He's not his friend, after all. He hates him.

"Look," he went on, "it's only a matter of time before the reporters find you. Don't answer the phone, don't go out. I'm leaving for Providence tomorrow morning. I'll give Billy a day to cool off, talk to him up there. I can fix this. I'll make it all go away."

"Sure," I said. "'No Witnesses Benedict', right? You make things disappear. Even people, sometimes."

There was a pause. "What is that supposed to mean?"

"Nothing."

"So let's go over this again," he said slowly. "You lay low—"

"Sure. But what if I need to go out for something? I've got to leave sometime. So these reporters, they'll ask me questions, and I'll say . . . what? Because I don't want to slip and say something I shouldn't. I need you to tell me what to say. Just like you've told me what to do. Every dancer needs a choreographer, right?"

"That's right," he repeated. He still wasn't sure if I was taunting him. "I know how to handle these things. And if you're smart, you'll listen."

"But I'm just a dumb kid," I said. "Remember? A dumb kid who doesn't know how to listen."

"That's enough," Nate said sharply. "I didn't say that you—"

264

"Just a chorus girl, dancing in a line," I said. "What do I know? My job is to show off my legs."

"Stop it." His voice was low. "Say what you mean."

"I'm not saying anything, I'm just talking. But I'm not supposed to talk, right? You see how dumb I am? I keep forgetting."

Another pause. "We're on the same side. Aren't we, Kit?"

"Sure we are. You call the shots. You have from the beginning. I was just too dumb to know it."

"I can see you're upset," Nate said. "Who wouldn't be? I'm telling you, I'll take care of this. Here's all you have to do. Sit tight. Give it the weekend. Don't talk to a reporter, whatever you do. Don't answer the phone. I'll find a way to get to you."

Quietly, I replaced the receiver.

Of course he would tell me what to do.

That was over.

I'll find a way to get to you. . .

Sweat had soaked through my nightgown. I hadn't been able to help myself. Scared as I was, I couldn't stop myself from taunting him. Risking his anger was a dumb thing to do, but for the first time I felt almost free.

Almost. And afraid. Still afraid. More afraid than I'd ever been.

I buried my face in my hands. That's when I heard the first knock at the door.

Trapped. All day, the reporters kept trying. Knocking at the door. Ringing the phone. Calling through the door.

265

"C'mon, Kit, doncha want to tell your side of the story?"

"You'll be on the front page!"

And then someone smarter, saying through the door, "I'm sure your family wants to know what really went on. You're a good girl, right?"

The super locked the lobby door and stood guard, so they couldn't get in that way. I stayed in the back of the apartment, in the kitchen, all afternoon. I tried to think. I had to act smart for once.

I had a little bit of time. Not much. Nate wouldn't come by with the reporters here. He'd head for Providence in the morning. I had a day or two to figure out my next move. I'd have to find a new place to live, pack my old suitcase and get out of here. I had enough money for a month, maybe two if I went back to eating apples for dinner. If I was lucky, Daisy would believe me about Nate. Or else she'd think having a mobster boyfriend wouldn't be a drawback in a room-mate.

Then I could write Billy a letter, give him my new address. And hope.

Is this what Delia had done? Had she sat here, making plans to get away from Nate? Had he caught her before she'd had a chance to run?

Twenty-nine

Providence, Rhode Island
April 1945

I waited until after school the next day and then I stood in front of the door so that Jamie couldn't go out to play.

"We're going to fix this," I told him. "We can't depend on Da."

"How can we fix it?" Muddie asked. Jamie just eyed me in that way he had, waiting for the pay-off.

"We're going to the only person we know who can make this go away," I said.

Muddie still looked puzzled as she bent over to buckle her shoe. But Jamie nodded.

"Mr Benedict," he said.

"We'd better leave a note," Muddie said. "Da will be back before we are. He's coming straight home from work now."

"We never leave a note," I said.

"Things are different now," Jamie said, and he got out the pencil and paper. "Now we're the perfect kids, remember? What if the social worker comes again, and Da doesn't know where we are?"

By the time we reached Atwells Avenue, we were hungry and my socks had disappeared into my shoes. We stood outside the plain brown building, hesitant. I had been expecting an office building, something impersonal. This looked like someone's house. The gold lettering on the window, NATE BENEDICT ATTORNEY-AT-LAW, made everything seem too serious. Would he help us?

I walked to the house, stood on tiptoe, and tried to peek through the slats of the blinds. I got a fractured image of a man sitting at a desk.

"Come on," I said to Jamie and Muddie. "We're here, so we might as well go in."

And before Muddie could think of a reason not to, I rapped on the door.

The door opened, and there he was, standing in his shirtsleeves and looking at me in surprise. "Kitty Corrigan," he said.

"Maybe you remember my brother, James, and my sister, Margaret. We've come to. . ." I hesitated. Why would he let us in if he didn't know we were serious? I had a sudden inspiration. "Hire you."

"I see. Maybe you should come in, then."

I beckoned fiercely to the others. We walked into a dark foyer. There was a closed door on one side, and a staircase facing us. To the left, the office door was open. Nate gestured for us to go in.

We stood uncertainly on the rug until he gestured again to a couch against one wall. We sat. He pulled up a chair and tilted his head to one side.

"Now. What seems to be the problem?"

I liked that, what *seems* to be the problem, like maybe the problem was in our heads and could be easily solved by someone like him.

"It's about our Aunt Delia," I said.

He reared back a bit, then knotted his fingers together. "Go on."

"She wants to take us away."

Nate got up abruptly and went to the table near his desk. "Would you like some cookies? I have cookies." He was already opening a bakery box and putting the cookies on a plate. With his back to us, he said, "Please go on, Kitty."

"She says Da is unfit, and she wants us," I said.

"We don't want to go!" Muddie burst out.

"She thinks we'll be better off," Jamie said. "But we won't."

"Is she suing for custody, then?" Nate asked. He stood, holding the plate.

"A lady came around and talked to us. And then a letter came in the mail."

"And your father opposes it?"

"Of course!" Jamie cried. "He told her to go away and never come back. She's already moved out!"

Muddie swallowed rapidly, her eyes on the plate. "So Kit thought maybe you would know what to do."

269

"Seeing that you knew our dad back when you were pals," Jamie added.

"And we don't have anybody else to turn to," I said. I'd heard a line like that in the movies; people in the movies were always saying they didn't have anybody to turn to. I pictured them spinning round and round, turning, as the people they knew became a blur, impossible to pick out.

He looked out the window. "When did this happen?"

"Last month. She came home early – we thought she was away, on one of her retreats, but she came home, and . . . she saw our dad. . ."

"He was fornicating with Elena," Jamie said. He looked at Muddie when she gasped. "Well, we might as well tell him."

"Elena?"

"She used to cook for us," Muddie said in a hushed voice. "In the summers, and weekends, when Delia was away. But now she's just our friend. She's . . . Portuguese."

"Anyway, she wants to take us away from him, and it's not fair at all," I said. "If you could only help us somehow. Da said you're important, that you know how to get things done. He says you're a great man," I added, even though Da had said no such thing.

Nate focused his attention on me. I clasped my hands together. The time had gone when I could rely on being cute. I was twelve, with bony knees and a skinny face. My red hair made me look freakish now, I was certain. But I

270

tried to conjure up some semblance of my old adorableness.

"If I help you, you'll owe me a favour," he said to me. "You understand?"

He was looking at me seriously, not humouring me, the way adults usually did. I nodded.

"Shake on it?"

I put my hand in his. I remembered to grip it hard. We shook.

"All right, then. It's a deal."

There was a sharp rap at the front door.

"Well," Nate said. "It appears that this is my busy day."

We heard the murmur of voices and we exchanged a panicked glance. It was Da. If we could have scrambled out the back window, we would have.

Da followed Nate into the room. One look told us how much trouble we were in.

"I'll deal with you lot in a bit," Da said to us. "Go outside while I apologize to Mr Benedict."

"Jimmy, it's all right," Nate said. "The children are upset. They have a right to be."

"It's family business, Nate, and none of yours."

"Why not, if he can help us?" I burst out. "It's not like you're doing anything!"

"Kitty Corrigan!" Da roared. "Mind your manners!"

"I'll mind them outside, if you don't mind," I said primly. I walked out with all the dignity I could. Nate Benedict had treated me like a grown-up, and I wasn't about to let Da turn me back into a child.

But we were desperate to hear what Da would say, and so instead of waiting outside on the sidewalk, we followed the concrete walk on the side of the house to a back yard, hoping to sneak near the open window.

On the patio was a round table and chairs, and a boy sat on top of the table with a camera, aiming it above at the sky. He heard our footsteps and turned, and I remembered him from the night we'd had ice cream. Billy.

We approached him warily. We knew, the whole city knew, that his cousin Michael had been killed in a car crash just a month or so before. He'd been sixteen, just two years older than Billy. Hundreds of people had attended the funeral. We didn't know his cousin and didn't know him, but the death of a young relative was serious enough to make us kinder than we might have been normally.

"Hello," I said. "That's a nice camera."

He looked down at us, and I figured he knew who we were.

Ignoring us, he put the camera back up against his face. That was OK, that was fine – we were in his neighbourhood.

He turned and looked at me through the camera. "Whatcha doing?" I asked.

"Shooting birds."

I'd never seen a camera like that before, with dials and gears and levers. And people didn't take photographs much – it was too hard to get film during the war.

272

"What kind of camera is that? A Brownie?" I asked, even though I knew it wasn't.

He snorted. "It's an Argus C3."

I hoisted myself next to him. "How do you get film?"

"My dad gets it." He lowered the camera.

I looked down at the camera, then back up at him. For a moment, we looked into each other's eyes. Something ran between us, like we each had hold of a string by the end and were pulling it level and taut.

"We came to hire your dad. Our dad's in there now."

"Yeah?" he said. "My dad is good at making things go away." He didn't say it in a bragging way. He said it in a way that made his mouth twist. "You got kicked out?"

"Yeah."

He regarded me silently for a moment. I'd never met a boy with a gaze like that, unblinking, like his camera, just taking me in. Most boys never met my eyes. They stared at the ground, or hooted at me, or pulled my hair, or ignored me completely even though I knew they were aware of me the whole time.

"You want to see what's going on in there?" he asked. "I've got a way."

I shrugged.

"It'll cost you a nickel."

I shrugged again. I knew better than to show too much interest.

"We need a lookout." Billy looked at each of us appraisingly. "Her," he said, pointing to Muddie.

273

"OK," Muddie said, relieved not to have to join in whatever he was planning.

He held out his hand for the nickel.

"Forget it, then," I said, even while Jamie fished in his pocket. "How about it'll cost you a dollar so I don't tell your father that you spy on him?"

He eyed me furiously, his face suddenly flushing a dark red. "Fink."

"Snake."

Jamie looked from one of us to the other, the nickel in his fist.

"You're just chicken," Billy said.

Well, that was that. I knew the rules. I couldn't back down now. I nodded at Jamie, and he put a nickel in the boy's hand.

"Gotta get something first," he said.

"Sure," I said.

He hopped off the table and I followed. He went to a half door in the side of the building, the old coal cellar. He paused on the top of the ramp going down. "What are you doing?"

"Following you."

He turned his back to me, but I shifted and watched him lift one of the bricks that lined the ramp and take out a key. He fitted it into the padlock.

The way he pushed open the door let me know he wouldn't stop me from coming in after him. That he *wanted* me to come in.

I'd been expecting just a coal cellar, made of stone and brick, filthy from years of the coal coming down the chute that was there before the slanted walk. Instead it was a workroom, with a light bulb hanging overhead, a table, and photographs stacked on it with wavy edges. A doorway led towards the cellar, shrouded in darkness.

Billy straightened a pile of photographs while I looked at the top of the pile closest to me. It was of a house with dark windows that looked like eyes. Another was of a man sitting on a chair outside in the sun talking to another man, except all you could see was their bellies and their hands. Somehow you knew they were having an argument, and maybe that they hated each other, and I didn't know why. I pushed that one aside and saw another, a view straight down some train tracks, the landscape blurred on the sides. Billy came over to stand next to me.

"This one is scary," I said.

"When I go someplace on a train, I like to be in the first car," he said. "I like to see what's coming at me. And I like to be the first one there. Subways in New York are the best. You can stand right up against the window."

"I haven't been to New York," I admitted.

I picked up one of a man shot through a restaurant window. He was holding a forkful of something, and he was looking off to the side. I could see this guy, how carefully he combed his hair, how his shirt was too tight but he thought he looked pretty swell. I laughed.

"I've never seen pictures like these," I said. It seemed

275

like a great and wonderful thing, to be able to look at the world through a camera lens. "You make everything look more real than it is, somehow."

"I develop them myself."

"With chemicals and stuff?" I tried to keep the admiration out of my voice.

"Yeah, this is my darkroom. My dad let me set it up here. I can only use it on weekends, though. Weekdays are for school."

"That's too bad." I touched one of the photographs. "If I could do this, I'd want to do it all the time."

We looked at each other, and I saw that I'd made him happy, only he was trying not to show it.

"Yeah." He turned to pick up a lens sitting on the table.

I moved towards the last stack of photos. This one was taken outside a window into a dimly lit room. I could see a woman from behind. She was pulling her sweater up, as though she was about to slip it over her head. I could see a couple of inches of white skin. A coat was thrown over a couch, I could just see the end of it.

I jumped back as he tossed the other stack on top of it. "Things get messy in here. Come on."

I followed him out. I saw relief on Jamie's face that I'd emerged. Billy led us to a tree in the sandy area near the garage and carefully screwed the lens into the camera while he asked, "Are you afraid of heights?" He pointed to the tree with his chin.

In answer, I grabbed the lowest branch and swung up.

Billy followed, then Jamie, who wasn't about to let me do this alone. Muddie looked up at us, her mouth open. I motioned for her to go out front and keep watch.

I sat on a high branch, legs swinging. Billy climbed on the branch above and motioned to us. We followed. We were at the roofline now, and the branch was wide, forking out so that there was room for the three of us to sit. I was conscious of his arm against mine. He handed me the camera. "Go ahead, look."

I put the camera to my eye. I couldn't see anything at first.

"Turn the lens to focus."

I turned the lens. I saw the rug in Nate's office. I shifted the camera slightly and saw Da's feet. I tilted upwards and saw Da standing in front of the couch, talking to Nate.

Da's face was hidden, he was turned slightly away. I could just see his hands moving, like he was trying to explain something hard. I could see Nate's face, frowning in concern.

"What do you see?" Jamie said.

"They're just talking," I said. "Hardly worth a nickel."

I swung the camera slightly upwards to the window over the office. The blinds were open and I could see a shadowy interior. I realized that I was looking at the same couch that I'd seen in the photograph in Billy's darkroom.

He pulled the camera away. "Let me focus it for you." He looked through the lens, his mouth slightly open. "You can tell a lot," he said, "by the way people stand. You can tell a lot by looking when they don't think you're looking."

I felt guilty, sitting in the tree, spying on Da. Jamie was looking at the boy with a fascinated, intent look in his eyes. Billy handed him the camera and showed him how to work the lens. I was jealous. Two boys absorbed by machinery, and the girl always got left out. Their heads were together, bent over the camera.

"Come on, Jamie." I sidled over on the branch, closer to the trunk. "Come *on*."

"Nate has his arm on Da's shoulder," Jamie said, the camera raised to his face. "Now they're shaking hands."

"That means the meeting is over," Billy said. "Gimme the camera."

We shinnied down the trunk, hanging on to branches and swinging, our shoes finally hitting dirt with a satisfying thump.

Muddie came tearing around the side of the house. "He's leaving! He's looking for us now!"

We dashed towards her, but for an instant I turned to look back. Billy was leaning against the tree, the camera up to his eye again, and I heard the shutter click.

We'd expected a courtroom, but instead we were just in a room with a judge and a few other people who didn't introduce themselves. We all sat silently, waiting, but we weren't sure for what. The judge looked at papers. He didn't seem friendly.

Da had brought the scrapbook with all our clippings. All the articles that said what a happy family we were and what a wonderful father he was. The pictures of us lined up on the couch, the first picture that was ever in the paper, Da with his arms full of three babies, a smile on his face, and sadness in his eyes. Da and the three of us at Maggie's grave site. We've only gone once or twice, and then because a photographer wanted a picture. Da couldn't stand the thought of our mother under the ground.

Da and the Corrigan Three at the Pennsylvania state fair. Da and the Corrigan Three at the Fourth of July parade. The Corrigan Three singing on the radio. On Decoration Day, on Thanksgiving, waiting for pie. Singing Christmas carols.

He tried to show the judge the scrapbook, but the judge waved it away. He looked down at his papers and looked at his watch and looked at his watch again. The minutes went by like long hours.

After what felt like an hour someone knocked on the door and came in and whispered in the judge's ear. Delia hadn't shown up.

We went down the courthouse steps and looked at each other in a daze.

"Something must have happened," Da said. "She'd never give up like this."

But what we didn't realize that afternoon, standing on the courthouse steps, was that she was gone for good.

Everything else was still there in her room: her winter coat, her good shoes, her hats, dresses, sheets. Her books, her radio, even her rosary.

He wrote to the convent in Vermont, but the sisters hadn't heard of her. Maybe we'd heard the name wrong. Sisters of Mercy, we thought, but could it have been something else?

"She'll come back," Da said.

"She'll send us a card," Muddie said.

"She can't just be gone," Jamie said.

Nobody looked at me. It was like Da's old story of our birth. Everybody knew who was at fault. Everybody knew who was guilty. I was the one, after all, who had made the deal with Nate.

Nate promised Da he'd had nothing to do with Delia's disappearance. He'd just talked to the judge and vouched for Da, for old time's sake.

We waited to hear from her. We thought surely she'd come at Christmas, or send word. Surely she'd send a card on our birthday. Surely. . .

There was a shift then. Strange how Delia was the fun-killer, the one who could flatten the fizz in the soda, could remind you it was raining, could tell you on a brilliant cold day that you'd catch your death. You'd think there would be more songs, more laughter after she was gone. You'd think that, wouldn't you?

When a family breaks you don't hear the crack of the breaking. You don't hear a sound.

Thirty

New York City
November 1950

Here was where Delia had moved and talked, read the papers, had a cup of tea in the afternoon. Maybe there was a whole other side to my aunt. Maybe she sang along with the radio. Maybe she painted her fingernails. Because I didn't really know her.

It was dark outside when I summoned all my courage and dialled the number. When I heard Muddie's voice, I almost hung up.

"Kit!" she said when she heard my voice. "Oh, the newspapers! It's all over, that picture of you. . ."

"So you saw it."

"What happened? How could they print such lies? Everyone in Providence knows you're Billy's girl."

I hung on, wanting to cry. Muddie's belief in me was a steady thing, no more noticed than the sidewalk underneath my heels. But now I was glad of it. "Did Da—"

"I don't know – he's not home yet. Any minute. Are you coming for Thanksgiving? I can meet the train. Anytime—"

"I don't know," I said, stalling.

"But you have to come! Is Billy with you?"

"No. I was hoping he was in Providence," I said, my heartbeat speeding up.

"Gosh, I wouldn't know. He hasn't called, but I'm sure he will," Muddie rushed to say. "I'm sure he won't believe any of this nonsense. Oh, here's Da! It's Kit on the phone! Hurry, it's long distance!"

"I know it's long distance!" Da shouted into the phone. "Kit? Are you there?"

"I'm here, Da—"

"I'm going down to that editor's office and stringing him up by his tie, do you hear me?" he roared. "I'm suing him for libel! How dare they print such a lie! So you're dancing with the man – you're a dancer, aren't you? Calling you a chorus girl—"

I was crying, leaning against the wall, tears sliding down my cheeks. He believed in me. Believed without my explaining or begging. "I *am* a chorus girl, Da."

"I know, but it's the way he wrote it. I've a mind to—"

"You can't do anything. It's in all the papers here. I'm just glad you don't believe it."

"Of course I don't!"

"Da, I have to ask you something. What happened between you and Nate?"

282

"What happened? What do you mean? I haven't seen him in years."

"No, I mean, long ago. Why didn't you stay friends?"

There was a pause. Then, cautiously, "Well, now, we're friends. Of a sort."

"What does he blame you for?"

I heard the hiss of the phone connection. I pictured Da, still in his work clothes and boots, standing in the kitchen. "This isn't something to be yelling into a phone long distance."

"Tell me! I need to know. Was it about Delia?"

"He asked for Delia's hand back then – when she was twenty and him twenty-two. And me being his best friend and her brother, he asked me. I said no. Well, of course I did! He was already mixed up with those gangsters up on Federal Hill. So much for his promises."

"What promises?"

"That he was out of the rackets. That he would take Delia and they'd move away, to Boston, or even further, to get away."

"Why would she listen to you?"

"Well, that's another question, isn't it? I think she listened to herself, more's like. But he blamed me, even though it was for the best. Anyone would say that. And he wasn't even a fine lawyer then, just a skinny kid saying he was *going* to be a lawyer. Who knew he'd turn out to be such a big man? But wasn't I right – isn't he still a gangster? Just look at the papers!"

283

"I thought you didn't believe the papers."

"Well, they get things right once in a while. Listen, everyone makes their own road, I'm not throwing stones at the man. I just didn't want him marrying my sister. That's enough of the past, now. What difference does it make?"

I choked out a half laugh, half sob.

"Darling girl, come home. Muddie is all sparked up."

I told him I would let them know, which he didn't like, and that long distance was expensive, which he couldn't argue with, and we hung up.

I was no further along than before.

If Nate had closed up this apartment after Delia disappeared in 1945, maybe there was more evidence of her having been here. I began to search. I had nothing else to do. I opened every drawer and felt behind it. I moved the rugs. I climbed on a chair to search the top shelves of the closet. I crawled on my hands and knees on the floor and ran my hand along every seam in the floorboards. I didn't know what I was looking for – a stray earring, a scrap of paper, a key . . . something left behind five years before that would have been overlooked the same way the powder compact had.

Nothing.

I suddenly sat up very straight, pierced by a thought.

There was one place I hadn't searched.

Down in the basement, there was no problem at all breaking the lock on the chain-link fencing for apartment

1A. The super kept his tools in the utility room, where the boiler sat. I broke the lock with a screwdriver and a hammer. Amazing the tips you could learn from growing up in a lousy neighbourhood.

The door swung open. I walked right through. I removed a box from on top of the footstool and then sat down to open it with the tip of the screwdriver.

The box was filled with women's clothes. Not folded and neatly put away, but thrown in and all jumbled together. I pawed through it and found expensive cocktail dresses with net and tulle and lace. Holding one up, I gauged the hemline and the style. A shorter hemline, out of date – the war years. A fox stole, a little black hat with a veil. Some rhinestone jewellery. And brassieres and underwear and girdles – all black, trimmed with lace, dainty things. Clothes to be seen in.

They couldn't be Delia's.

I pressed my nose to a sweater. Delia had never worn perfume, but a scent clung to these. . .

But wait. During the war years, there had been a bottle on her dresser. A little bottle with a gold top. Toujours Moi. I'd never paid attention in French class, but I knew that meant *Always Me.*

I breathed in again. Suddenly, my eyes smarted with tears. Delia burst into brisk, purposeful life, her fingers resting on top of my head, bending down to adjust a scarf or fix a button. I *smelled* her.

I slipped into a little gold jacket, nipped in at the waist

with a small peplum. It fitted perfectly. I vaguely remembered this one.

So this was why Nate knew how to buy clothes for a woman. He'd had years of practice with Delia.

A small chest was wedged against the grating. I opened all the drawers. Empty. I pulled them out and searched underneath and behind. Nothing.

Another box. This one, handbags and shoes. Platform pumps in kid and sandals in black. Summer shoes. Shoes to dance in. And tiny bags, a clutch in black satin and one in red leather. A small beaded one for evening. The shoes had scuffed bottoms but seemed barely worn, and there was nothing inside the handbags except a crumpled tissue. At the very bottom of the box was a green quilted rectangular box, the kind ladies kept their silk stockings in, instead of rolling them into balls and tossing them in a drawer. I opened it – nylons and silk stockings, tumbled together. I shut the box, then opened it again. Underneath the stockings, I'd caught a glimpse of white.

An envelope addressed to Nate at his office address on Federal Hill. In Delia's handwriting. But there was no stamp, no postmark.

I opened it.

Do you remember the night of the hurricane, when you picked me up and carried me through the water – do you remember? We said we could never walk away from something so true. We did once and we found each other

286

*again and so we'd never leave again. That's what we
said.*

*Are you afraid of me now? Is that it? Do we have too
many secrets to keep?*

*I thought my heart had been broken every Sunday
afternoon we parted. Every Friday night you put it back
together. My life was full of waiting.*

*And now it ends with waiting. I'm waiting for you
here and you aren't coming. I know that now. You're
shedding your mistress. You are making that clear. Yes, I
said mistress. I know, I was never allowed to use that
word. I wasn't your mistress, I was your love. How many
times did you say that to me over the years? How could I
have known that the language was as false as the
promise?*

*I wish I could take back every tear I shed for you. I
wish I could take back every kiss. I wish I could take
back the years.*

*Keep your money and your clothes. On my forehead,
the words are written in ash, and I am wearing scarlet
and purple and I am leaving because*

The letter stopped there. I could see Delia writing it, maybe
wiping tears away while she did it, putting down her pen
and picking it up again. I had no way of knowing if Nate
had ever read it. It seemed the kind of letter you'd tear up
if you found it.

The air was so chilly down here. The light was dim. I

287

was suddenly aware of how alone I was, and how much time had passed.

Turning to go, I saw something I'd missed. A trunk, an old one with leather straps. Pushed to the very back, with an old rug tossed on top.

I stared at the trunk. Suddenly, fear seized me, a hard, cold fear that made it impossible for me to move, or even think for a moment.

Are you afraid of me now?

Do we have too many secrets to keep?

What would his *mistress* know about his business that no one else might know? What part of his life could she threaten if she became *emotional*? If she showed up where she wasn't supposed to show up, like in a theatre when his wife was there? If she suddenly brought a legal proceeding against her own brother, what would she do to Nate?

I knew it from the movies, and I knew it from Fox Point, where windows and doors were flung open and fights were like opera in other houses – men were afraid of desperate women. They'd do anything to shut them up.

I needed somebody else to open that trunk, because I was too afraid.

I felt the screwdriver in my fist. I made my legs move. *All I have to do is break the lock and lift the lid. Just glance inside, quickly, and put it back down. Don't think about what you'll see, just do it. Because you have to know the truth.*

I walked over to the trunk. I fitted the screwdriver in the lock. My hands were perspiring and the screwdriver kept slipping. The clatter of the noise made my heart pound. It took long minutes before I was able to pop it open with a clatter that made me jump back.

I put my hands on the edges of the trunk. I tried to find courage, but could only come up with some sort of tattered determination and the knowledge that I couldn't go to the police with a story like this unless it was true.

I pulled at the lid. It stuck for a moment, and I knelt on the floor and pushed harder. The lid sprang open and scraped against the fencing like a scream.

The trunk was empty.

Closing the lid, I sagged backwards, placing a hand over my heart in a futile attempt to slow it down.

But if Delia wasn't in the trunk, she was *somewhere*. Nate was involved in her disappearance, or her murder. Why hadn't we gone to the police at the time? Because in our family, you didn't poke at things. You just accepted them. Delia was angry, Delia moved away. There had been a short investigation, but it was clear that Delia had been rejected by her family and had chosen to go. We didn't know where she'd kept her money; she'd handed over the rent to Da in cash every month. It made sense that she would just go. Never darken our door again, like in some melodrama.

If we suspected that Nate had done something terrible, we pushed the thought away, because it meant we were responsible for it. I'd been only twelve, so of course I would hide my head under my pillow and try to forget. But Da?

What was his excuse? Was the answer so easy – that Da hid from everything?

I remembered his loyalty to me, how he believed in me, and I felt helpless against the great tide of his love. Delia had been right – he took the easy road. But he loved us and protected us. He was all kinds of things in one – liar and charmer and schemer. He was my da.

He wasn't alone. We all chose to believe that Delia had left. We didn't believe it – we *chose* to. We saw there was a mystery, but we decided to believe the easiest thing, the thing that made us the most comfortable. My father had led a whole life by that principle. Maybe choosing to believe the easiest thing was the worst sin of all.

And what about me? I had taken the easy road, too, accepting the apartment and the job and clothes. . . How many things did I turn my face from, afraid of losing something?

I put everything back the way I'd found it and left. As I reached the stairway I realized that I was still wearing the jacket. The light was better here, and I looked down at it. For the first time I saw a stain on the front, near the waist. I slipped it off and looked at it closely. Dark brown, faded now, but an irregular stain that had splattered a bit, faint drops in a trail.

Wine?

Or blood.

Suddenly, I heard the whirr of the elevator. I looked over at it, my heartbeat thudding. It was between me and the stairs. Any minute the small round window would reveal a face.

I bolted backwards, turning and running silently back towards the storage room. I heard the thunk of the elevator settling, then the sound of the heavy door opening.

I'd have to hide. There was no telling who it could be – a zealous reporter, or something worse . . . Nate. Footsteps headed towards me.

I carefully opened the door to Nate's unit. The gate squeaked.

The footsteps stopped.

I reversed direction and glided across the concrete floor. Maybe there was another exit towards the back. I slipped down the corridor, but it ended at a bare wall. I doubled back. There was a side room with a washing machine and dryer, and another where carriages and bicycles were stored. I took a cautious step forward when the lights went out.

It was like someone knocked me to the ground. I couldn't see, and I was afraid to move. I tried to orient myself. How close was I to the first storage unit? How many steps to the door? I inched over, holding out a hand. When my fingers met cold metal I kept a hand there lightly as I moved forward. As frightened as I was, I was more frightened of standing still.

Inch by inch, I went forward. I heard a slithering noise, a footstep, but it was impossible to tell where it came from. I was breathing hard, I realized, and I tried to slow down.

As my eyes adjusted, the blackness dissolved into greys. I could make out shapes. Faint light from the barred window in the laundry room illuminated part of the basement. At last I could make out the shape of the door to the stairs.

The air and the darkness made panic surge. I ran. As fast as I could, eyes on the stairs. I collided with another body and went down. I screamed and tried to roll away.

"Kit!"

It was Hank. He was on his hands and knees, staring at me through the gloom, his eyes wild.

"*What are you doing?*" We both screamed the question at the same time.

I rolled on my back on the hard cement floor, gasping. "You scared the living daylights out of me!"

"Me, too. Why were you hiding?"

"Why did you turn out the lights?"

"I thought—" He got up and put out his hand to me, pulling me upright.

"You thought what?" I asked, dusting off my trousers.

"Never mind. Mom sent me down for the Christmas box," he said, gesturing to a box by the elevator. "She puts the Christmas stuff up the day after Thanksgiving. Everything has to be done the same way, every year, even this one. She's crazy."

Hank wasn't meeting my eyes. He'd seen the headlines, too, of course.

"Well," he said, "I guess I'll see you around. Happy Thanksgiving."

I could see that he could hardly wait to get away. He must have hated me. And of course he was afraid of Nate.

Afraid of Nate. . . With everything I'd been thinking, I'd forgotten about that meeting with Hank. What had that been about? Nate's hand on Hank's shoulder, whispering. . .

"It's not true," I said.

He half turned. I could only see the side of his face. "What's not true?"

"I'm not Nate's girlfriend. I already told you he's Billy's father. That's why he gave me the apartment."

"It's none of my business."

"You've got to believe me!" I insisted. "I was mixed up with him, but not that way. And Hank – I think he might have killed somebody."

"Well, that's reassuring," Hank said. "Just one?"

I closed my eyes for a second. "Please don't joke right now. Please."

"I wasn't joking."

"I just wanted you to know that I'm not . . . what they say I am. I'm not the best person, but I'm not . . . that. Look, out of everyone in New York, your family should understand. Sometimes what they say about you? It just isn't true. No matter how true it looks."

He frowned. "Please don't cry. It's really hard to talk to you when you cry. Here." He offered me his shirttail, and it made me laugh.

I wiped my tears with the back of my hand. "The reason I'm down here – I'm looking for evidence. I think my aunt

293

was Bridget Warwick. I think she took that name – and she lived in my apartment with Nate." I spilled out the story as fast as I could, afraid he'd walk away. But I could tell that he wouldn't, that he was believing me, every word.

"You thought she was in the trunk?" he asked, his eyes wide. "And you opened it?"

"I had to know. Hank, what happened that day with Nate? Did he threaten you about something?" Hank hesitated. The air down here was chilly and damp, and I felt goosebumps on my arms. "I didn't send that message to come to my apartment. You saw how surprised I was to see you. Please tell me. I might be able to help you. Did he threaten you that day? About what?"

"I was there that night," Hank blurted.

Slowly, I realized what he meant. "You're the witness."

"I just wanted to walk you home. I didn't know if your boyfriend would come. I waited and you didn't come out. Everybody else came out, and I just kept waiting around the corner. I wanted to talk to you, I guess. Make sure you were OK or something."

"I didn't see you."

"Finally I decided to go in and look. I used that door you told me about—"

"—the door to the lounge—"

"It was dumb, I know. I peeked in the dressing room but it was empty. I was just going out when I heard a noise. So I opened the door and saw – I saw it happen. I saw it, the whole thing." Hank's face twisted. "It happened fast – he

294

got shot in the head. I don't think he knew it was coming, because he didn't try to get up. Or maybe he did know it. I don't want to think about that part."

"Was Nate there?"

"I don't know! I couldn't see anything, no faces or anything. All I saw were men in suits. Except for the killer. The big guy they caught? He did it."

"So just tell the cops you didn't see anything but that."

Hank looked at me as though I were a transfer student from the dumb class. "It doesn't matter if I didn't see anything. They think I did. So that day Nate was just telling me that he couldn't protect me. He could only get me out of town. He has contacts in Cuba."

"Cuba!"

"I'd just have to go for a year or so, he said. And my parents . . . they were just . . . well, you can imagine. And they don't trust the government, either. Trust the FBI? They think if we go to the FBI, they won't protect the son of two Commies."

"So what are you going to do?"

"I don't know. They went to go talk to my uncle. They're trying to figure it out. We thought we had it bad before. Now I got us into a worse mess."

"I'm sorry. It's all my fault. But, Hank, if I could prove that Nate killed Delia, you'd have something on him. And maybe you could make a deal."

He looked puzzled. "Make a deal? But I have to tell what I know eventually."

"Why? Then they'll really be after you!"

"Because it's the right thing to do. My parents are just trying to figure out how to do it. So that I'm protected. If I go to the wrong cop, he could inform, and then . . . it's curtains." Hank pulled a funny face and drew a finger across his throat, but I knew how scared he was.

"And you're in a mess, too, I guess," he said. "Billy saw the headline?"

I nodded, biting my lip.

"Those reporters . . . I think they've given up."

"They'll be back tomorrow."

"But it's Thanksgiving!"

I snorted. "You think those guys have families?"

Hank looked down at the box. "Want to help me decorate for Christmas?"

"No, thanks." I didn't think I could bear ribbons and bells. "I'm just going to go to bed."

He walked me to my door. Without my asking, he went inside and looked around, in closets, under beds. He put a chair under the handle of the front door. Then he hesitated at the kitchen door.

"I'm so sorry," I said. "It's all my fault."

"It's not. It's nobody's. You couldn't know I'd be there that night. Even you wouldn't think I'd be such a drip."

"Not a drip," I said, touching his arm. "Just a good guy, that's all."

I closed the door behind him and locked it.

I climbed into bed that night, praying for sleep. I had one more night to feel safe. One more night.

But I didn't sleep, of course. I tossed and turned, trying to escape my dreams. I woke up when it was still dark, not even seven a.m., which was the middle of the night for me. I knew I wouldn't sleep any more.

I rolled out of bed and went to the kitchen. I reached automatically for the radio, but stopped. I didn't want to hear the news.

I heard it now, the soft insistent knocking from the door to the street. Would reporters be out this early? I tiptoed to the door and leaned over the chair under the knob to get closer.

"Kit? Kit, are you there? Let me in."

My heart lifted, and I felt giddy as I grabbed the chair and pushed it aside. I flung open the door.

I didn't know why he was there, it was just a miracle that he was. I put my hands on his lapels and pulled him inside. Then I fell forward until my forehead hit against his chest.

"Jamie. You have no idea how good it is to see you." My laughter bubbled out, fast and nervous. "Oh, I just remembered – it's Thanksgiving! Did they send you down to make sure I'd come?"

Laughing, I pulled back from him, but he only hugged me harder. Suddenly, I realized that he wasn't holding me in an embrace. He was holding me up, or preparing to, and the first alarm began to clang inside me.

His mouth was close to my ear and his voice was so much softer than the blow.

"Billy was killed last night."

Thirty-one

New York City
November 1950

The agony of the minutes. To go from one to the next. To hold on to Jamie as I started to fall. And Jamie's eyes were wet, crying again as he saw me absorb what he was saying, trying to tell me though a curtain had slammed down in my brain – *No, it must be a mistake, no, I don't understand you, no, this is not happening* – that Billy was on a train going to Long Island, did I hear about the big train wreck? He was on that train, and something had gone wrong, a signal or something, they didn't know, and his train slammed into the other, and seventy people were dead, and one of them was him.

Jamie had heard the news from Da. Da had borrowed a car so Jamie could drive down to tell me in person. I tried to ask details, and could only manage one word at a time. *How. But.* And finally got out the sentence that was roaring in my head.

"Are they sure?"

At the look on Jamie's face something tore inside me, and I screamed.

It was later that he coaxed me into the bathroom. He put the seat down on the toilet and bathed my face with a washcloth. I looked at him as he did it, as he concentrated on the movement of the cloth on my skin.

He was thinner, and he needed a shave, reddish stubble on his cheeks. There was a muscle I'd never noticed in his jaw that jumped.

We went back to the couch and he sat, his hands clasped between his knees. For some reason I held the washcloth now, and I felt water soak my robe as I squeezed it, over and over. I felt my hands and my legs shake. I couldn't stop. Even my teeth chattered. Jamie put a blanket over me and took the washcloth away.

"But why was he on a train to Long Island?" I asked. "He was staying in Brooklyn. And he was going home for Thanksgiving, he said."

Jamie shrugged. "I guess he got on the wrong train."

"Maybe it's not him," I whispered.

"Nate identified the body last night. It's all over Providence. Nate drove up to tell Angela. Someone called Da to let us all know. I'll make us some tea. Do you have tea?"

I nodded numbly. I sat waiting, listening to the normal noises in the kitchen of running water in a kettle, the clatter of cups. It seemed impossible that tea could be drunk on such a day.

When he came back in, holding the cups, I noticed what he was wearing for the first time.

"Why aren't you in uniform?" I asked.

"Da wrote to my commanding officer and told them how old I was. It took a while – everything takes a while in the army – but I got sprung. Muddie wanted to surprise you at Thanksgiving."

"The last time I saw Billy . . . he was here. We had a terrible fight. There's a story in the papers—"

"I know. I saw it in the *Journal*."

I couldn't look at him. "Do you believe it?"

"Of course not."

"Billy believed it." I gasped, feeling it again – the deep, sharp pain.

He leaned forward, hands clasped. "I know from Fox Point, from school, from the army. . . There are some guys who are always spoiling for a fight. Billy . . . he was always ready to be betrayed. He was always *waiting* for it. It made it hard on the people who loved him. That summer you were down at the beach, that summer. . . we saw each other every day. . ."

I saw the muscle in his jaw jump again, and his face suddenly changed, went transparent. I could see the muscles under his skin, and I saw how thin and stretched the skin was, how hard he was working to keep his expression. And then in the next second his mouth opened. His sob was deep and breathless, just one, full of agony.

"I'm sorry," he said, and a series of sobs tore out of him.

I didn't know where to look or what to do. I wanted to comfort him, but wasn't he here to comfort me? Wasn't it my place to grieve? Inside I felt myself shrink from this rawness. I didn't want to see Jamie's pain. I didn't want to think about what it meant.

"Stop it." My voice was harsh. "Just stop it!"

He stopped. He wiped his tears with the back of his hand, swiftly, and then on his trousers. He got up, clearing his throat, and went to the bathroom. I waited, hating him.

When he came out, he was composed, but his face had gone back to looking like a mask.

"Do you want to pack a few things? The car is outside. The funeral is tomorrow."

"I can't go to the funeral," I said, and laughed. "I'm his father's mistress. Don't you read the papers?"

Jamie left.

There had never been such a silence between us. Never such a distance. I was afraid I didn't understand him, and how could we still be close if I didn't? I thought of Delia and Da, facing each other across the room, saying things that should never have been said. Did I just lose him the way Da had lost Delia? Had we got to a place where we didn't know each other any more?

Outside this apartment, people all over New York were cooking. Cream and butter were set on counters. Crystal

302

was examined against the light. Pumpkin pies were baking, and card tables were set up for the kids. Cars were packed with grandmothers and casseroles. All of it, all of that stirring, laughing life . . . and Billy was dead. I couldn't hold that thought next to the idea of the world still spinning.

Later that morning I was lying face down on the bed when I heard Hank softly call my name. He was at the kitchen door.

I turned over and tucked my knees under my chin. He would go away. I couldn't talk to anyone now. I didn't think I could walk out into the world, see people, open my mouth and have words come out instead of screams.

But he wouldn't go away. The knocking would stop and start again. He knew I was in here.

I dragged myself to the door and opened it.

"I think I know where she is," Hank said.

I blinked at him. I felt as though I were swimming through a murky sea. I had to push the words out. "Who?"

"Your aunt." Hank walked past me into the kitchen. He held up an envelope. "I found this in the Christmas box. Remember I told you that my mother was a Christmas maniac? She saves cards for *years*. She keeps a list. She exchanged cards with Bridget Warwick in 1946 and 1947. So if Bridget Warwick is your aunt, she could be still alive."

I sat down heavily at the table. He pushed the card in front of me. "*This friendly card is sent your way, to wish you peace on Christmas Day.* Hank. . ."

"Is it her handwriting?"

I looked at the card, the slash of the B in "Bridget", the way the t was crossed. The commanding W. "It could be . . . I don't know."

"She lives out on Long Island," Hank said.

I turned slowly. "Long Island? Where?"

"Babylon. Which is strange, because—"

"*On my forehead, the words are written in ash, and I am wearing scarlet and purple. . .*"

"What?"

"It's something Delia wrote. I remember now. It's from the Book of Revelation . . . the whore of Babylon. That's just the kind of thing Delia would do, pick a town for its name. She *is* alive." And then I remembered. The two thoughts, side by side, clanged inside my head. "Hank, did you read the paper today? Did you hear about the crash? The train, where was it going?"

"That's what I was about to say. It's a strange coincidence. One of them was going to Babylon," Hank said. "It's awful, isn't it? Hey, are you all right?"

I had started to cry again. It wasn't a conscious thing, the tears just fell. "Billy—" I had to stop and take a breath. "He was on that train. He was killed. Last night."

Hank stared at me. "Last night? He . . . I'm sorry, Kit. I'm so sorry. Shouldn't you be . . . with family or something? Is there anything I can do?"

I pressed my hands against my forehead. It was so hard to think, so hard to reason around the grief. Billy didn't get lost. He always knew where he was going. He knew his way to Brooklyn on the subway. Why would he be on a train to Long Island?

I looked up. "I have to see her. I have to see her today."

"There's no train service out there today. But I've been thinking about it. I knew you'd want to go. I have a car. My uncle loaned it to my parents – he talked them into driving to Boston tonight. He's got a friend who's a lawyer, the only one they'll trust. He's a federal prosecutor. They don't trust anyone in New York. Anyway, I have the car. I can drive you to Babylon this morning. There's time."

I shook my head. "Thanks for the offer, but no. You don't know how dangerous it could be. Nate's got nothing to lose now that Billy is gone. He could be after me, too. I passed information about Ray Mirto to him. I could link him to the guy."

"Well, what do you know?" Hank said. "We finally have something in common."

Thirty-two

New York City
November 1950

There were still a few reporters out front, so we went through Iggy's apartment. We passed through the kitchen, where the turkey was cooking, past the dining room, where the mother was setting the table. It was a glimpse of a normal world, where families sat around a table and said a blessing, and there was plenty of grace to go around.

On a table I saw the paper, and I quickly turned away from the screaming headline.

75 Known Dead in L.I. Wreck in Richmond Hill
Toll Mounting in Crash of Eastbound Train

"Hi, Mrs Kessler," Hank called.

"Hello, Hank. Tell your parents happy Thanksgiving!"

"Will do!"

A few minutes later we were in a grey Ford and heading

towards the Midtown Tunnel. I looked into every car, pressing back against the seat. If I saw anybody who seemed suspicious I would nudge Hank, and he'd take off fast from the light. But mostly I saw families in their good coats, or couples not talking, or someone fiddling with the radio.

I didn't breathe easily until we left the city. Hank took a road that curved along the East River, and you could see the skyline of Manhattan bristling on the other side. Then we drove past dunes and marsh grass and seagulls. We passed Coney Island and Idlewild. I hadn't quite realized how close Manhattan was to sand and sea.

I tried to think about what to do when we got there, but instead I kept thinking about the day I'd left Providence. I thought I was going like a smart person, with my bills rolled up in my underwear. I'd thought I had enough money to stake me, enough looks and talent to get ahead. I'd thought that was all I needed to meet the world. How I'd hated Da for the speeches he made, walking into my room and shaking his finger. He had said things about "the characters you'll meet" and "when you think you have all the answers, you're just dumb". I'd never thought I'd get to a place where Da would be right.

We saw the sign for Babylon and Hank followed the curving road to a small, pretty town. He ran into a gas station to ask directions. I felt the first vibrations of nerves, and my stomach dropped away.

He slid back into the driver's seat. "It's just a few blocks away."

I cranked down the window and gulped in some air. "The air feels different here."

"We're near the ocean," Hank said.

"Delia liked the ocean," I said. "We went once. She said" – and suddenly the memory was fresh and alive, Delia sitting on the beach, her dress tucked around her legs as the wind whipped tendrils of hair around her face – "that it must be the luckiest place to live."

The house was small, more of a cottage, really, with a white picket fence and a red door. The shutters were painted a blue that was close to violet, cornflower blue, Delia's favourite colour. I knew just looking at the house that Delia lived there. She was alive.

My mouth was dry and I swallowed hard. "Could you just drive by? Drive by, please?" I added urgently, sliding down in the seat. Hank drove to the corner, pulled over, and parked.

"Kit, it's not too late. We can just drive back to New York."

"I can't."

"Well. We'll have to go forward, then."

That made sense. Except I couldn't seem to get myself out of the car.

I twisted in the seat and looked again at the house. It looked spare and small in the grey light, a little narrower than most of the houses on the street, with its high peaked roof. There was a dried yellowish plot of grass in front and no porch or stoop, just irregular slabs of slate for a pathway to the door. They were placed too far apart, so that you'd have to have a wide stride to make it to the door without stepping in mud.

A woman turned the corner, walking briskly, dressed in trousers and sneakers and a navy coat, a wool cap pulled down to her eyebrows. She looked like a sailor.

When I got out of the car, she stopped in her tracks. Slowly, she pulled off her cap.

We stared at each other. I guess the changes were bigger for her. I was twelve when she left, with knees like door knockers. She had short bangs now, and her hair was the length of mine. She was dressed in a baggy grey sweater and khaki trousers. The hems of her trousers were wet – she must have been walking on the beach. Despite looking like she had thrown on some men's clothes in the morning and despite the fact that she had to be over forty, she looked almost shockingly beautiful and wild.

"Kit," she said.

"It's me."

"All grown up." She put a hand out, and then flinched as I took a step back. "You're lovely."

"I came to see you."

"Well, you'd better come in, then."

She opened the door to the house. To the right I could see a living room with a small hearth and a couch facing it. There was one long table against the wall with books and newspapers and magazines arranged in stacks on it.

I saw all this in a flash, all of it unfamiliar and strange, because I'd never seen Delia pick up a book in her life. Besides the Bible.

"I like to read now," Delia said. "Comes with the job. I work at the library." There were two deep, dented lines on either side of her mouth. Laugh lines, they were called. Did she still have cause to laugh?

Hank stepped forward, holding out his hand. "Hank Greeley. I'm a friend of Kit's."

"Greeley." Delia frowned, as if the name tickled a memory. She shrugged out of her coat. "Come in, I was just about to light a fire. Take off your things."

It was a blessing, to have the fire, for Delia busied herself with kindling and newspaper and matches, so I was able to look around and get my bearings. A bookcase covered one wall, its shelves stuffed with novels and biographies. There was a small pastel of a beach scene framed and hung on one wall. On the mantel was a row of small vases, each of them with a bit of beach grass or dried roses in it. On the window sill, beach stones were arranged in order of size, white and smooth. Between each one was a shiny new penny, heads up. The reference to Jamie made me bite my lip and turn away.

How different it was from our apartment in Providence, chock-a-block with shoes thrown about and papers, sweaters left on chairs, blankets thrown over the worn spot on the couch, forgotten glasses of milk and cups of tea. I remembered Delia's room, the plain lines of the wooden table she'd dragged out to the back yard and painted white, the white chenille bedspread, one brass candlestick. Delia had always liked things plain and spare. Back then we'd seen it as evidence of her need to show us up with her own superiority, neat in the face of our messiness.

I guess I thought I'd cry, but I felt strangely numb. Maybe I was just all cried out. By the time Delia turned away from the fire – taking longer than she needed to, I was sure – I'd gone through relief and curiosity and pleasure and had settled right back into anger, my most comfortable place.

"We thought you were dead," I said.

Delia looked startled. "You did?"

"Of course we did! You disappeared without a trace! You didn't send one word to us."

Delia put a hand on the mantel like some fancy grande dame. She must have thought better of the pose, because she dropped it. "Your father told me I was no longer welcome—"

"He had every right to!"

"Yes," Delia said, "he did." She took a breath. "Why don't I make us tea?"

"I don't want your tea. I want answers."

"Well, how about tea *and* answers?"

Hank looked from me to Delia. I hadn't taken off my coat yet. I had the feeling I should just run out the door.

"Hank," Delia said, "there are books to read – you look like a reader, somehow – and you can sit by the fire for a bit, is that all right?"

311

"That will be fine, Miss Warwick."

"How do you keep track of all your names, Delia?" I chewed on nasty like it was chocolate, sweet in my mouth.

"Have a seat, Hank. I think my niece will have an easier time berating me in private."

How could she stay so cool? Delia walked out of the room and down the hall, looking back to see if I would follow.

"If you need me, I'm here," Hank said.

I hesitated just a moment, and when I went into the kitchen, Delia was setting the tea things on a breakfast table, a small round one by a window that looked out on another patch of dried, dreary grass. There was a package of butter on the counter, along with apples and brown sugar and a sack of flour.

"I'm making a pie this morning," Delia said. "I've been invited to Thanksgiving dinner at a neighbour's."

"That sounds cosy."

She pushed her hair behind her ears, a gesture I remembered. She crossed to fill the kettle.

"You've got a right to hate me," she said over the crash of water hitting metal. "I know that. But you came for answers, too. Wouldn't it be easier if we were civil?"

She put the kettle on the stove and lit the burner with a match. She couldn't light it the first time; her fingers were trembling. She struck another one and this time it worked. It was the tremble in her fingers more than her words that allowed me to sit down.

"Did you know he was coming last night?" I asked.

"Who?"

"Billy! Did you know he was coming to see you?" Was it only yesterday?

"What?"

"He was on the train, the Babylon train."

Delia's face went white. "Billy was on. . ."

"He was killed."

"Oh. Oh." Delia said the word over and over in short exhalations of breath. "I went to church early this morning – we've lost several in the town. The funerals start on Saturday . . . Billy."

"Why was he coming to see you?" I asked.

The blast of the whistle from the kettle made us both jump. Delia hurried to the stove and took it off the burner. She carefully poured the water into the pot and warmed it, moving it around in her hands. Then she measured out tea and poured the rest of the water in. She did it slowly, as though she had to concentrate.

"He must have been . . . eighteen?"

"Nineteen. He enlisted in the army."

"That poor, broken little boy." Delia wiped her hands on a dish towel and brought the teapot to the table.

It was the word *broken* that did it. I started to cry again. The tears just leaked out, like air from a tyre. I couldn't seem to stop them. "He asked me to marry him a few days ago."

She looked startled. "You and Billy. . ."

313

"You didn't know?"

"I didn't know." She reached out instinctively to grab my hand, but I pulled away.

"I was with him just yesterday morning. Before he left he was upset. He said he just wanted the truth. That he had to stop the lies. Why would he come here?"

Delia looked down at her hands. "I'm not sure. I expect it has to do with his father."

"I know you were his mistress, so don't bother lying."

"I wasn't going to."

I felt dizzy and sick, and though I'd been planning to refuse Delia's tea, I took it. She had already added the cream and a half teaspoon of sugar. She knew just how I liked it. Funny how family is. You know how somebody takes their tea, but you have no idea about their heart.

"I've done my confession," Delia said. "I've been forgiven. I've lived my penance."

"Oh, good. I'm so happy to hear you're square with God. Have a ball in heaven."

She looked down and creased a napkin with her fingernail. "You're old enough now to hear about it. You're seventeen. I was about your age when I first met him."

"At Buttonwoods Cove, in Warwick."

It was like I hadn't said anything. "Have you been in love yet? In love like you thought you would stop breathing when you saw him? Did you feel you were only truly in the world when you were with him?"

I didn't answer, and I didn't think Delia meant me to.

314

"That's how it was. Of course, we parted back then. Nate blamed Jimmy for it, but it was me. I knew I couldn't marry him. I couldn't fit into his world. Irish and Italians . . . we look down on each other, don't we, for no reason at all, and I knew I'd be in the middle of that. So there was that, but there was also – I don't know, fear. I didn't know what he'd be. Bootlegging in Rhode Island . . . well, lots of people did it. Police looked the other way, the speakeasies were roaring, there was money to be made. But it started getting rougher, and I saw that Nate didn't turn away from it like Jimmy did. So I told Nate to go away, and he did. I still think it was the right decision. You can't save people, you know."

"So how did you meet again?"

"The day of the hurricane. Do you remember, I was caught downtown? I ran into Benny – he was Nate by then. He saved my life that night. I don't mean it in a silly romantic way. I was trying to cross Westminster Street, fool that I was, and my feet went out from under me, and I would have drowned if he hadn't hauled me out. We laughed about it later, how I was swept off my feet. He took me to a friend's office to dry out and wait out the worst of it, and that's how it started up again. At the time I thought thank God it did, because I was dying without him. I didn't go a day without thinking of him for ten long years. He got me that job with Rosemont and Loge. He helped our family and he made me happy. He made me happy, Kit. He made a world for us as though we were married, and for a while it was easy to believe it."

I looked away, out at the yellow grass. "What about Billy?"

"I'm getting to that. I just have to explain how it was. When the war came and Nate got that apartment, I went, God help me."

"You never had a job in Washington."

"It was like we were living the life we were born to live, married. It was lovely, most of it."

"So that was it? Moonlight and roses, tra-la? Lying to your brother, to us, violating the sacrament of matrimony, mortal sin, all of that?"

"I said it was lovely. I didn't say it was easy. I didn't say it was right. That summer we were together, it made us reckless. So that fall I started to see him in Providence. I'd go to his office. One night, one Sunday night, it was snowing, and we were . . . together, and we saw Billy run past, down the alley by the house. We knew he'd seen us – he was probably looking in the back window."

No, I thought. *He was in the tree with the camera, looking.*

"Then we saw someone else run by. Nate went after them, but it took a few minutes, because of course we had to—"

"—put your clothes on," I supplied.

"And so I followed Nate, but I kept a bit away, you know, in case there was anyone around. But Sunday nights are quiet, and there was this snowfall, and it was bitter cold and everyone was home. I saw Nate's car down the street, and Nate chasing it. He always left the keys in the

316

car – nobody in Federal Hill would dare steal Nate Benedict's car. It was like the world went still except for that car and Nate chasing it. The car was going so fast, like an aeroplane, like Billy wanted to just take off into the sky. It was like a dream, so white and quiet except suddenly I heard the tyres spinning. And then it just . . . moved sideways, it spun like a toy and smashed sideways into a tree. I started to run. Nate got there first, and Billy was already getting out – he was driving. He had blood on his forehead and he was dazed, but he was all right." Delia stopped talking. She placed her hands around her cup but didn't drink from it.

"His cousin Michael," I whispered.

"He was already dead." Delia took a sip of tea. "A patrolman suddenly showed up, and he was kneeling in the snow over Michael. Nate pushed Billy towards me and said, 'Take him away.' So I did. I brought him back to the office and I cleaned his cut – it was under his hair. There wasn't a mark on his face. He was crying – he was only fourteen, and his cousin was dead and he'd been driving and he thought his life was over. Nate came by an hour later and said, 'It's done.' And it was. No one ever knew that Billy had been driving that car. Nate made it go away because that's what he could do. He told Billy it was better that way. That one boy was dead, but if the other boy's life was ruined, it would be even worse for the family. The family would fracture – how could his Aunt Laura ever look at her sister again, knowing that Billy had been driving the car? He said all this while he was hugging Billy. They were both crying."

"When was this?"

"In 1945, in February."

"When you took me to the play in New Haven—"

"I knew he'd be there with Angela. I hadn't heard from him in weeks. I'd gone down to the apartment like always, and he hadn't come. I had to see him. And I guess that day we both realized that Angela knew. And I made him afraid of me, afraid of what I might do. I was afraid for myself. I was afraid I was losing my mind."

"Why did you try to take us away?"

For the first time, Delia looked uncomfortable. "I went a little mad. I wasn't sleeping, I was staring at my life and I saw how every choice had led to the next, that it wasn't some big fall but a series of steps, each one of my choosing. I could see Jimmy doing the same with Elena and I didn't want that for you. Think about it, Kit – could he have married a dark-skinned girl? Could that have worked?"

"Was that up to you? We loved Elena!" I drew in a breath. "You were jealous of her, jealous because we loved her."

She looked down. "I was jealous of anyone who had love and wasn't going to lose it. But it wasn't just that. I thought I" – she pressed her lips together – "I thought I should be the one to raise you. Because I'd renounced him, and I had nothing, and I could dedicate myself to all of you."

"That doesn't make any sense at all."

"Of course it doesn't – I said I went a little mad, didn't I? One night, I . . . well, never mind. Terrible things were in my head."

The night I'd seen her in the tub, Da's razor on the edge. I realized I hadn't understood anything that night.

"It was the look on your faces that destroyed me. The fact that you didn't want me – no, that the idea of my having you would be a terrible, dreaded thing."

"You were taking us away from our father!"

"I was like a mother to you!"

"A mother who left every weekend! You got what you wanted, and it wasn't us. It was never us!" Now we were shouting at each other, finally, and I felt satisfaction in it.

Delia controlled herself with an effort. "It is a terrible, terrible thing, Kitty, not to be loved by those you love. I hope you never find that."

"This isn't about love. This is about *possession*." I shook my head. "You're just like him. You're just like Nate."

I saw her recoil. "That's not true."

"Do you really expect me to feel sorry for you?"

"No, of course not. I don't feel sorry for myself – why should you? I left everything because I had to. He made it clear I had to leave town. He was afraid of what I would do. So I made another life."

"The whore of Babylon?"

She gave a small, private smile. "You got that, did you? I meant it as a taunt to him, but I like this place. Nate and I took a holiday once. We drove out to Fire Island and I saw this town, and I remembered it. I couldn't risk staying in Rhode Island. But I wanted to be near the sea."

I didn't want to hear about Delia's life. I reached into my pocket for the letter. "I found this."

Delia looked over at the letter but didn't touch it. "Where. . ."

"I guess Nate packed up all your stuff – he threw it into boxes. It was in the storage unit at the apartment."

Delia shook her head. "The apartment – how did you—"

"Nate offered it to me when I moved to New York."

Delia's glance flicked to the living room. "The Greeleys – that tall boy is their son." Her chair scraped back. She went to the sink and gripped it, her back to me.

"He said the apartment was just sitting there, and that I could take it until Billy came back from the army and we could be married."

"And you accepted?"

Delia's voice had risen, and I stood up to face her as she turned.

"You think you have a right to judge me?"

"Not judge you, just point out a particular piece of idiocy! What did you think you were doing, getting mixed up with Nate Benedict?"

I laughed. And, suddenly, Delia barked out a surprised laugh, too. We were bitter and angry and lost, but we both saw what was ridiculous in what she said.

"Oh, Lord, Kitty." Delia dabbed at her eyes.

"So you wrote the letter and didn't send it," I said.

"I don't think he saw it – I found it in your stocking box."

"I thought I'd be going back, one more time."

"'Keep your money and your clothes,' you said."

"Well. When you leave a man, that's what you do, I thought. To prove you aren't a kept woman. I didn't need the clothes; they were clothes to go out to restaurants and things in. I wasn't going to do that. But I took the money. If someone pays you to leave town, it only makes sense to keep the money."

The matter-of-factness took my breath away. She'd taken money to leave us. She could call it something else. But it was a pay-off.

"So you're still bought and paid for, then," I said. My whole body shook. I looked at her small, neat kitchen, with the apples and butter on the counter, and rage filled me up. I remembered Billy describing his anger, how it made him blind, and now I knew blindness and hatred and how it felt.

"Why did you come?" Delia asked quietly.

"Not for your mea culpa!" I swept the butter and the apples and the flour off the counter. The apples bounced and rolled, and the sack burst, sending up a puff of flour that settled over our shoes like ash.

Mea culpa. The words in the Mass where you beat your chest three times. *Through my fault, through my fault, through my most grievous fault.*

But Delia didn't look humble. She looked *fine*. She hadn't

321

said the word *sorry*. She hadn't asked about Jamie or Muddie or Da.

Why was I here? It was so clear that we didn't matter to her, so why would I think she could help us? She didn't know why Billy was on that train. I'd come for nothing, I thought, and a vast and helpless emptiness opened up inside me. I would have to leave here and face my grief again. I would have to face the fact that Billy was coming here and not know why. I would have to think of him on that train, dying with a heart full of anger and desperation.

"There are some sins that even God can't forgive," I said. "Go back to your new life – your library and your books and your apple pie. You're right. We didn't want you then. We don't want you now."

I heard Delia calling me, but it was as though from a far, far distance, and I was running, flinging myself out of the house as though pestilence was there.

Thirty-three

New York City
November 1950
The good news was that I was done with crying. Delia had stopped my tears.

All the way back into Manhattan, I thought about air-raid drills, disaster raining from the sky. They said that if the Bomb hit Manhattan the living would envy the dead. I knew how that felt now. All I wanted was to close my eyes and not hear another word, see another sight. When I looked out the car window and saw people walking, I hated them for their smiles, their scamper towards a meal, a hissing radiator, pumpkin pie. The whole world, it seemed, was in a holiday mood.

How had Billy lived with that, killing his cousin, attending that funeral? No wonder he'd been so afraid of his anger. So afraid that he clung to me desperately, wanting me to make everything all right.

Hank gave me space to think on the way back. He was

good at that. The sound of the tyres was like an easy beat if I closed my eyes. When I opened them I saw we were leaving the tunnel. The circle of grey light ahead grew and grew until we hit open air. Hank followed the signs for uptown.

"What are you going to do now?" Hank asked.

"The right thing," I said. "However it falls."

"What's that?"

"I've got to be braver than I want to be," I said. "And that means going home."

I hitched a ride with the Greeleys. It was a long drive and we drove without stopping, eating turkey sandwiches in the car. Mrs Greeley had got up at four a.m. to roast a turkey, because that's the kind of mother she was.

If the Greeleys felt it was my fault that Hank had got involved in a murder at a nightclub, if they resented me or despised me, they didn't let me know it. They shared their sandwiches and their thermos of coffee, and they drove me through the streets of Providence straight to my front door.

I got out of the car. Hank rolled down the window and I leaned in to look at them all, Mr Greeley at the wheel, his eyes red and tired, Mrs Greeley, tense but summoning up a smile for me, and Hank, who just looked bewildered. I didn't know what I'd done to deserve their kindness. I think they were the kind of people who just gave it out for free.

"Thank you for this," I said. "I owe you more than I can repay."

What was left to say? I'm sorry? Good luck? Take care?

I looked at Mr and Mrs Greeley, and I silently promised them that nothing would happen to their son.

And then I shut the door.

I stood on the sidewalk and looked in the lighted window of the apartment. The shades were up. Muddie passed by the window in a navy dress. I could glimpse Jamie sitting on the couch. I couldn't hear the radio, but I knew it was on. They'd probably already had the turkey and the dressing and the pie.

I walked up the stairs and pushed open the door. Muddie turned, startled.

"You came!" She rushed forward to hug me.

The hug lasted a long time. Usually, in our family, we gave quick, fierce hugs that resembled strangulation.

Over her shoulder, I met Jamie's eyes. He dropped his gaze as he got up to greet me. "So you came after all."

Da heard the commotion and hurried into the room. Muddie finally let me go and Da hugged me quickly. "You're where you belong," he said.

I wasn't sure where I belonged any more. But I was where I wanted to be.

I noticed that Da was wearing a suit, the only one he owned. "Where are you off to?" I asked him.

"The wake, of course."

"You're going?"

"Yes, I'm going," he said. "I've got to pay my respects. We're all going. You should come, too. You were his girl."

"I can't go. Everyone thinks—"

325

"What difference does it make that the paper prints a lie about you? You are what you are."

"I'm afraid of Nate," I said. "I'm afraid I'm mixed up in everything, and he knows it. I'm afraid he might do something."

"He's not going to do anything," Da said. His voice was firm. "The Corrigans and the Benedicts are family friends."

"I've got something to tell you all first," I said. "I found Delia."

The news seemed to freeze them in a tableau, as if they were on a stage and had hit their marks and they were waiting for the director to tell them where to move. Over a storm of questions from Muddie, I spilled the story of finding out that Delia had lived in my apartment, about her romance with Nate. I had to tell the story between a chorus of "No!" and "I don't believe it!" from Muddie.

The words tumbled out, about her house, and the way she looked, and how bitter I'd felt when I left. I looked at Da. "You knew about Delia and Nate, didn't you?"

He pulled at his tie. "I didn't know anything for sure," he said. "I suspected plenty. But it was her life to live."

"Delia and Nate Benedict," Muddie breathed. She sat down abruptly on the couch. "Cross of Christ about us. I don't believe it."

Jamie shook his head. "Well, that explains all those weekends away."

"Do you still think it's a good idea to go to the wake?" I asked Da. "Considering?"

"It was five years ago, and it's got nothing to do with us," Da said firmly. "Nobody knew, did they, until now?"

"Angela knew," I said.

"Well, that's between Nate and his wife," Da said. "Anyway, I've heard Angela won't leave her bedroom, so we won't see her at all. I've known the man for twenty years. I'm going, and whoever comes along, that's fine with me."

In the end I went because I couldn't stay away. You did this for people you loved, you went to honour them at wakes and funerals. That had been embedded in me since childhood. I would go, and I would kneel and say a prayer, and then Billy would be put to rest, and I would have a part in the grieving. Nate and I were in our proper places now, both of us mourners. Both of us dead inside.

The house on Broadway was glowing with light. Cars packed the street, and we saw a steady stream of people going in and out. The temperature had dropped, and the wind was cold, the kind that cut through your clothes. A wet, thick snow had begun to fall. We hesitated in our little clot of nervousness and gravity until Da took a breath and climbed the porch steps.

We passed through the front hall into the living room. Folding chairs had been set up, most of the furniture cleared out or pushed to the sides. The room was full of women in black and men in dark suits. There was a strong smell of coffee. I could see into the dining room, where

327

there were platters of sandwiches and pastries crowding the table, their edges overlapping.

The closed coffin was at the far side of the room. Were we supposed to be comforted by the luxury of it, the satiny wood, the gleaming brass? Should a coffin beg for admiration? It was an insult to grief. I felt the horror of it in my knees and I would have fallen if Muddie hadn't gripped my arm right then. I turned and counted the spoons lined up next to Angela's fine china cups and saucers until I felt like I wouldn't faint.

Something took me over, an underwater feeling. Sound was muffled. This wasn't real, my feet moving on the carpet, the people moving away as we passed, parting in front of us like a school of balletic blackfish.

Nate sat in the corner, an untouched cup of coffee in front of him. Three men in suits sat with him, men I didn't recognize. Their hard glances put up a wall between us and Nate.

Da went up. We clustered behind him. "Benny," he said. "I am sorry for your loss. He was a grand boy, and a hero. I don't have words for you, just the sympathy of my family."

Nate stared at him as though Da didn't exist. Like there was just air where we were standing.

Da hovered uncertainly for a moment, then moved jerkily away. We filed past the coffin, crossing ourselves.

The room fell silent, down to the sniffles and sobs. A heavy presence seemed to be at our backs as we knelt in front of the coffin and bowed our heads. I tried to pray, I tried to think of Billy as I knew him, as I loved him, but I could only think of the silence pressing against us.

After a brief time Da got up, crossed himself again, and started out. We followed in a single line. Past the mourners in back. Past the corner where Nate sat. We only began to breathe again when we hit the sidewalk.

We started down Broadway. No one said a word. The sidewalk was slick with the wet snow and Muddie slid into me, clutching my arm.

We heard quick footsteps behind us and as one, we turned. Nate was heading towards us, quickly, hurrying to catch up with us, crossing his lawn instead of using the walkway. The same three men walked more slowly, keeping him in sight but giving him distance.

He came within a few feet and then stopped, as if coming any closer would contaminate him.

He was clutching something in his hand, a wadded-up mess of newspaper, wet from the snow.

Muddie huddled next to me, her arm still in mine. I pressed it. Jamie moved closer to Da. We felt the threat, the violence in the way Nate stood, feet apart, breathing heavily.

In a motion so quick it caught us off guard he threw the wadded-up paper at Da. It hit his face and fell to the sidewalk. Da didn't flinch.

I saw part of a headline.

WILLIAM BENEDICT DEAD IN NYC TRAIN DISASTER

"He was in the first car," Nate said. His voice shook.

Yes. He always liked to ride in the first car.

"He was decapitated." The word was torn from his throat, it shredded in the telling, and yet I saw and felt it like he'd struck me. Muddie cried out. I thought of the coffin, the lid closed, and I felt sick.

"They wouldn't let me see him. They had his dog tags. They said a father wouldn't want to see him."

I put my hands over my face.

"Benny—" Da started.

"They wouldn't let me see him!"

I felt terribly sick. Sweat broke out on my forehead. Billy. I couldn't envision the horror of it. His beauty, his face, his hair, his skin. That last morning in my bed, his slow, sleepy smile.

"You took my son from me," he said.

Da looked confused. "I—"

"I can trace it all back, you see," Nate said. "You wouldn't let me have Delia. I wasn't good enough for you."

"That's not—"

"And then my boy wasn't good enough for you, either. My boy!" Nate let out a sound so anguished Da took a step forward. Nate held up a hand to stop him.

"You took my heart!" he cried. "And then you took it again!"

"Benny, let's be reasonable—"

"I curse you," he said. "It's because of you and your

330

children that my son is dead. So one of your children will die."

"What are you saying?" Da asked, confused. "You don't know what you're saying. It's the grief talking—"

"*I'm* talking!" Nate shouted. "I'll do it, Mac, God knows I can, and I have a right to. You won't know which one I've chosen. But one of your children will die. James. Margaret. Kathleen. It doesn't matter to me which one. Nothing matters any more. An eye for an eye. A child for a child. Do you understand?"

"No. Benny . . . Nate – you don't mean this!" Da cried. "You don't!"

Nate turned and walked back. Alone, but with the three men at his back, protecting him.

Thirty-four

Providence, Rhode Island
November 1950

"Nate isn't a killer," Da said to us. "He's out of his mind with his grief, and who could blame him for that? He didn't mean what he said."

Muddie nodded, her eyes wide with fear. Jamie and I said nothing.

But Da decided we would go to a friend's anyway. The Learys lived over on Power Street, in a big square house that looked like it was squatting on its lot, holding on against any stray hurricane that might try to blow it away.

The day of Billy's funeral was a grey day, with a sky like steel and clouds scudding across the sky. The papers said that hundreds had come to the church and people lined up outside. I could picture it: the heavy smell of flowers in the church, and the pools of water from people's umbrellas. Billy was a Korean War hero, never mind that he had never gone to war; he had enlisted and died in uniform, and that was enough. His mother, they said, was in a state of collapse, but there was a photograph of Nate, ashen-faced in his suit, going into the church.

It all had nothing to do with Billy. Billy was somewhere else in my mind.

I remembered the day we went with Jamie to Roger Williams Park. The cherry trees were in blossom, and under the trees the light was so pink you felt you were nestled in the heart of a flower. Billy took my picture, and Jamie's, because he kept saying how perfect the light was. After a bit the weather changed and the wind blew and suddenly the petals were flying in the air, thick as a hard rain. We ran through the trees and the petals nestled in our hair and our clothes, and we brushed each other off, laughing because we were so happy to be all together, and it was spring.

Jamie stayed on the sunporch the afternoon of Billy's funeral, and I knew he was thinking what I was thinking, of the cold, frozen ground and the coffin, and the graveyard, and the mourners with their black umbrellas.

I thought of that night in the parking lot, how Jamie's arms had gone around Billy and he'd rested his cheek against Billy's back, and how I should have seen that he was managing to calm Billy with his embrace, with his words, in a way that I never could. I thought of how he'd driven all night to get to me, how he'd bathed my face and brought me a blanket and made me tea, and how I'd paid him back by ordering him to stop crying. I could hear the exact tone

333

of contempt that had been in my voice, and I thought that out of every bad thing I'd done, that could be the worst.

Quietly, I went into my purse, and Muddie's. In my fists I carried the coins, and I walked on to the cold porch. Jamie's eyes were on his book but he wasn't turning pages. I moved around the room, placing the pennies, heads up, on the window sills and the bookshelf and the arms of the chairs. I felt him watching me. I saved one last penny and opened his hand. I put the penny heads up in his palm, then closed his fist over it.

Then, without looking at the title, I took a book from the bookshelf. I sank into the couch on the other end, nudging his stockinged feet aside. I wiggled into my space, put my feet up, and opened my book.

I thought of the first day we'd spent together, of Billy kneeling in the sand with his camera, grinning at us, the wind whipping his hair. It was a good thing to know and to remember: this was joy, and he had known it.

Jamie and I stayed there together until the light faded, our books open, not reading a word, waiting until dark, when we knew Billy would be buried, and all the mourners would be gone. What could we wish for him but that? To sleep without dreaming. To rest in peace.

The house was quiet when I rose from the bed I shared with Muddie and slipped out. I tiptoed down the stairs, holding my shoes. The house seemed full of breath – the quick pants of the Leary children, dreaming in their beds, the uneasy sleep of Da, the mound of Jamie under a blanket on the couch.

I quickly pulled on my coat and Muddie's black beret. I slipped out of the sunporch door. I hurried to the back yard, where I climbed a short fence. No shades flickered, no shadow moved as I took off to the crown of the hill.

I crossed over into the streets that ran through Brown University. I had forgotten my gloves, and I tucked my hands in my armpits to keep them warm. It was close to midnight. The Brown campus was deserted, most of the students gone for Thanksgiving weekend. I walked faster, knowing I was outside Fox Point territory now.

I don't know where my courage was. I didn't feel brave at all. I just felt scared. But doing nothing was worse. Da didn't believe Nate would put a contract out on one of us and I did. So it was up to me to stop it.

I took the trolley downtown. A few people were waiting at the stop, a woman and a man I'd thought were together. But she got off, and the man stayed on. He wore a hat that shaded his face and he was thin and not too tall, a man nobody would notice unless you were alone and afraid.

When I got off, he got off, too. With every nerve screaming, I wanted to walk fast, but I didn't. I strolled down Westminster Street, past the Chinese restaurant, turned again, and headed for Washington. He was still behind me. There were people on the street, but not many, not enough.

335

When I came to the Riverbank Club I ducked inside and nodded and smiled at the hostess who'd replaced me. Sammy was over at the bar, and he hurried to greet me.

"Kit! Gee, you look swell. What brings you here? Tony will be glad to see you; the new girl can't find a punchline with both hands."

"Sammy, I'll come back and see you, I promise, but right now, can I use your alley? I'm trying to ditch some joker who followed me."

"You betcha, kiddo, don't give it a thought. I'll make sure he doesn't go after you." He gave me a pat on the shoulder and turned, shielding me from the door.

I walked out through the kitchen into the alley, surprising a busboy emptying trash. I hurried down the alley and turned on to Snow Street. Then I headed up Federal Hill.

I crossed the street when I got close to the Benedict house and walked on the opposite side, turning my collar up. The lights were still blazing, and cars were parked outside. Relatives and friends sitting with Nate and Angela. They would come for weeks with casseroles and fruit, they would sit in the kitchen and make coffee and soup. Life would go on, no matter if Nate or Angela wanted it to.

I slipped through the dark streets towards Atwells Avenue, grateful for the clouds that covered the moon. There was no one around, as if every family on Federal Hill was paying their respects to Nate by staying home.

Nate's office was dark. I hurried down the side walkway to the back.

336

It had been five years, but I remembered every detail of that day. I counted the bricks and lifted one and there it was, the key, dull and crusted with dirt. I fitted it in the padlock and I heard the click.

Billy had wanted me to follow him that day. He'd known about Delia. Had he wanted me to know, too? *I liked you because you liked my pictures. Before that . . . you were my enemy.*

His enemy because of Delia. That photograph I saw that day – of a woman pulling off her sweater – he'd wanted me to see it. He'd wanted me to know about Delia. But something had stopped him. Maybe because I liked the pictures so much? I'd never know.

I could only guess that it hadn't been friendliness that day that had led him to bring me inside. It had been something else. Some impulse to share a knowledge of a grown-up world that was wrong and painful. So he wouldn't be alone.

I switched on the light, but the place was bare. Billy's darkroom had been cleared out years ago. Later he had developed his photographs at college. But today, on the day of his burial, the bare planks of the tables felt wrong. It was as though he'd been erased. When I thought of that boy, down here alone with his trays and his solutions, tears burned my eyes. I wiped them away fiercely. I couldn't do this if I thought about Billy. I had to save who was left. I turned off the light again in case it would shine through the cracks of the coal cellar door.

I walked slowly through the basement. The darkness was almost total, and I kept my arms outstretched. I could just make out a wooden stairway in the gloom.

I walked slowly up the stairs, testing each one before putting my weight on it. I couldn't hear a sound from the house, and when I paused at the top and cracked the door, I could only see more darkness.

I made my way to the office. I had no way of knowing if I could find anything that would bring Nate down. I didn't even know if I'd know it if I saw it. He was a lawyer. He knew how to cover his tracks.

But it was my only chance.

I couldn't switch on the lights and I had no flashlight, but I could just make out the desk and filing cabinet. I opened the drawer and began to flip through the files. I took some out to read them by the window, where a small shaft of light entered from the street light. Financial transactions, arrest records, several wills . . . I had no idea what to look for.

Frustrated, I wanted to wad up the papers and throw them around the room. Trash Nate's office, destroy everything.

Instead, I carefully returned the papers and put the files back. I opened the next drawer and flipped through.

I hadn't heard a thing, not even the front door, so I was taken completely by surprise when Nate opened the door and switched on the light.

We stared at each other for a moment. Never have I seen grief mark a man like it marked Nate. He looked like a

338

ruin, like his clothes should be smoking. He didn't say a word but crossed to the phone and dialled a number.

"I found her. I'm at the office." He paused. "Do that." He hung up the phone but kept his hand on it, his back to me. "I don't know what you think you're doing, but you can't change anything. And if you think I keep anything here that could incriminate me, you really are a dumb kid."

"Da had nothing to do with Billy's death," I said. "Neither did I. But did you ever think that you did?"

He whipped his head around. "What are you saying?"

"That morning Billy said he just wanted truth. That he was going to stop everything. I think he meant he was going to stop you, somehow. Didn't you ever think of why he was on that train?"

"He was lost, he got on the wrong train. . ."

"Billy didn't get lost! Don't you know where that train was going? It was going to Babylon. He was going to see Delia. Why?"

I'd succeeded in rocking him. "I don't know." He crossed to the window and pulled back the curtain.

From behind him, I could see a man across the street standing underneath a street lamp. The same man who'd been on the trolley.

"It's time for us to go," he said. "What does any of it matter now?"

"I'm not going out there," I said. "You'll have to drag me out."

"I can do that."

339

"Why do you hate us so much?" I whispered.

We heard a noise and turned to see Delia and Da in the doorway.

"He doesn't hate you. He hates me," Delia said.

"Dee," Nate said. "What are you doing here?" His face flushed red, but whether from anger or emotion, I didn't know.

"I called Mac last night," Delia said. "He told me what you said. Is it true, Nate? You want to kill one of my family? A child?"

"They aren't children," Nate said. "Do you understand? My heart was cut out! He has to pay!"

"It's Jimmy's fault? Is that how you see it?" Delia glided into the room, stripping off her gloves and tossing them on the desk in a gesture that rang with such ease I knew she'd done it countless times before.

Da moved into the room and stood beside me. "Why did you come here?" he said in an anguished whisper to me. I could see his problem. He couldn't send me out there, out into the streets of Federal Hill, where a killer might be waiting. But he didn't want me here, either.

Nate was still staring at Delia. "How did you get in?"

"Through the kitchen door," Delia said. "The key you gave me so long ago. Did you forget? You should have changed the locks."

"I don't want to see you again. Haven't I endured enough on this day?"

"I want to make a deal," Delia said.

340

"I thought we were done with deals."

Delia crossed in front of me. She stood, blocking me slightly, facing Nate. "I'm sorry about Billy."

Nate said nothing.

"There is nothing else on earth worse than what you're feeling," Delia said. "What I don't know is why you would get pleasure out of giving that pain to someone else."

"Not pleasure," Nate said. "Satisfaction."

"You take satisfaction in killing? Is that what you've become?"

"What does it matter what I've become—"

"It's what I was always afraid of in you, this . . . hardness. Billy was coming to see me that day. Why don't you blame me?"

"Maybe I do," Nate said. "Maybe you're not safe any more, either."

"Did you tell him where I lived?"

"Of course not. But he worked in the office in the summers. He must have seen a cheque, an address."

"So he knew you paid off your mistress. The three of us were locked in a lie, weren't we?" Delia took another step towards Nate. "You buried him today. Hundreds of mourners were there to bury William Benedict, soldier, scholar, hero. Not the killer of his cousin who lived with that lie—"

Nate took a step towards her and stopped.

"Do you want to bury him a hero or a killer?"

"He *is* a hero!"

"He was a poor boy who lost his head one night and crashed a car. A boy was thrown from the car into a tree. Was it Billy's fault? Yes. You told him that night that it wasn't. That was one lie he couldn't live with. You told him it was *your* fault. You told him you'd never see me again. You told him that you could make it all go away. That was the second lie. Was that the right thing to do, Nate?"

"He couldn't have lived with it."

"He did!" Delia shouted. "He lived with it every day!"

Nate sat down, as though his legs couldn't support him.

"I know you're afraid I'll be getting a subpoena from Kefauver," Delia said. "That's why you sent someone out to check up on me a few weeks ago, isn't it?"

He didn't answer.

"I figure I owe you this – telling you to your face that I'll testify. I'll spill every detail if you don't call this off."

"You've got nothing to say that would hurt me."

"You'd like to believe that, but it's not true," she said quietly. "Let's start with obstruction of justice when it came to the death of your nephew. I don't blame Billy – he was just a kid. But you should've known better."

Nate laughed, a mirthless bark. "You've got to be kidding me. You think you can threaten me? You think I'm going to back down? You don't have one shred of evidence that Billy was driving that car."

"I have a police report."

Nate was silent, and I looked at Delia. She didn't look triumphant, she just looked sad.

"Remember, you took Billy home and you said, 'I'll be back.' You left me here. And I waited for you. A bottle of wine was delivered from the police commissioner. Wrapped around it was the original police report. The one the patrolman wrote that said Billy was at the wheel. You must have paid him well. It was a very nice bottle of wine. I drank all of it."

The air in the room seemed to compress and flatten, making it hard to breathe. Nate stood up. He was very still, but I knew from dance how stillness could explode into movement.

"So what do you say, Nate?" Da asked. "Why don't you let us walk out of here, free and clear? Why don't we just end things here?"

"Sure," Nate said. "But we'll end them my way."

Delia casually took off her coat and draped it over the couch. She pushed up the sleeves of her sweater. "That night you told me to wait? I was used to waiting for you, so I waited a long time. I was wearing a gold jacket you'd given me. I tried to get the blood out. There was no soap up here in the bathroom, so do you know what I did?" Nate stared at Delia, a puzzled look on his face. She had his attention now. "I went downstairs to Billy's darkroom. I found the soap. I couldn't resist looking at his photographs. Maybe a little bit of torture – to look at Christmas pictures of you and Angela and Billy, that sort of thing. Clues to see if you loved her. I found something else." Delia reached into the pocket of her trousers and handed a small snapshot over to Nate. "Do you know what you're looking at?"

"A bad photograph of a car."

"Bad because of the angle? Do you notice the licence plate? Because I think that's the point of the photo. There were others like this. They're all dated. Photographs of cars, of men meeting in a secluded house . . . taken by a boy who was supposed to wait in the car. That's what I'm betting anyway. That meeting that the Kefauver Committee is so interested in – the one in 1945? The merging of the Boston mob and the Providence mob – these are the photographs."

"Why would Billy—"

"He followed you, Nate. He followed you around and took photographs. And I took them all that night, to protect you. Poor scared Billy knew it, of course, but he wasn't about to ask for them back. Until a few nights ago, when he got fed up with the lies. I think I know what he was going to do with them. Don't you?"

I took a sharp breath. "He was going to testify against you," I said to Nate.

"That's impossible."

"Is it?" Delia asked. "I think back then, when he took them, he had some sort of crazy scheme in his head – he was going to blackmail you with them – but only so you'd go straight. Blackmail with an innocent heart. He just wanted you to stop. Then one day, while he was following you, he found me."

Nate suddenly put his hands over his face.

"Why was he here that night with Michael? They were close, like brothers. I guess he just wanted to show off. And here we were . . . together, and they saw it. I don't know what all the pictures prove. Maybe nothing. Maybe you'll skate away on taking the Fifth. But the fact that these photographs exist . . . friends of yours aren't going to like that."

"And the commission might not like knowing you were involved in a certain murder at a certain nightclub," I added. "I may not have been your moll, but I was your spy. It's not enough to convict you, I'm sure, but it will sure make you uncomfortable. And Mr Costello won't be happy, either."

Delia waited for Nate to speak, but he didn't. She pointed to the phone.

"So. Call off the hit man. Leave my family alone. The photographs are in a safe-deposit box. I'll mail one a year to you if you stay away from Mac. And Kit. And Jamie. And Muddie."

"And Hank Greeley, too," I said. "Stay away from him and his family."

"Do it, Nate," Da said. "Or by God I'll kill you myself if you harm my children."

But Nate ignored him and just looked at Delia. "Dee. Is this what's become of us, threatening each other like this? The day of my son's burial?"

"I'm doing this for Billy, too," Delia said. "I'm just carrying on what he planned."

345

For a moment I thought Nate was going to hit her. The heavy threat of violence had been in the room with us but now the air was alive with it.

"You don't know anything about my son." The words were forced through his teeth. I could feel my father tense next to me, ready to spring at Nate if he had to. "It makes me sick to hear you even say his name."

Delia didn't flinch. "I know you, though. I know you, Nate. And I have nothing to lose."

She picked up the receiver and held it out.

Nobody moved or breathed. It seemed to take a lifetime before Nate took the receiver from her hand. He dialled a number. "Call it off. Yes, that's exactly what I mean. Not just for tonight, for good. Yeah. Tell him to get lost fast."

As soon as he hung up, Delia said, "You were never a killer, Nate. I think I just did you a favour."

He didn't answer. He gave her a look of such hate that this time she turned away.

We waited, not speaking, until the soft sound of a car came from the street. Nate went to the window and looked out behind the curtain. We heard a car door slam.

"He's gone," he said.

Delia went to the window and looked out. Then she picked up her coat and brought it to me. "It's cold," she murmured. "Take this – your jacket isn't warm enough." She felt me shaking and so she did the buttons herself, like she used to when I was a kid. Then she put on my jacket.

"Ready, Jimmy?"

"Ready."

"We're going home now," she said. "Goodbye, Nate."

Nate sat at the desk, looking down at his hands.

Delia led the way to the door. She shoved her hands in my jacket pocket and took out Muddie's beret. She pulled it on. She turned slightly and smiled at me, a smile I didn't understand.

She opened the door and went out first.

I heard a sound like a branch snapping, and then another, and at the same time Delia must have missed a step on the stairs to the walkway, because she stumbled. She went down on one knee. One arm outstretched back towards me, as if for help.

A man in a dark overcoat hurried by, his hat pulled low, his collar up.

I caught the outstretched hand. I dropped to the ground in time to catch Delia, to cradle her head in my lap.

Da cried her name and fell to his knees. "No!" he said. "No."

Delia looked up at me, her eyes green and clear.

"I figured I could trust him," she said. "I just wasn't sure."

Thirty-five

Providence, Rhode Island
December 1950

We really hadn't expected anyone to show up at the funeral. But people came, people I hadn't seen in years, people who I'd never met, Delia's old bosses, Mr Loge and Mr Rosemont, and their wives. Helen Rosemont hugged me and told me how after her son had been lost in the war Delia had stopped in every day on her way to work to bring her the newspaper. Peter Arnot had said she'd given him a lecture when she caught him lounging on Wickenden Street, telling him if he didn't use his brains he was stupid, and now he was the first in his family to go to college. Story after story, not so much of her incredible kindness, because it wasn't that, it was that she said her piece and moved on, but it was a choice piece. Or she noticed if someone needed an extra hand. Flowers came from Long Island, too, from the library where she worked, from a neighbour, from the man who ran the bookstore, from a man down the street because Delia walked his dog for him.

Was she trying to make up for her secret life? Did it matter? We didn't discuss it any more than we discussed how she'd died, how she'd taken the bullet meant for me.

I didn't know if Nate had tricked us, if he'd wanted one last revenge. We didn't know if it had just been a mistake. Nate was in seclusion somewhere and scheduled to testify in New York.

Everyone was back in their houses. Everyone had breakfast in the morning and dinner at night. The moon rose, and the stars came out, and the milkman delivered the milk in the morning. And Billy and Delia were dead.

The day after Delia's funeral, an envelope arrived at the house on Hope and Transit addressed to me. It was large and thick, and whoever had sent it had taped the back shut.

I put it on the kitchen table. The family sat and stared at it.

"Delia's handwriting," Da said.

"Postmarked the day she died," Jamie said.

I slit it open with a knife. Photos tumbled out, pictures of men laughing, holding cigarettes, men leaning forward in conversation, a man leaving a car, cars pulled up into a driveway, their licence plates visible. Nate Benedict, walking down a snowy driveway, smiling at the boy who held the camera.

Da didn't have a TV, so we went down to the bar on Wickenden to watch the hearings in New York. Thirty

349

million Americans watched, too. Movie theatres in New York showed them, and people dropped in and out during the day, whenever they could. Every television, it seemed, was tuned in. When Frank Costello testified, he wouldn't let them show his face, so the cameras focused on his hands. They never stopped moving, and people watched, fascinated, hearing the voice and seeing the nervous hands. That was enough to tell a story.

Virginia Hill came in her mink stole and picture hat and told the committee that sure, she got presents and cash from men, and what of it? On the way out, she slugged a woman reporter.

Nate invoked the Fifth Amendment twenty-seven times, plus attorney-client privilege. He wasn't a crook, he said, just an honest attorney. And he had no personal knowledge of Miss Delia Corrigan, who lost her life so tragically on Atwells Avenue.

Billy stayed a hero.

The day after Nate's testimony, I called the number on the card the man had given me outside the apartment in New York. I realized now that it hadn't been about the Greeleys; he was trying to warn me about Nate. He told me what to do, and so I took the trolley downtown and personally delivered the photographs to the office of the FBI.

Time passed, but not enough. Muddie fed me soup and pudding and her terrible stews, Jamie took me to the

350

movies, Da bought me records, and I was grateful for every scrap of their caring, even though it didn't quiet the howl of grief inside me. I couldn't imagine going back to school, and Da didn't suggest it. I visited Madame Flo, but I didn't take a class. I couldn't even walk into the diner on South Main without seeing Billy at the table, his head bent over his books. Every day I would decide to look for a job, and every day, I would walk the streets instead. I couldn't find a way to return to my life. I couldn't find my way anywhere good, and panic was beginning to alternate with grief.

When you learn to sing, you learn to keep a reserve of breath in your lungs. It's there when you need it, at the end of a phrase, to hold the note strong and clear. Did I still have a reserve somewhere deep inside? Would I ever find it?

An evening came when Da looked at me across the kitchen table and shook his head sadly.

"It's time, darlin'," he said. That night, he took my suitcase out of the closet, and left it in my room.

The second time I left Providence for New York City, my family took me to the station. Da hugged me, and Muddie did, too. When Jamie hugged me, I whispered, "Come live in New York, I need you there."

When I pulled away, he nodded.

"First I have to finish high school," he said. "One of us should get a decent education."

"You'll get settled in your new place?" Da said.

351

"Daisy will be waiting for me. She says the residential hotel is a safe place – lots of dancers and actresses live there. All girls," I added, smiling. "No men after ten o'clock."

"No men, period, is more like it," Da said. "A nice boy now and then, maybe."

I climbed on the train and found my seat. They walked along the platform until they found me, and they waved until I was out of sight.

It was almost spring. The branches were fuzzy, as if you needed glasses to see, but you knew it was really the buds of the leaves ready to poke their way out into the world. One day those edges would be sharp and clear and startlingly green.

As the train picked up speed, I thought of Billy. This time, I thought of him as a boy, standing at the front of a subway car, watching the rushing tracks. On the night he died, did he see the light of the oncoming train coming towards him? That brilliant light, that flash, and then everything changed.

There were accidents in life, collisions, damage, and some happened through no fault of your own and some happened because you invited them. I had barely escaped the wreckage. Maybe I'd be haunted by Delia's death for the rest of my life. Maybe I'd never get over Billy.

I'd been thrown clear of the wreck. I was alive.

The train pulled into Pennsylvania Station and I walked up the stairs into that great vaulting space. People rushed by with places to get to. I was in the middle of it, and I

352

stopped, closed my eyes and let my tears fall. I listened to the footsteps until I could swear I'd picked up the rhythm of a dance – triple-time steps, shuffles and shim shams. My heart lifted for the first time since Billy died. Just a flicker, just a quarter note of a moment, not enough to hang on to, but still, I had felt it.

I was a girl crying in the middle of a crowd, and nobody noticed. Maybe there was something awful about that, but there was something good, too. I would dry my own tears. I opened my eyes and kept on walking.

Things can fall from the sky, it's true, anything can, from radiation to salvation, a bomb raining fire, packages of food into outstretched hands in a desperate city.

Or on an ordinary day, nothing sinister. Nothing noble. Just balloons.

Acknowledgements

I hereby acknowledge that without the editorial guidance of David Levithan on this book I would have been face down in the clam chowder. Most profound thanks to him for taking his red pencil and stabbing it right at the story's heart. I am grateful to everyone at Scholastic who worked on this book, and those who were kind enough to read it. Special thanks to Becky "Bex" Amsel, who is so tolerant of my crazy, even when I make her miss trains. And thank you to the gifted and gorgeous book designer Elizabeth Parisi, whose vision I trust.

Thank you to Molly Friedrich, the agent who doesn't do lunch, for being a champion of writers and readers. Thank you, too, to Lucy Carson for the thoughtful reading of this manuscript.

Research for this book was a treat. I lost myself in the pleasures of a Manhattan we've lost. For a taste of it, pick up E. B. White's *Here Is New York*. I watched movies for ambience (*All About Eve*, of course, and *Sweet Smell of*

Success) and haunted used bookstores for autobiographies of actors and dancers who began in the nightclubs and theatres of the early fifties. Ethan Mordden, wherever you are, thank you for all your brilliant books on Broadway musicals – you bring every era alive. And of course there are the treasures on YouTube. If you want to see dancing, take a look at Bob Fosse and Gwen Verdon in "Who's Got the Pain". Or Carol Haney in "Steam Heat". I'm sure Kit was at least half as good.

Thank you to John Sefakis, president of Dancers Over Forty, who got me in touch with the lovely Norma Doggett Bezwick, who started on Broadway in 1947, danced the choreography of Jack Cole and Michael Kidd, and was willing to talk to me about it. And thank you to my theatre friends, John Bedford Lloyd, Anne Twomey, Larry Hirschhorn, and that walking Broadway encyclopaedia, Mark McCauslin, for sharing tales, bringing books, and sending me down some fascinating paths.

Mary Cantwell's memoir, *American Girl*, was a wonderful trip back in time to the Rhode Island of the thirties and forties. Thanks also to the Rhode Island Historical Society for answering my questions and for access to their library.

A shoutout goes to Ethan Marcotullio, who knows how to tell a girl he loves her with style, even in kindergarten.

Any mistakes in history or geography are my own. I admit to fudging one historical event for the sake of my own chronology – the citywide air-raid drill took place a year later, in 1951. The horrifying Thanksgiving Long Island Railroad train wreck is an actual event. I did not exaggerate the way the threat of the Bomb permeated American life in 1950, nor the chill of the blacklist on teachers in 1950s New York.

I offer here inadequate thanks for the patience of friends, family and random acquaintances who listened as I anguished and languished for way too long over this manuscript. Thank you to Julie Downing, Katherine Tillotson and Elizabeth Partridge for their daily unflagging support. Thanks especially to Betsy for her keen editorial advice early on, when I wanted to throw the proposal into any random river. Thank you to my dear Donna Tauscher, for everything she is in my life. And to Jane Mason, for saying over and over that I could do it. Thank you to fellow author and Clue hunter Peter Lerangis for one particular pep talk that helped.

I borrowed names, but not characters, from my Irish great-aunts and -uncles. Thanks be to the dear departed – the original Muddie, who never wrote a book but should have, and my beloved grandmother Kathleen, called Kit, with her collection of red dresses – her "slashers" – that she wore to every party. Thanks to my parents, who threw the parties.

There are no words for what Cleo Watson and Neil Watson bring to my life. I just know they hold me up.

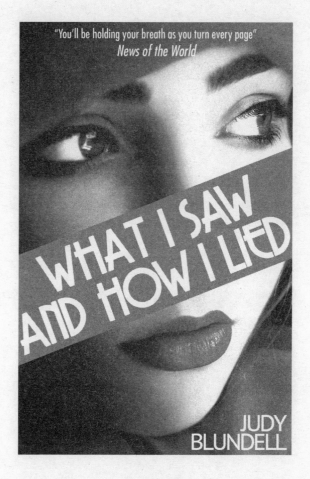